THE RETURN OF THE DUKE

Her gaze traveled over him slowly and thoroughly, assessing his merits—causing him to straighten his spine, hating the notion that she might find him lacking in any manner—before she began striding toward a delicate rosewood sideboard that housed several crystal decanters and an assortment of glasses. "Marcus Stanwick. I believe your preference is scotch."

Devil take her for knowing who he was as well as that little truth about him. But it boded well that if his sire had shared those intimate particulars of his heir then perhaps he'd also confided the pertinent specifics regarding his nefarious plans.

She poured the amber liquid into two tumblers, glided over as though she walked upon clouds, and extended one toward him. "I expected you sooner."

By Lorraine Heath

THE RETURN OF THE DUKE
GIRLS OF FLIGHT CITY
THE DUCHESS HUNT
SCOUNDREL OF MY HEART
BEAUTY TEMPTS THE BEAST
THE EARL TAKES A FANCY
THE DUCHESS IN HIS BED
THE SCOUNDREL IN HER BED
TEXAS LEGACY (novella)
WHEN A DUKE LOVES A WOMAN
BEYOND SCANDAL AND DESIRE
GENTLEMEN PREFER HEIRESSES (novella)
AN AFFAIR WITH A NOTORIOUS HEIRESS
WHEN THE MARQUESS FALLS (novella)
THE VISCOUNT AND THE VIXEN
THE EARL TAKES ALL
FALLING INTO BED WITH A DUKE
THE DUKE AND THE LADY IN RED
THE LAST WICKED SCOUNDREL (novella)
ONCE MORE, MY DARLING ROGUE
THE GUNSLINGER (novella)
WHEN THE DUKE WAS WICKED
DECK THE HALLS WITH LOVE (novella)
LORD OF WICKED INTENTIONS
LORD OF TEMPTATION
SHE TEMPTS THE DUKE

Waking Up with the Duke
Pleasures of a Notorious Gentleman
Passions of a Wicked Earl
Midnight Pleasures with a Scoundrel
Surrender to the Devil
Between the Devil and Desire
In Bed with the Devil
Just Wicked Enough
A Duke of Her Own
Promise Me Forever
A Matter of Temptation
As an Earl Desires
An Invitation to Seduction
Love with a Scandalous Lord
To Marry an Heiress
The Outlaw and the Lady
Never Marry a Cowboy
Never Love a Cowboy
A Rogue in Texas
Texas Splendor
Texas Glory
Texas Destiny
Always to Remember
Parting Gifts
Sweet Lullaby

THE
RETURN
OF THE
DUKE

ONCE UPON A DUKEDOM

LORRAINE HEATH

AVONBOOKS

An Imprint of HarperCollinsPublishers

THE RETURN OF THE DUKE. Copyright © 2022 by Jan Nowasky. All rights reserved. Printed in the United States of America. No part of this book may be used or reproduced in any manner whatsoever without written permission except in the case of brief quotations embodied in critical articles and reviews. For information, address HarperCollins Publishers, 195 Broadway, New York, NY 10007.

First Avon Books mass market printing: July 2022
First Avon Books hardcover printing: July 2022

Print Edition ISBN: 978-0-06-311459-3
Digital Edition ISBN: 978-0-06-311460-9

Cover design by Amy Halperin
Cover illustration by Victor Gadino

Avon, Avon & logo, and Avon Books & logo are registered trademarks of HarperCollins Publishers in the United States of America and other countries.

HarperCollins is a registered trademark of HarperCollins Publishers in the United States of America and other countries.

FIRST EDITION

22 23 24 25 26 BVGM 10 9 8 7 6 5 4 3 2 1

In loving memory of Dora,
who stole our hearts with her gentle nature
and is now chasing bunnies on
the other side of the Rainbow Bridge.

CHAPTER 1

September 1874

ONCE UPON A time, Marcus Stanwick had been heir apparent to the prestigious, exalted, and powerful Dukedom of Wolfford, born into a family that had been a favorite among royalty since the days of William the Conqueror.

Once upon a time, he'd had friends aplenty with whom he'd enjoyed carousing, imbibing the finest liquors, and wagering on the fastest horses. He was respected among his peers as well as his father's and considered to quite the catch by the ladies of the *ton* who vied for his attention. Adored, admired, and expected to live an easy and rewarding existence.

Once upon a time, he'd wanted for nothing and taken every aspect of his good fortune for granted, as his due.

But that was all before betrayal had shattered his life. Before the Crown unmercifully stripped his family of everything they possessed—including their good name—and condemned them to fight for their survival on the streets with nothing but their wits, courage, and determination. Before the father he'd once sought to impress was hanged for treason during the summer of 1873 and the genteel mother he'd loved had died shortly thereafter—a result of the unbearable shame and heartbreak of her husband being found guilty of plotting to assassinate Queen Victoria.

Before Marcus had become someone he hardly recognized, someone swallowed by fury, hatred, and a need for revenge, someone with a guiding purpose much darker than the frivolousness it had once been. Someone burning with a need for retribution.

It was that terrifying purpose that kept him awake at night and presently had him standing at the mullioned window in the sophisticatedly furnished parlor of the elegant terrace house. He fought not to catalog the plush carpets that it appeared few had walked upon, the rosewood credenza that sported not a single scratch, the exquisite and tasteful artwork that adorned the walls. He struggled not to wonder how much of it had been purchased by his dishonorable father for his notorious mistress—with an abundance of coins from the family coffers, back when the coffers had overflowed. Before they were barren of silver and gold. Before their contents and everything of importance were seized by the Crown.

For a little longer than a year, Marcus had avoided coming here, of confronting *her*. But desperation had finally driven him to knock upon her door. A well-appointed and stately butler—with a crooked and slightly off-kilter nose that hinted at a fight he'd possibly not won—had opened it and proclaimed the hour too late for visitors. Marcus had merely scoffed. The whore who lived within these walls would be accustomed to gentlemen arriving whenever the itch struck, no matter the hour's proximity to midnight. Therefore, he'd simply given the servant a scathing glare and the words, "Fetch the *mistress* of this household," his tone one that didn't invite argument, one befitting a man who would one day be a duke. The tone he'd once used when his future was secure, and he'd known well the path upon which he trod and where it would lead. While none of those situations applied any longer, old habits were difficult to break.

Without further ado, he'd barreled past the startled gent to take up his vigil by the window. He would see his father's former mistress. He wouldn't leave until he garnered every iota of information she could provide that would assist him.

He'd only ever seen her once, and then from a distance, while his father was handing her up into a carriage. Sitting astride a black steed he no longer possessed, Marcus had followed the vehicle through the bustling London streets. He'd observed her entering this residence and when later he'd confronted his father, the scapegrace had admitted her leading role in his enjoyment of the night. Marcus had come to despise the woman for her part in deepening the cool disdain that had often marked his parents' relationship, because after his heir had challenged him, the Duke of Wolfford had made no secret of his infidelity. The whole of London had soon learned he was cavorting with a woman young enough to be his daughter. As far as Marcus was aware, his father had never strayed from honoring his marriage vows until this brazen harlot had worked her wiles on him.

At that precise moment, the object of Marcus's scorn swept gracefully into the room, immediately taking ownership of it. With her fiery red hair piled artfully on top of her head and held in place with pearl combs, a few strands dangling to tease her long swan-like neck, she was striking— and taller than he'd realized, only a few inches shy of his six feet and two. Highlighting the voluptuousness of her body, her crimson gown daringly revealed a good bit of her cleavage, clung to her ribs, cinched at her narrow waist, and flowed out over wide hips in a smoothly draping manner that hinted perhaps no petticoats resided beneath. A man could ride this woman hard, fast, rough, and she'd enthusiastically welcome his fervent attentions and return the favor.

It irritated the devil out of him because he understood why she would appeal to his father, to any man with blood coursing through his veins, blood she could cause to boil. Christ, she had his cock reacting with such swiftness that for all of a heartbeat he was light-headed. He wanted to plow a fist into the wall at his own body's unexpected betrayal. But it was only animalistic lust, not desire, not want, not attraction. Since his tumble from grace, he'd possessed neither the time nor the temperament for fornication. Besides, the sort of women who would deign to lower themselves to be taken by the son of a traitor held no appeal to him. Unfortunately, this harlot did appeal. She was a female who understood her worth and flaunted it, a woman who wasn't shy about giving the impression she knew her way well around a man's body.

Her gaze traveled over him slowly and thoroughly, assessing his merits—causing him to straighten his spine, hating the notion that she might find him lacking in any manner—before she began striding toward a delicate rosewood sideboard that housed several crystal decanters and an assortment of glasses. "Marcus Stanwick. I believe your preference is scotch."

Devil take her for knowing who he was as well as that little truth about him. But it boded well that if his sire had shared those intimate particulars of his heir then perhaps he'd also confided the pertinent specifics regarding his nefarious plans.

She poured the amber liquid into two tumblers, glided over as though she walked upon clouds, and extended one toward him. "I expected you sooner."

Such conviction in her tone, such confidence. She was not a woman to cower before him and tell him everything he required and demanded to know. He was going to have to alter the strategy he'd considered employing when he'd thought she'd be impressed by—and perhaps a bit fearful of—who he'd once been. And he'd imagined she'd be more wary that his eyes revealed who he now was: a man who took what he wanted without shame or remorse. When he strode down the street, people avoided him as though he wore a sign about his neck: *Approach at your own risk*. But if she was aware of any of that, she appeared determined to ignore it.

She was more mature, older than he'd realized, somewhere north of thirty, he'd wager. As for himself, he'd only just reached his thirtieth year. With a measure of disgust at her for being so beautiful and himself for finding her so, he took her offering but let none of his emotions gush forth into his voice, keeping his tone flat and uncaring. "You have me at a disadvantage as I don't know your name."

"Esme will suffice." She lifted her glass, took a sip, and licked the full lips of a wide mouth that had been designed to give a man pleasure. Turning her back on him, her hips swaying provocatively, she wandered to a dark blue wingback chair near the fireplace and eased slowly into it, and he imagined her daringly easing down onto other things. A bed. A lap. A cock. *His* cock, damn her.

With the elegant hand holding the glass, she indicated the chair opposite her. He shouldn't. He should stay where he was, reestablish his dominance, lord over her as he had the bloody butler, but she'd left in her wake the fragrance of crisp cleanliness and a freshly bloomed rose, both of which had been sadly lacking from his life for much of the past year. No time for strolling through gardens, no interest in kissing perfumed necks. So, he followed where she led and dropped unceremoniously into the chair like the uncouth monster he'd become.

He fought not to be embarrassed by the sad state of his clothing, worn and frayed. He had spared a few of his precious coins to visit a bathhouse for a wash and a shave before coming here, but he'd walked, and now reeked of his journey. He doubted this woman ever reeked. Taking a sip of his whisky, he nearly groaned at the familiar flavor. Coming from the finest of Scottish distilleries, it had once been his favorite. It seemed she had expensive taste in all things.

"Is there some man upstairs awaiting your return?" he asked begrudgingly, not bothering to hide his distaste for how she'd chosen to make her way in the world.

"I don't see how my bed is any of your concern."

"My apologies. It's not." He sighed, remembering a time when he wouldn't have sat in judgment, when he would have welcomed a woman such as she into his arms and been grateful that she didn't observe Society's strictures. The sooner he got to the matter at hand, the sooner he could leave and forget her. "You were once my father's mistress. Did he tell you anything about his plans . . . his comrades . . . his fellow treasonous snakes that might help me find them?"

For the first time, she seemed taken aback, her golden-brown eyes widening the tiniest fraction. She tilted her head slightly as though taking a new measure of him, like a puppy accustomed to being kicked suddenly finding a hand willing to pet. "You're searching for the other men involved in the plot to assassinate Queen Victoria? For what purpose?"

"To restore a bit of honor to my family name," he stated succinctly. Or at least to his own name, hoping to regain some of the respect his father's actions had stolen from him. Being associated with a traitor did him no favors. "To see them tried and hanged as my father was, to see the country rid of them."

She studied him intently as though she could see into his blackened heart, one that had rotted and shriveled until he feared nothing that he accomplished would be enough to restore it to what it had once been or to recast him into the man he should have been. "Your father didn't really come to me for conversation."

He leaned forward, resting his elbows on his thighs, gripping the glass between both hands.

She was his last hope for a reckoning, for proving he had no role whatsoever in his father's misguided attempt to put another on the throne. Other than his brother and sister, everyone he'd ever known or cared about shunned him now. His other relatives, near and far, as well as those individuals he'd once considered friends, wanted naught to do with him. He was a pariah, avoided at all costs. Even she treated him with cool disdain as though he was beneath her. His jaw clenched. Beneath *her*, a woman with no morals. "Perhaps he mentioned something that didn't blatantly regard the plot, something innocuous, a name, a portion of a conversation that made no sense or was without context. Tidbits of information must be burrowed in that beautiful head of yours that could at least place me on the correct path. He can't have fucked you every second he was in your company. Some words had to have been exchanged. Think, woman."

"Think? How presumptuous of you to believe I've not already given considerable contemplation to every syllable uttered by your father." She came up out of the chair in a flourish of righteous indignation, and never in his life had he felt so looked down upon, so trivial. "You and your brother were dragged to the Tower. I was hauled to Whitehall where Scotland Yard's finest and most ruthless had a go at me. Interrogated. Intimidated. Accused. Then to Newgate for a spell in the hopes of breaking me so I might, too, confess to being involved in this ill-conceived conspiracy.

Doubt thrown upon my reputation. My association with your father has ruined my life."

Surging to his feet, he took a menacing step forward. "Yet you live in this luxury while I dwell in squalor."

Caught in a storm of emotions, not wanting her to witness or decipher them, he marched the three steps to the fireplace and stared at the empty hearth that so reflected the fruitlessness of his life. He was unwilling to accept that his quest was a waste of his time and efforts. He would never regain what he had once possessed, but by God he could at least ensure the next generation didn't have to hang their heads in shame, that his father's embarrassing actions were overshadowed by his own more heroic ones.

"Why now?" she asked softly, almost gently, when he would have sworn the woman didn't possess an ounce of tenderness. "Why your interest in finding the culprits now?"

He tossed back his scotch before admitting, "I've been trying to find them from the beginning."

As a result of the dangers involved in his pursuit, he'd been forced to abandon his younger brother and sister, occasionally giving them money when he secured some but for the most part leaving them to fend for themselves. Althea had worked—*worked*—in a tavern, for God's sake. Until she'd crossed paths with Benedict Trewlove, and he'd offered her other employment. Eventually she'd married him, and from what Marcus had been able to gather, was blissfully happy. Before she was under the protection of Trewlove, Griff had lived with their sister, overseeing her well-being, and toiling on the docks. But once free of his responsibility to her, Griff had joined Marcus, for a short time, in his endeavors. However, his brother was not as suited to the shadows, nor did he have the patience for a resolution that was so slow in coming. He'd left to pursue his own quest and was now a club owner and husband. While Griff was willing to finance his brother's obsession, Marcus couldn't bring himself to take more than had already been given. Returning to the chair, he set his empty glass on the delicate table beside it, waiting until she'd once more lowered herself. "Did Father ever mention Lucifer?"

"As in the devil?"

"Possibly." He heaved a great sigh, rife with frustration. "I don't know. A man, a woman, a place, a thing. It's a name that crops up from time to time."

"In what manner? Where have you searched?"

He shouldn't confide in her, but where was the harm, especially if he could unlock in her mind something his father might have told her? "There had to be others involved. Father didn't have the mental acuity for strategizing. He was a follower, not a leader. Therefore, it is possible the plotters are still preparing to strike. With that in mind, I've been striving to hear whispers of another attempt. I began by spying on my father's friends among the aristocracy. No joy to be found there.

It occurred to me that if another noble is involved, he wouldn't do the deed himself, but would hire someone with the skills, a dodgy background, and other misdeeds in his past. I've made my way through the darker corners of London, even letting it be known the Wolf was open to selling his services in hopes the schemers might hire me."

She raised a finely arched auburn eyebrow. "The Wolf?"

"An homage to the title that should have come to me." The Duke of Wolfford. Only later did he realize the moniker didn't suit. Wolves traveled in packs, were part of a group, a family—while he prowled and hunted alone. "I suspect I came close to discovering something. I had to submerge myself deeper into the shadows to avoid those who wished to end my ability to breathe."

Most women might have gasped or paled or appeared horrified, but she merely sipped her scotch, her gaze level. "You were attacked?"

"Multiple times."

"Yet here you are."

"Here I am." He'd left London for a while. He'd only recently let Griff know he'd returned, but he'd never shared the details of what he was doing with Althea. Although her husband knew the darker parts of London as well, Trewlove had more pressing matters to attend to these days as he'd recently discovered *he* was heir to a dukedom.

"You must be very skilled at evading danger."

"I've learned a few things, but not enough. Lucifer. Does the name mean anything to you?"

"I'm afraid not."

"You can think of nothing that my father might have uttered when lost in the throes of passion?"

"Fucking me usually leaves men quite speechless."

He grimaced at her crudity, but he'd set the combative tone for this meeting, and he was rather regretting that he'd taken that tack. "I deserve that."

"Yes, you do. I have a tendency to give men what they deserve."

A small smile played at the corner of her lips indicating she was referring to pleasure as well as comeuppance. He had the absurd thought that he wished he'd discovered her before his father had.

"I'm sorry I can't be of help," she said, regret lacing her words.

"Well, it *has* been more than a year . . . perhaps if I'd come sooner."

"Why didn't you?"

Because I couldn't stand the thought or sight of you. "I'd hoped to spare you the bother."

He came to his feet, and she followed suit, so gracefully. At some point in her life, she'd been well tutored. "I apologize for disturbing your evening."

"I had nothing pressing on my schedule. Should I recall something that might offer some assistance, where would I find you?"

"You shan't. But leave a message with my brother at the Fair Ladies' and Spare Gentlemen's Club." Griff owned the establishment where unmarried people sought companionship. "He'll see that I get it."

"Ah, yes, I've heard rumors about the Fair and Spare. It's quite the scandalous place from what I understand. Is he working with you then?"

"No, but he knows how to get in touch." A lamp in an upstairs window signaled when Griff placed a message behind a loose brick in the facade at the rear of the club. "I shall see myself out. Good night."

"I'll walk you to the door."

"Not necessary."

"What sort of hostess would I be if I left you to simply wander off?"

He was tempted to ask how she'd met his father, how they'd come to be, why she'd gone with an old man—but based upon how she lived, his father had done well by her, or someone had. Did she have a lover now? A woman such as she wouldn't go long without a protector. Before he could indulge his curiosity, he strode for the door. She easily kept pace with him. The advantage of a woman with long legs, and he fought not to envision them wrapped tightly around his hips. It angered him that he should be so drawn to the vixen.

He opened the door, crossed onto the landing, and when he would have pulled the door shut, he discovered she'd wedged herself into the opening.

"Take care of yourself, Marcus Stanwick," she said quietly, and yet, it still sounded like a command.

He wondered where she gained her confidence, wished some other reason had brought him to her, one that would allow for all the exploring of her in which he wished to indulge. He gave a curt nod before jaunting down the steps, through the small wrought iron gate, and into the night.

HAVING RETURNED TO her chair by the fireplace in the parlor, Esme Lancaster was soon joined by more pleasant company: Laddie, her black-and-white cocker spaniel. After bringing her companion to her lap, she allowed her thoughts the luxury of contemplating her recent guest.

Marcus Stanwick was certainly more handsome than his father. His midnight-black hair had been recently trimmed. His eyes were a deep blue but when he'd come close to her with a fury that caused them to burn an even deeper hue, she'd realized that within the irises were the tiniest streaks of gray. They'd made him more intriguing than he should have been. She liked that she had to tip her head up slightly to meet and hold his gaze. Unlike his father, he had yet to go to fat, although she suspected he might never follow that route. In spite of the fact that his clothing didn't fit him particularly well, he was a fine specimen of toned muscle and brawn. He'd certainly not been idle since being tossed onto the streets.

It was also obvious that he loathed her, not that she blamed him. Her association with his father had painted her as a scarlet woman, and it had been a role she'd had no choice except to embrace. She'd gone to a great deal of bother to ingratiate herself to the duke, to intrigue him, and ensure he wanted to spend time in her company. Much to her chagrin, however, their relationship had been on public display for much of the time they were together, which had been a little over two months. Most married men preferred to keep their liaisons secret, but for some reason, Wolf-ford had felt a need to boast. Perhaps because he'd been nearing the ripe old age of sixty and wanted it known that he still had it within him to attract the attention of a much younger woman. He'd squired her around London as though he didn't have a wife and grown children to embarrass. His behavior had always baffled her, but because of it, his elder son had now made an appearance at her door. She had guessed at his preference for scotch, had seen the flash of irritation cross his features, and known she'd gotten it right. She wondered what else regarding him she might guess correctly if given the opportunity. Figuring things out about people was one of her strong suits, had been ever since she was a child.

Her mother had spent a good bit of time whipping Satan out of her when she was a wee one, although she'd never fully understood what she'd done to deserve the punishment. She'd begun to suspect it was the manner in which she struggled to make sense of the world, the way she focused intently on anything or anyone she found puzzling until she was able to fit what she knew into some semblance of order that put all her questions to rest. A vicar who visited her mother far too often when Esme's father was away; a sweets shop owner who paid far more attention to boys than girls; an inordinate number of children in the village who so closely resembled the eldest son who lived in the large manor house on the hill.

From her father she'd learned to be observant. Whenever he wasn't off fighting for queen and country, he would take her on strolls and periodically question her about their surroundings. What color was the frock worn by the blond-haired girl with the ringlets who'd just gone into the bakery with her mother? How many lads were crouched and playing marbles in the alleyway they'd passed a minute ago? Once, when she was eight, he'd taken her into a toy shop in London to purchase her a doll. She'd been mesmerized by all the choices, had finally found the porcelain one she wanted more than she wanted to breathe—when her father had suddenly knelt beside her and said, "The shop is on fire. People were crowding through the door, and now they are stuck. How do we get out?"

They weren't in danger. There were no flames, but his urgency had her heart racing. She was expected to know the answer, didn't want to disappoint him. He was one of Britain's heroes, but more importantly, he was hers. "Through a window. And if it won't open, we'll throw something at it to break the glass, so we can climb out."

"What if we get cut?"

"Better than getting burned to death."

With a grin, he'd rubbed her head. "So which dolly would you like to have?"

The doll wearing a fancy pink frock and large bonnet adorned with flowers had gone everywhere with her through the years and now sat on a corner of her vanity. It served as a reminder to always have an escape plan in case danger arrived. And danger had arrived, in the form of Marcus Stanwick. Yet the very last thing she'd been thinking about while he was in her parlor was escaping.

Light footsteps sounded just before her butler stepped into the room and hovered slightly beyond the threshold. "I lost him."

"How far did he allow you to follow him?"

"He didn't *allow* it."

"Without a doubt he did, Brewster, or you'd have not lost him when he was of a mind to end the farce that he didn't know you were about."

Her *assistant* more than butler was extremely skilled at tracking but had never been particularly talented at hiding his disgruntlement when she had the right of a situation at hand. "Only a couple of miles or so. Moved at a bloody quick pace, though. Fair wore me out. I caught a hansom back, after he disappeared."

"Hmm. Farther than I would have thought." Although he may have done it out of spite. "I don't suppose he left you with an impression as to where he was going."

"He seemed to do a lot of circling and backtracking. For a while there, I thought he was lost."

A man such as Marcus Stanwick never became lost. She'd wager all she owned on that.

"What are you going to do about him?" Brewster asked.

"I haven't decided."

But she was fairly certain they'd not seen the last of each other.

CHAPTER 2

"Marcus Stanwick paid me a visit last night."

"Why?" The disembodied voice came from the deepest shadows in the farthest corner of the dimly lit area. It was a game he played, as though not being seen made him more formidable or menacing. She suspected it had something to do with the fact that the top of his head barely reached her shoulder. Or perhaps it was the hunch of his back. Men could be such sensitive creatures. Especially this one. He went by many names, but she referred to him as O.

"He wished to know if his father had ever confided in me regarding the planned assassination, if I might know some information that could help him track down those involved in the plot."

"What did you tell him?"

"That I knew nothing."

"Good. We don't need him mucking up our plans."

"It may be a bit late for that. He asked if I was familiar with Lucifer."

"Devil take him." In his agitation, he came partially into the wavering light provided by a half-dozen torches nestled in iron sconces on the stone walls. The alcove, one of many in a network of tunnels beneath the city, had few amenities but hidden away as it was lent itself well to clandestine endeavors, especially those that involved nefarious plots to end the reign of a queen. "What did you tell him?"

She sighed with impatience at his constantly questioning that to which he should already know the answer. They were a few months shy of having worked together for two years. By now he should fully comprehend that she had the wherewithal to know what she was doing. "What do you think I told him? Nothing."

"And he believed you?"

"Why would he not?"

His smile was the sort that might make a more delicate flower's skin crawl. But she was immune to that sort of thing. She had no feelings whatsoever. The *heartless harlot* they called her—if they bothered to call her anything at all, those who thought themselves above her in station. Although she'd certainly *felt* something troubling, a reawakening of aspects to her she'd thought long dead, as she'd sat across from Marcus Stanwick.

"I wonder if it might be to our advantage for me to get a little closer to him," she said as flatly as possible, even though the mere thought of seeing Stanwick again caused her heart to beat a little harder and her stomach to quiver as though it was suddenly home to an assembly of acrobats, tumbling and jumping and messing about. "Determine all that he does know or suspect."

"He's unimportant and we're closer than ever to accomplishing our goal." He walked to a table that had probably seen two hundred years, and it wobbled as he lifted something off it. "There is to be an . . . *affair* at Lord Podmore's Wednesday next. I've secured you an invitation. No names will be asked. Everyone will be wearing a mask. It is our hope that you will find the opportunity to search his study for what we seek."

"If it is there, I will find it." She should leave matters as they were, should leave him where he stood, but couldn't shake off the sense that Marcus Stanwick might prove to be a danger by interfering with their plans. "Stanwick believes the plot to assassinate Victoria is still afoot."

That sly grin again. "We shall soon prove him correct."

CHAPTER 3

$\mathcal{I}$T WASN'T OFTEN that Esme disobeyed orders, but in the two nights that had passed since Stanwick invaded her home—her peace—she'd been unable to rid herself of thoughts of him. He possessed a hunger, a way of prowling about like a caged animal waiting for the moment when it could break free of its constraints—and God help anyone in his path once he gained his freedom.

Her gut told her that O had the wrong of it. Stanwick might provide some answers. She'd allowed him to interrogate her, while she'd questioned him little. Truth be told, she was now standing across the street from the Fair and Spare because she'd come to realize that the man had somehow managed to steal her wits not two minutes after she'd greeted him in her parlor. With his commanding presence or his devilishly handsome features or the depth of his loneliness, one that she'd recognized only because it mirrored her own. She couldn't afford to become close to anyone, to let so much as a solitary person mean anything at all to her. Danger was her stock-in-trade.

However, it wouldn't limit itself to her but would reach out with deadly tentacles to destroy anyone for whom she had a care. Therefore, it had been years since she'd known the warmth of a gentle touch, since she'd enclosed her heart in ice and her soul had evolved into little more than a shell that allowed her to do what was demanded of her without remorse or regret. She was like a cog in a machine at a factory—she had a single purpose and saw to it with an intense focus until nothing else mattered.

Marcus Stanwick, however, was a distraction. She needed to know the reason, needed to understand what it was her survival instincts were striving to tell her.

After crossing the street, she marched up the steps to the broad, towering man who barred entrance. She imagined him hefting a broadsword while dressed in the pelts of animals he'd slain. Habit had her calculating how she would take him down if need be. "Let me pass."

"Ye gots to show me yer membership card."

"I don't have one."

"Ye wants to be a member then."

"No." She had no use for a place where people gathered to enjoy each other's company. She arched a brow. "I want in."

He furrowed his brow. "I can only let in members and them wot's want to be."

"I need to have a word with Mr. Stanwick."

"'Bout membership?"

She gave him a hard glare that promised retribution.

Finally, he gave a curt nod. "Righto. Follow me."

Opening the door, he led her inside, and she was immediately struck by the gaiety echoing from rooms along the hallway and up the stairs. The people she could see were smiling and laughing, having a jolly good time. She couldn't recall the last occasion when she'd smiled or laughed. The man who probably seemed a giant to most but simply large to her escorted her to their right and into a grand chamber with an enormous crystal chandelier and a woman sitting at a large desk. Near the window a man occupied a smaller desk. She immediately took a liking to Griffith Stanwick for ensuring this room was dominated by a female.

"Gertie, she wants a word with Mr. Stanwick," the bruiser said.

Standing, Gertie gave her a thorough examination. "Right then. Wait here."

While she walked out, the guardian of this establishment braced his feet apart and crossed his arms over his massive chest. Was he open to being hired by someone else? Herself, for instance?

She rather doubted it. The gentleman by the window had taken pencil in hand and based upon his movements was busily sketching.

She glanced around. Although austere, the room had an elegance to it. She'd expected that a place where people came to fornicate would appear tawdry, but Stanwick had taken measures to ensure people could walk out of here without their faces turning red in shame. She knew a great deal about what it was to walk in shame, mortification thrust upon her by those who had judged her a sinner before she was one, judged her when, until those long-ago horrendous few weeks of her youth, her worst offense had been snitching a biscuit from the tin when the cook wasn't looking.

After circling the room, her gaze returned to where it had begun: the man at the small desk. He smiled tenderly, almost gently, and extended a card toward her. "Here you are."

Ensuring her shoulders were pulled back, her posture intimidating, she approached and took his offering. It wasn't a sketch of her face . . . and yet it was. Her features were all sharp angles, brittle—not by nature's hand but by her own unwillingness to reveal a modicum of softness. He'd drawn the facade but had somehow managed to capture what lay beneath it. She nearly wept because there was only the barest hint of the trusting girl she'd once been, the one who had longed for love and acceptance. "What am I to do with this?"

"Keep it." He picked up another piece of parchment. "I draw the likeness of the members on their membership card so they're able to enter more quickly and can't loan it to someone who hasn't a membership."

Turning over the card, she saw that the other side had lines for inputting pertinent information such as name, age, and dues expiration. Clever. "Your talents are wasted here."

"I'll take that as a compliment."

"I do not compliment. I speak but the truth."

"Few would pay me as well as Mr. Stanwick does for so simple a talent."

"It's not a simple talent. You see what escapes the notice of most."

"But not yours."

"No, not mine." Lives were put at risk if she didn't notice everything.

"You wished to have a word, Miss—"

She quickly spun around to face Griffith Stanwick. He was blond, fairer than his brother but he possessed the same shade of eyes.

"—my father's *strumpet*."

The disgust woven through the last word was no doubt shared by Marcus Stanwick as well and accounted for his not coming to her sooner. Opening her reticule, she placed inside the card the artist had given her and removed a small envelope, sealed with purple wax. "I need you to see this delivered to your brother."

He dropped his gaze to the thick vellum before lifting it to hers. "For what purpose?"

"If I wished you to know that information, I

wouldn't have gone to the bother of writing it out and sealing it."

"You don't think I have the means to open the letter?"

She took a step nearer until their breaths fairly collided. "I don't think Marcus would want you to know and would be most disappointed in you for making his private business your own."

"How private?"

"That is between him and me, but he offered assurance you could be trusted with my missive should I have a need. I do hope you won't make a liar out of him."

He narrowed his eyes. "You've spoken with him?"

She merely arched a brow.

"When?"

"Two nights ago."

With a hardened glare, he snatched the correspondence from her. "I'll see he gets it. Unopened."

She gave a half nod. "Good evening then, Mr. Stanwick." She edged past him—

"You made a fool of my mother."

His harsh words caused her to stop in her tracks and glance over her shoulder. "On the contrary. I believe that honor goes to your father. He was the one to brag about his conquest of me. I prefer discretion when it comes to such affairs." She should leave it at that but couldn't quite bring herself to do so. "For what it is worth, however, which I suspect is very little, it was not my intention to bring any hurt to your family. I believed my relationship with your father would remain a secret, known only to us."

His jaw tightened. "That doesn't excuse what you did."

"No, I suppose it doesn't."

"I'll not see you ruin my brother."

Such conviction, such devotion, such . . . love. For a few brief seconds, she envied Marcus Stanwick. "He's already lost everything, Mr. Stanwick. What worse harm exists for me to inflict upon him?"

Esme knew what it was to lose everything. Lying on her bed, with the fingers of one hand buried in Laddie's fur, the other holding the drawing of her face, she wondered if Marcus Stanwick had seen her as clearly as the artist had. She was extremely bothered by the hope springing within her that perhaps he might have. He seemed an intuitive sort.

She was counting on that intuition when it came to the missive for him that she'd delivered. The thought of him reading and deciphering it sent a thrill through her. The possibility of seeing him again, matching wits with him, filled her with excitement. She felt as though she'd merely been existing before she walked into her parlor and saw him standing there. He'd made her feel as though she'd been struck by lightning and re-animated, much like Frankenstein's creation.

She wondered how the artist might have drawn

her face at that moment, when her gaze had first collided with Marcus Stanwick's. She was probably being very foolish to initiate contact. But she welcomed the opportunity to outwit him and gain what she needed.

CHAPTER 4

$\mathcal{I}$T WAS LATE, the establishment closed, when the light appeared in an upper window, one that was part of Griff's private rooms. Marcus's chest swelled with his triumphant satisfaction. It had been only two nights since he'd seen her. Esme. Yet already she was beckoning him.

For a while each night since leaving her, he'd stood in the mews outside his brother's place of business hoping—no, not hoping, merely checking—to see if curiosity would get the better of her, if she would remember something or at least wish to meet with him again. He'd regretted not lingering longer in her presence, not questioning her further, delving into her origins, her past . . . her present. He'd considered watching her abode, but if she truly knew nothing, his time was better spent elsewhere.

Yet no matter how deep and dark the alleys he

roamed, how dangerous his surroundings, how wicked those he encountered, the Ice Princess haunted him. It was how he'd come to think of her. Cold and calculating. He suspected she'd gathered as much information from him as he had from her.

He shouldn't be intrigued by her and yet he was. A disappointment to himself.

Looking around the mews, ensuring he was quite alone, he crossed over to the building, removed the loose brick, slipped his fingers inside the vacant slot that had housed it, and discovered nothing within. His brow furrowed.

"Care to explain why you're spending time in the company of Father's tart?"

He didn't give a start at his brother's voice, didn't give any reaction at all to the words. Simply slowly returned to its place the means by which Griff passed him messages. If he had anything for Griff, he merely picked the lock, went inside, and left it on his desk. "You and I are not supposed to meet."

"We're not to fuck Father's whore either."

He spun around. "I'm not. I wouldn't. Even the thought of touching her turns my stomach." Although the thought of *not* touching her created a vivid sense of loss that he'd rather not examine, but it hovered at the edge of temptation.

"Then why is she bringing me a message for you?"

The desperation with which he wanted it in his hands, his eyes upon her words, astounded him. Not because they might help him, but because she'd penned them. Fighting back the urge to demand the letter be given to him, he leaned against the wall and folded his arms over his chest. "I visited her, yes. I thought perhaps Father might have inadvertently revealed something to her. But she could think of nothing although perhaps something came to mind after I departed."

"She's more beautiful than I recalled."

At one point or another, each of the duke's children had caught sight of his mistress. "I hadn't noticed."

"Liar."

His brother had the right of it. A man buried six feet under would notice. "You mentioned she brought me a message. Where the devil is it?"

Griff held out an envelope so pristine white as to be visible and a stark contrast to the night as it caught light from the nearby windows and far-off streetlamps. Exhibiting extreme restraint, Marcus did not snatch it from his brother's fingers and tear into it in order to see what she'd written. Casually, as though not filled with immense anticipation, he took it and tucked it into a pocket inside his jacket. "So how are you?"

Griff studied him for several heartbeats. "Happy, if you can believe it. I no longer miss the old life."

"Good. What I'm doing won't return it to you."

"Then why not give up the quest?"

He couldn't put it into exact words. "Do you remember what it was like to be dragged from our beds in the middle of the night? With no warning or explanation? Those two weeks rotting in the Tower? Treated like traitors, interrogated every day? The fear, the confusion? The shame of it? Then after we were released, the agony of watching Mother withering away in mortification at her husband's betrayal of his country, until she lost all will to live and died shortly after he was hanged? Helpless to stop the immense tide that was taking us all under until we could scarcely breathe, were on the verge of drowning? I want to know the why of it. What did he think he would gain that was worth the risk of losing everything our forebears had accomplished? Who convinced him to take that path?"

"Perhaps his mistress."

Unexpectedly, he felt as though he'd been struck with a battering ram to the chest and had a strong need to defend the one woman whom he'd long loathed. "They arrested her as well."

"Doesn't mean she wasn't involved." He shook his head. "She seemed a rather cold fish to me. I can't imagine why she appealed to Father."

"A few minutes ago, you were complimenting her visage."

"I've admired beautiful marble statues. Doesn't mean I want to fuck one. I prefer warmth in my bed."

"Perhaps I'll be able to decipher more regarding her appeal to him when I've read her missive."

"I very much doubt that."

The hairs on the back of his neck rose, and he experienced a moment of irrational anger. "You read it?"

"What there was to read."

He had an urge to slam his brother against the wall for intruding on something he considered private, personal. What the devil was wrong with him? Griff had saved his life, had killed a fellow who had sought to put an end to Marcus's ability to breathe. He had earned the right to any information Marcus uncovered. "Spare me the suspense. What did she have to say?"

"Very little. The only thing she wrote was an *E*. I suppose that means something?"

A wide grin formed, the movement of his mouth strangely odd-feeling, as though unaccustomed to those muscles being used. "It means she didn't trust you."

He was also fairly certain she wished a meeting.

MARCUS HAD CONSIDERED slipping into her residence, into her bedchamber one evening. But he wasn't convinced she didn't have a lover and he had no desire to witness her fornicating with another. Griff might believe her to be cold in bed, but Marcus suspected when it came to fiery passion she could compete with a volcano. Perhaps it was only his own desire shading the way he viewed her. If she was all ice at all times, he had an urge to see her melted, to be the one causing the frigidness to thaw.

Then he'd curse because his father had gone before him, and he had no yearning to furrow what his father had plowed. In the end, he'd decided on

arranging a meeting in neutral territory and had
paid a street urchin a shilling to deliver his missive:
The Mermaid and Unicorn at 10 o'clock tonight.

He expected she'd have the wherewithal to
find it. She proved him correct. Sitting at the back
of the tavern in Whitechapel, he watched her
walk in one minute before the designated hour in
a simple dark blue frock that left nothing of any
interest exposed. The collar rose up to her chin,
the sleeves ran down to her wrists where dark
gloves continued on to the tips of her fingers.
Her hair was a simpler style, lacking in pearls
or any adornment at all. Along with her reticule,
she carried an umbrella. It certainly hadn't felt or
smelled as though rain was in the air, but then
in London one could never be completely certain
that it wasn't lurking about.

Her gaze immediately went to the rear of
the tavern as though she'd instinctually known
where she'd find him. She began wending her
way among the tables crowded with boisterous
customers enjoying a pint. One fellow, well in
his cups, reached out to her. She stopped, her
glare causing him to straighten and tuck the of-
fending hand beneath his armpit. With a nod,
she carried on.

He didn't want to admire her for the impression she gave that she'd tolerate no nonsense
whatsoever when it came to her person. Was she
that commanding in bed? Had she ordered his father about?

For any other woman, he would have stood as

she approached, but she didn't deserve the courtesy, and so he would stay lounging back—

Ah, sod it. She'd contacted him, had answered his summons. Shoving back his chair, he came to his feet. "You had no trouble finding the place, it seems."

She glanced around. "An establishment owned by a Trewlove? I sincerely doubt there is a person in London who doesn't know every business owned by a member of that infamous family. Did you think to shock me?"

"No. This tavern carries the best spirits." Before he'd given it much thought, he was pulling out the chair for her, inhaling her rose fragrance, and enjoying the grace with which she lowered herself. He returned to his place, mesmerized as she set her reticule and umbrella on the table before slowly removing her gloves, tugging one finger at a time until a sliver of pale skin at her wrist became visible, inviting a man to press a kiss to the pulse thrumming there. Did she remove all her clothing as slowly, provocatively?

What the devil was wrong with him? It was only a hand, then two. Long fingers, well-manicured, not a blemish or callus in sight.

"I'll have a brandy," she said, and it was only then that he realized the barmaid had approached.

He pointed to his tumbler. "Another scotch, Polly."

"Aye, sir." She gave him a saucy wink before scurrying off.

"Come here often, do you?" Esme asked.

"No, but when I first arrived, she introduced herself, was quite flirtatious actually, until I mentioned I was waiting for someone."

"You were so confident I'd come?"

"You were the one who requested a meeting."

"I wasn't certain you'd understand my message."

"Are you always so careful not to give away anything?"

"My experience with your father has made me a frightfully suspicious and more cautious wench."

He wished his sire didn't have to constantly intrude and wasn't the reason they were here. "You thought of something."

Polly returned and set their drinks before them. Marcus handed over the coins. "Keep the extra for yourself."

She bobbed a quick curtsy. "Thank you, sir." Then she was dashing off to see to someone else.

Esme took a sip of her brandy, licked her lips. "Not really, no."

Fascinated with watching as the pink tip of her tongue journeyed over her lush mouth, he needed a moment to realize she was responding to his earlier comment. "Then why the missive?"

"It occurred to me that we didn't have the best of beginnings. Perhaps if you shared a bit more of what you've uncovered thus far, it might trigger a memory of something of import. Your father's actions put us both through a trial of sorts—well, it put your entire family through hell. I would like to assist you if I can."

"Why do I have the feeling there's more to it than that?"

"Not a very trusting fellow, are you?" He arched a brow. "I don't suppose I can blame you for that. I'm not very trusting myself."

"So I determined when you wrote only your first initial on the missive."

Her lips moved in a toying, teasing manner. "Did your brother open the letter?"

He merely nodded.

"What a naughty fellow."

Somehow, she made it sound like a compliment, a characteristic she admired, and he was tempted to show her exactly how naughty he could be. He didn't like remembering a time when he had teased, when he'd been adept at enjoying all the pleasurable pursuits that life had to offer. When he wasn't filled with such loathing, a great deal of it directed toward faceless men who had lured his father toward his end. "I might say the same of your butler. He followed me when I left you."

"Brewster is a protective chap and didn't trust you. You gave him a time of it, didn't you? I rather suspect you prolonged his misery, leading him hither and yon like a wayward child."

He didn't much like how it pleased him that she'd known exactly what he'd done. He'd had a jolly good time doing it, too. "Is it possible my father might have mentioned something to him?"

"Hardly. Like most of the nobility he paid scant attention to servants, certainly wouldn't have confided in one. How many have you told your deepest secrets?"

She always spoke directly, and yet she'd managed to thread an undercurrent of disappointment in the ones just uttered. As though she knew he'd once viewed servants in the same manner he did a pair of well-made boots: to serve him. Not one of his finer qualities. He'd certainly never take household staff for granted again, should he ever be in a position to offer employment. "It stands to reason then that he wouldn't have confided in you."

"I never would have allowed myself to be viewed as someone to only cater to his whims. I demand respect and equal footing from those who associate with me."

"Will you be having another?" Polly had arrived again.

"Yes," Esme said. "One for each of us."

After the barmaid left, Esme opened her reticule.

"I'll pay," he said, reaching into a pocket.

She gave him a commanding smile that fairly froze him in his place. "As I said, equal footing. My coins will be used this time." A pocket watch was removed and set aside before she reached farther into her purse.

"You strike me as being too elegant for a pocket watch, especially one that appears to be made of nickel." Gold or silver, perhaps, but not something as cheap as nickel.

She looked up at him, over at the watch, closed her fingers around it, and slipped it back home before setting coins where it had been. "It was my father's. I carry it with me for sentimental reasons."

He had no idea what had happened to his father's. Perhaps he'd used it to bribe a jailor for a better cut of meat or as payment for the hangman. Or maybe it had simply been stolen by a guard.

Polly returned with their drinks. Offering another quick bob, she took the coins Esme handed her.

"What was your father's occupation?" He didn't know why he bloody well cared but was curious regarding what had placed her on the path toward becoming a man's plaything.

"Village drunkard." Lifting her snifter, she tipped it toward him before taking a slow swallow. "The watch serves to remind me of my origins and how I never wish to return to them. Whereas I suspect you would very much like to return to yours. Hence your quest."

"It's not going to return anything to me, except honor." But with his demonstration of loyalty to the Crown as a stepping-stone, he could secure success elsewhere and might even regain some respect among the nobility.

"Your father's planning to murder his sovereign took you completely unaware?"

He wasn't pleased by the doubt reflected in her tone, as though she suspected he had known something was afoot and had either ignored it or was complicit in it. "We weren't particularly close. He did grumble from time to time because Victoria became such a recluse following Albert's death, and he often complained that, in his opinion, she wasn't giving the country the attention it deserved, but I can't countenance that he considered killing her to be the solution."

She seemed to ponder his answer, chewing it over, before giving a little nod. "He did once tell me that he didn't believe a woman should sit upon the throne, but I can't imagine he wanted Bertie lounging upon it. The Prince of Wales seems more interested in fun than rule."

"None of it makes sense. She's provided an entire line of heirs. Did they intend to kill them all?"

She paused, her glass halfway to her lips. "That would have been quite the undertaking. Or perhaps someone controls Bertie. Or maybe they merely wish to sow chaos for something more nefarious. To rid the country of a monarchy altogether? To replace it with a dictatorship?"

He'd not expected her to have given it so much contemplation, but she'd probably had little else to do while awaiting her release from Newgate. "You agree then he wasn't working alone?"

"As you said the other night, he wasn't particularly clever."

"He was loyal, however. If there were others, I don't think he gave them up."

"He's fortunate they no longer use the rack. He would often leave me to go to a meeting, although he never told me with whom or where or what it entailed."

"You didn't send your butler to follow him?"

"To be honest, I didn't care enough to go to the bother."

He wasn't going to interpret her sentiment to mean she did care about his goings. "But you had him follow me."

"You're more intriguing. By your clothing, I'd say you've had a rough time of it, but I'd wager that's by choice. You're well educated. You can find employment in any number of occupations and yet you are searching for what you may never find. It seems a waste of your talents."

"You know nothing at all about my talents."

OH, HE HAD the wrong of it there.

Esme had learned at an early age how to judge a situation. When her mother was so melancholy that a wrong word would set her to tears. When she could be enticed to frolic among the bluebells. When the vicar would be raining down hell and brimstone in his sermon. When he would talk gently of lambs and children.

So she did indeed know a good bit about Marcus Stanwick's talents. He was skilled at evading followers, could disappear into the mist before the person trailing him knew the mist had even arrived. In spite of his clothing, he reflected a mien that matched his surroundings and allowed him to blend in seamlessly. In her parlor, he'd been the son of a duke, arrogant and proud. Within this establishment, he would be mistaken for a laborer as he did nothing to draw attention to himself.

Yet he was watchful, his eyes sharp and alert, and anyone with half an ounce of intelligence would know he was not one to be trifled with.

He also possessed a tactile nature. If he wasn't stroking his glass with a long blunt-tipped finger, he was rubbing his bristly jaw or using his thumb to draw a non-ending circle around a knothole in the scarred wood of the table. She fought not to imagine him stroking her nape, rubbing her shoulders, drawing circles around her nipples.

And he savored. He didn't toss back his scotch but sipped slowly and allowed it to wander for a time along his tongue. She knew because she watched his throat just above his perfectly knotted neckcloth to determine how long he went before swallowing. She couldn't help but think he'd take the time to savor a kiss as thoroughly, was tempted to test her theory. It had been a good long while since she'd been tempted by any man to do anything other than what was required of her. He was temptation, dark temptation, wicked temptation. In the end, probably a devastating temptation, one that could fracture hearts, if a lady had a heart to fracture.

Perhaps O had been correct, and her coming here was a fool's errand. Yet, she couldn't seem to regret it. "Do you think anyone still cares what your father did?"

"I care."

Resolute, she'd give him that. "Your father often mentioned a Lord Podmore. It seemed they were firm friends. Could he have been involved?"

"Podmore?"

"Do you not know him?"

"I know the viscount. I can't see Father having much in common with him. The man seems to have an interest only in plotting wild escapades."

"Conspiracy makes for strange bedfellows, I suppose."

"Did Father ever take you to one of Podmore's affairs?"

"No. Perhaps because he knew it wouldn't be to my taste."

"What did he say about him?"

"Only that he was off to see him. Has his name come up during your quest?"

He slowly shook his head. That was disappointing. She'd hoped to garner some information before she attended that particular lord's latest affair. "It probably means nothing then."

She finished off her brandy. "I'm sorry I couldn't have been of more help."

He narrowed his eyes. "You went to all that bother to arrange this meeting to toss out one name? You could have provided that information in a missive." Placing his elbows on the table, he leaned forward until she could see the silver in the blue of his eyes. "Why did you want to see me?"

She licked her lips, then cursed herself for doing so when his eyes darkened with desire. It stemmed from her youth when she would become nervous, sometimes going so far as not to lick but to gnaw until she drew blood. "I just thought the name might prove helpful." And perhaps he might do some investigating, learn of the upcoming affair, and attend to determine if he could garner any information. Although for the life of her, she didn't know why she wanted him there. His presence would simply interfere with her task.

He came half an inch closer, and yet given the manner with which her heart thudded, he might as well have touched his nose to hers. "Liar. What did you hope to gain?"

"To put my past with your father to bed."

She shouldn't have mentioned that particular piece of furniture because now his eyes smoldered.

"My father . . . or me?" he asked in a silky voice as though they were already locked together, her arms wrapped around those broad shoulders, her legs around those narrow hips as he pounded into her. "Perhaps you want to put me in your bed."

Another lick of her lips. A hard swallow.

"You're drawn to me," he said huskily, and she imagined that rough voice whispering naughty words into her ear.

"Don't be ridiculous." Did she have to sound so damned breathless as though she'd just spent the last of the air in her lungs crying out his name in ecstasy?

"Let me be absolutely clear, Ice Princess. I would never partake of my father's leavings."

As HER CARRIAGE rumbled through the streets, Esme was disappointed that she'd finished off her brandy before he'd uttered his horrid and ugly words. She'd have taken immense pleasure in tossing *her leavings* in his darkly handsome face. Instead, she'd laughed caustically and said, "How arrogant you are to think you appeal to me in the least."

When he appealed to her on far too many levels to count. Then she'd stood, bid him *adieu*, and with her head held so high she was bound to have an aching neck come morning, she'd stormed from the establishment.

Why had his words smarted? Why did his opinion matter? She was accustomed to not feeling, to never experiencing remorse, regret, or doubt. Dear Lord, she'd gotten something in her eye. Both of them as a matter of fact because they each stung. How careless of her.

Her upset was a result of the ordeal she'd endured for the past year, that was all. The aftermath of Wolfford's deception. She vaguely wondered how Marcus Stanwick would react if he knew the truth of things, of how it had truly been between her and his father. Probably wouldn't care in the least. She was a fool to find herself attracted to him. It had been a good long while since she'd been a fool.

The carriage came to a stop. A footman handed her down. She strode into her residence, passed off her reticule and umbrella to the waiting butler, and then held out her arms, welcoming Laddie as he leapt into them. She hugged him tightly. Unconditional love. Would that people gave it as freely.

"Did you learn anything of significance?" Brewster asked.

"He knew you were following him. He questioned me about it." She wandered into the front parlor, set Laddie in a chair, went to the sideboard of decanters where she poured two brandies, and offered one to her most trusted ally—which meant she trusted him just a hair.

"Blast him," Brewster muttered before sipping. "Anything else?"

"Not really." She lowered herself to the chair. He hadn't reacted to the name Podmore so she suspected the viscount might not be as involved as O thought. She'd probably find nothing at all within his residence. "He wasn't as tidy."

She'd wager he'd not taken a razor to his face since the night he'd come here. His unkempt state was rather appealing, made him appear more rugged and dangerous. Or perhaps that was a result of his disgust for her.

"What are you thinking?" Brewster asked.

She released a long, slow, drawn-out sigh. "That I'm ready for this matter to be done with."

CHAPTER 5

$\mathcal{I}$T WAS A blasted orgy. The affair at Podmore's.
Marcus had been able to slip in through a door
that led into the gardens instead of coming
through the front where he would have had to
show an invitation he didn't possess.

After making some discreet inquiries of the
servants beforehand, he'd known people would
be wearing masks, so he'd be unidentifiable,
could move about with a measure of anonymity.
However, in addition to the mask, he'd expected
people to wear clothing. Especially after he'd
gone to the bother of borrowing evening attire
from his brother. It was a slightly tight fit, not that
anyone was going to notice as they were too busy
shedding their own apparel.

In all honesty, most were not nude, not completely anyway. A couple of ladies were gallivanting about in gossamer sheaths as though they

were wood nymphs. Three men had thrown in-
hibition and their clothing to the wind and were
chasing after them.

Marcus was no prude but certainly preferred
privacy in his intimate encounters with women.
One clad creature, untamed moon-shaded hair
flowing around her, came up to him and trailed a
slender hand along his chest.

"I'm Aphrodite. Whom might you be?" Her
voice was soft and refined. Was she of the nobility? With the domino hiding three-quarters of her
face, he couldn't be sure if he'd known her in his
previous life.

"Zeus."

She laughed, the sound ringing out like crystal bells within a cathedral at Christmas. "Zeus
is over there."

Following the direction of her tilted head, he
saw a man lounging on a huge pillow resting on
a dais, scantily clad women spread out over other
pillows feeding him what appeared to be grapes
and olives. He wore trousers and unbuttoned
shirtsleeves. No mask, but then he was the host
and was expected to be here. Podmore.

As Marcus began to swivel his gaze back to
Aphrodite, he caught sight of someone else he recognized, someone he shouldn't. He narrowed his
eyes. He had to be mistaken. It was only because
he'd hoped she'd be here, and yet she moved as
gracefully as Esme. But the hair trailing along her
back was a mahogany shade that glistened in the
wavering light provided by the flickering flames

of the candles that adorned this room. No gas-light to illuminate the surroundings more clearly but then decadence preferred darkness.

He couldn't take his eyes from the not-so-mysterious woman as she wended her way among the guests. She wore a gold domino with feathers at the side, the shade matching her loosely flow-ing golden satiny attire that was cinched at the waist by a thin braided rope. He knew that chin, shaped like the bottom of a heart. More, he knew those lips. They'd visited his dreams often enough since he'd first met her, with more deliberation since she'd joined him at the Mermaid. And oh, the wicked things they did to him when he was lost to slumber would cause Satan to blush.

"Excuse me," he said to the goddess beside him, before cutting a swath that would put him directly in Esme's path.

She was adept at avoiding reaching hands that would have brought her in for a passionate em-brace. Everything within this chamber, no doubt within this residence, was done passionately, and he resented that she was here, probably search-ing for someone to replace his father's role in her life, at least for the night. What did he care who crawled into her bed? He'd made his position clear, and yet he'd never regretted the utterance of words so much. He could have used a differ-ent phrasing to indicate he would never fancy her, but the hell of it was he did. And it angered him to be so drawn to her.

So he'd been deliberately cruel and crude in

order to send her running. The man he'd been a year ago would have never done such a thing. Perhaps he should stop trying to understand the past and just move on with his life. He was weary of the frustration and the fury. Of the cold permeating his soul, of never knowing warmth. Of distrusting everyone—especially her.

As he made his way to her, she sidled between two gents, and he noticed the pocket watch dangling from the braided rope at her waist. What an odd adornment for an affair such as this. Was she obsessed with time or merely the memory of her father?

Slowing his pace, he decided against confronting her immediately in favor of observing her more closely. With her head slowly moving from side to side, she was taking in her surroundings, apparently making mental notes of where she was less likely to be noticed. Periodically, she changed her course, skirting areas with gentlemen who were busily engaged with other women. While she seemed to be part of this soiree, he also had the impression she was striving to blend in and not be detected. But he was certain it was her. Esme. The height, the curves. The grace with which she glided among the guests.

But the lustrous shade of her hair confused him. Had the other been a false piece? Or was this one? The vibrancy of the red would certainly make her stand out. This one not quite so much. Still, she was not one to not shine. Her confident bearing was almost a physical presence. Like that of a royal. When one entered a room, people immediately noticed. Royals commanded attention, as did she.

She glanced around, a soft smile turning up the corners of her mouth as though she was exceedingly pleased with how the night was going. He fought the urge to duck. With his black trousers and tailcoat, ivory waistcoat, pristine white shirt, and gray cravat not resembling those of someone who came from the streets, and the simple black domino mask covering the top half of his face, he thought it unlikely she'd recognize him. If she had spotted him, she certainly gave no pause before floating into a nearby corridor and disappearing from sight.

Keeping his gait quick but measured so no one would think he was giving chase, he followed, entering the hallway in time to see her slipping into a room at the far end and shutting the door behind her. He peered over his shoulder. Because the grand salon was naught but flickering shadows and this passageway even darker, it would be difficult for anyone to see what was going on in here. Not that anything was. It was deserted.

He marched forward until reaching the chamber she now occupied. He considered rapping on the door or simply bursting in or abandoning his need to confirm that the woman he'd spied was exactly who he thought she was.

And if she was? If she was engaged in a secretive tryst within those walls? Did he truly want to witness a man enjoying the delectable fruits she offered? Those lush lips, that wide mouth, that succulent body, those legs that judging by her height had to go on forever? Perhaps she was auditioning a new lover. He should return to his own efforts to discover why his father might have mentioned Podmore, if the viscount had somehow been involved in leading his father to his ruin. He turned on his heel—

Hell and damnation.

He gripped the latch, shoved open the door, and crossed the threshold. She glanced up from where she was hunched over the desk—her discarded mask resting beside the lone lamp providing light—and studied him, one second, two before returning her attention to whatever she'd been doing when he strode in.

"Get the hell out, Stanwick," she commanded in a tone that would brook no argument from a gentleman, but then he'd long ago given up claim to being one.

Therefore, he quietly closed the door behind him and cautiously approached. She appeared to be holding her father's pocket watch . . . only it seemed to have a minuscule telescope attached to it. Quickly she took something out, put something similarly shaped in, and peered down. *Click.* Rapidly she went through the motions again. *Click.*

He came around to stand beside her. A bit of foolscap was flattened on the desktop, and she was moving that odd contraption over it. *Click. Click.* "What the devil are you doing?"

"None of your affair."

Another *click* sounded, this one louder and more ominous. The opening of the door.

"Demonstrate your intelligence," she demanded just before grabbing his lapels, falling back upon the desk, bringing him with her, and latching her mouth onto his.

THAT BEAUTIFUL MOUTH that had her tossing and turning in bed with frustration most nights since he'd first shown up at her door was as dark, rich, and flavorful as she'd imagined. Scotch, probably. Perhaps even a cheroot. He was decadence, pure and simple.

She'd spied him shortly after he arrived and had decided that once she was done with her task here, she might take a bit of time to flirt with him, tempt him, make him regret his words from the other night. She'd even considered indulging her fantasies, to make him want as he'd never wanted before. No one would find it odd if she'd kissed him in the main parlor. She could only hope whoever had opened the door would feel the same about coming upon them now. She also prayed that Marcus Stanwick understood her instructions and comprehended that he needed to play the part of a lover caught in a tryst.

He tore his mouth from hers. The flame in the lamp revealed eyes smoldering with desire. "Struggle against me," he rasped so low she almost couldn't make out the words.

He covered her nose and mouth with a large

hand, which effectively served to make her less recognizable. Squirming, she pushed against his broad, sturdy chest but not with any strength, not that she could have shoved him back if she put all her force behind it. Solid muscle greeted her, and she wanted to run her hands over every inch.

He skewered with a gaze the one who had opened the door. "A little privacy, if you please."

"No one is supposed to be in here," a male voice said a tad hesitantly.

"She's been teasing me all night and I'm near to bursting."

"Be quick about it then." The door slammed shut.

Marcus lifted his hand and his weight. "What—"

When she shoved this time, he moved. Knowing it would be unwise to linger after having been spotted in here, she quickly gathered up all the attachments of her camera, including the tiny bits that held the images, dropped them all into a black velvet pouch, and tucked it into her corset so it was nestled snuggly between her breasts. Picking up what had normally looked like a pocket watch, she pressed the lens until it collapsed into place, snapped the cover shut, and left the object to dangle from her waist. Rolling up the foolscap, she crouched and slipped it back into a hidden compartment beneath the desk where she'd found it. Straightening, she snatched up her mask and tied it into place.

"I'm going out through the terrace doors." She hadn't been able to come in that way because of the crowd mingling about on the terrace, but if she rushed from this room now with a coy smile anyone who noticed her would no doubt think she'd been engaged in a little tryst or was striving to escape the notice of an ardent admirer. "To throw that lout off my scent, I need you to go back into the hallway and tell him you sent me out through the terrace doors to shield my identity."

"Wait for me out there."

She nodded brusquely, grabbed his cravat, rose up on her toes, and gave him a quick, hard kiss on the mouth. "Thank you for putting your revulsion for me aside and playing along, Marcus Stanwick." Before he could respond, she blew out the flame in the lamp, dashed over to where she knew the outer door waited, drew the draperies slightly aside, and escaped into the night.

REVULSION? YES, MARCUS should have been repulsed while kissing her. Instead, he'd become lost in the sensual movements of her lush mouth and the tantalizing flavor of her tongue.

Now he quickly made his way to the corridor where the masked intruder was leaning against a wall. He immediately straightened. "Where's the bird?"

"She never should have been in my arms." But damned if she hadn't felt right there. "I sent her out via the terrace to protect her reputation."

"Every woman here is fair game. Her only loyalty should be to pleasure."

"The one who brought her would no doubt disagree and I've no desire to face a pistol at dawn."

The man shrugged. "You should be able to find a replacement easily enough."

Marcus almost told the man Esme wasn't so easy to replace. "I'll take a look around then, see what I can find."

"Be sure to use someplace else for your next encounter." He moved to the door and slipped a key inside the keyhole. "This door should have been locked."

It no doubt had been before she'd required entry. Marcus headed outside where people were wandering around or frolicking about like wood nymphs. Even though most were silhouettes, he knew he'd recognize her if he caught sight of her. He moved quickly through the gardens, checking behind bushes and rose trellises, interrupting one couple engaged in a frenzied coupling against a tree. He'd never much liked Podmore, had heard rumors about his proclivities and entertainments, and was grateful he wore a mask to disguise his features. Although it only now struck him that she'd still known who he was, just as he'd been able to identify her. It seemed they were attuned to each other. He didn't want to contemplate the reasoning behind it—or how much he'd enjoyed kissing her.

The glare he'd given the fellow who had opened the door had not been feigned. He'd detested the interruption, had wanted to slide his hands along her long legs, lifting her skirt as he went. He'd wanted to taste more than her lips, had wanted to taste all of her. The thoughts bombarding him now infuriated him, almost as much as the fact that she'd lied, hadn't waited for him, but had effectively made her escape.

He reached the rear of the gardens. If she remained, he suspected he'd have little luck finding her, but he knew where she'd eventually appear— her residence. Shoving on the gate, he stepped out into the mews. A host of carriages were lined up, awaiting the return of their travelers. Weary coachmen and footmen would probably be standing about until dawn. He approached a liveried footman, leaning against the door of a coach and smoking a pipe. "Did a woman wearing a golden mask pass this way?"

"Like decadence personified. She went that way, guv." He tilted his head toward the left side opening into the mews.

"Thank you." Trying not to recall a time when he'd have had a coin to flip toward the servant, he raced to the mouth of the mews and onto the brick walk that lined the street.

There she was, a considerable distance away, walking briskly but managing to give the impression she wasn't in any rush. Somewhere along the route, she'd discarded the mask and acquired an umbrella. The fog was beginning to roll in, silent and thick, but he detected no whisper of rain. He was beginning to find her far more intriguing out of bed than he thought he might find her in it. He'd looked at her and seen a woman whose value resided in what she was capable of delivering while lying on her back. But she was multifaceted, a conundrum that made her worth exploring while vertical as well as horizontal. Her relationship with his sire made no sense. He couldn't imagine the duke being captivated by every mysterious aspect of her, and what a waste that would be—to focus only on what she provided between the sheets.

Striding more quickly than she was, he tossed his own mask aside and fought to give the appearance he wasn't chasing her, she wasn't his target, and his ultimate goal wasn't reaching her before she could disappear again.

Continuing on, not breaking her stride, she glanced back and hailed a hansom cab. As the driver brought the horse to a halt slightly ahead of her, Marcus broke into a run, reaching the conveyance and climbing in after her before the front doors could swing closed. She gave no indication she was surprised by his appearance, but neither did she glance over at him. She merely stared straight ahead as though she had the power to cause the encroaching fog to dissipate.

"What were you doing back there?" he asked. "At Podmore's. In his library."

"Kissing you."

Was that the reason she'd run? Because she'd enjoyed it as much as he had? Because she'd felt the fire igniting between them? "Before that. At first blush, I'd say you were taking photographs, but I've never seen a camera that small."

"I suspect there are a good many things you've not seen, Marcus Stanwick." The cab began to slow. "I'll be getting out here. You should carry on."

As the carriage came to a complete stop, she handed up coins through the opening to the driver. After the doors sprung open, she gracefully leapt to the ground and began walking at a fast clip. He jumped out and hastened to fall into step beside her. "You'll not be rid of me that easily. I have questions."

"Your curiosity does not mean I have the answers or if I do, that I'll divulge them." Abruptly, she turned on her heel and started down another street.

There was a time when he'd known only the posher, more exclusive areas of London. Now he was intimately familiar with the dodgier corners, knew she was leading him farther into the bowels of danger. What surprised him was the confidence with which she traversed along the dimly lit cobblestone streets, as though she reigned over this world of ruffians and cutthroats who barely gave her a passing glance, in spite of her provocative attire. She ignored the dollymops—with skirts lifted to brazenly reveal an ankle, a knee, or a thigh—leaning against brick walls, hoping to earn a few quick shillings in a nearby alley or room let by the quarter hour. She appeared to be a woman with a purpose, and he was fairly certain it involved evading him. Not that he blamed her. He'd rather badly ended their time at the Mermaid, and her words before she left Podmore's library ate at him. "A few streets over is a pub. Let's go there, talk things out."

"Don't look back, but we're being followed."

It took every ounce of willpower he possessed not to glance over his shoulder. Now he understood her mad dash and frequent turns onto other streets. Going around corners gave her a chance to look out the side of her eye, without appearing to do so, in order to get a bead on who was trailing them.

Abruptly, she ducked into an alley. As he trailed after her, he angled his head only slightly but enough so he caught sight of a rough-looking fellow, maybe two or three, in close pursuit who would be upon them in no time at all. Enough light bled in from the street that he could see she'd come to a stop and was facing the mouth of the alleyway, fairly bouncing on the balls of her feet, like a boxer preparing for a bout within a ring.

"Race to the other end, escape, head to your residence," he told her, reaching around beneath his jacket to pull free the two wickedly sharp knives from the leather scabbards he'd secured at his back. "I'll dispatch this lot and catch up with you there."

"Don't be ridiculous."

Was there a more stubborn wench in England? "Esme—"

But his argument was cut short by four men— he'd obviously overlooked someone—running into the alley and staggering to a halt. A malicious grin spreading over his face, the largest one took a step forward, while the others fanned out behind him—all brandishing knives. "We're gonna have some fun 'ere, ain't we?"

The whisper of steel sliding against steel echoed between the buildings. Darting his gaze to the side, Marcus was stunned to see Esme holding a sword—not a sword, more like a rapier—her umbrella nowhere to be seen. Had she been hiding the weapon in the long handle, just as she'd hidden a camera in a pocket watch?

She took a fencer's stance. "Give it your best."

Challenging the blighters was not the tactic Marcus would have taken, but he had no time to contemplate further as he lunged in front of her, blocking the two who had decided to come for her. Surprise was on his side because they'd expected to be battling a woman, had anticipated an easy victory. He managed to bury a knife in one and slashed with his remaining blade across the soft belly of the other. When the second ruffian groaned and bent slightly to protect himself from another swipe of the deadly dagger, Marcus took him down with a balled fist to his jaw.

Turning for the two who were now engaging her, he fought not to become mesmerized by her agility at warding them off, at the cutthroats' grunts and cries of surprise when she managed to slice a cheek, an arm, a hand. Marcus grabbed the largest fellow, the one he wanted to never again smile, spun him around, and brought his knife down.

But the ruffian blocked the blow and shoved Marcus back. It took him two steps to regain his balance. The lout hurled himself and rammed into him. Marcus clutched the man's shirt, bringing him along as he fell to the ground, rolling. Fists were flying, sharp-edged blades slashing at air and flesh, so fast, with such purpose, there was little time to think, to strategize, only to react. To roll away, to come to his feet, to kick the other man in the face before he was standing. Marcus delivered one blow, two.

As his foe managed to swing his lower body around, Marcus found his legs suddenly knocked out from beneath him. The man jumped on him, fists pummeling. Marcus stabbed him in the side, but still the blows came. He pulled the knife free, intending to aim for the heart, but the enemy grabbed Marcus's hand that clutched the weapon and levered himself so his weight gave him the advantage and, smiling deviously, guided the sharp point toward Marcus's throat. Marcus resisted, tried to buck him off, but something was amiss, his strength seemed to be waning.

Suddenly his nemesis went still, his eyes bugged, and blood gurgled from his mouth. He dropped down onto Marcus like a ton of bricks toppled from a scaffold. Looking past the man's shoulder, Marcus saw Esme standing over them, rapier in hand. He couldn't see beyond her, but where was the fourth fellow?

Dropping to her knees, she shoved the formerly grinning man off him, touched her fingers to his shoulder, causing pain to ratchet through him. "You're hurt."

At some point, although he vaguely recalled it, during the melee, his last attacker had gotten lucky with his knife.

"If you want to return to the residence with me, I can tend to your wound," she said calmly.

Ruffians. Blood. Gore. She took it all in stride. When most ladies would be in tears, swooning, or have already run off. Ice Princess. But even that moniker he'd bestowed upon her no longer seemed appropriate. With a groan, he shoved himself up to a sitting position and studied her. "Who the devil are you?"

"Esme Lancaster."

He wasn't asking for her name, for God's sake. He was asking for so much more. "*What* the devil are you?"

"It's complicated."

"I'm an intelligent man with the ability to comprehend complicated."

She glanced around the alleyway at the carnage, and he thought for a heartbeat he saw a bit of regret, perhaps remorse, wash over her features before she quickly hid anything she might be feeling, almost as though she couldn't dare risk being viewed as soft. She brought her gaze back to his, resolve reflected in the shadowed depths of her eyes. "An agent of the Crown and presently protector of the Queen."

CHAPTER 6

TWO OF THE ruffians were dead. One by her hand, one by his. That of the gentleman who now sat at the thick blocked wooden table in her kitchen as she warmed some water. He'd knocked one thug out cold. The other would survive the wounds she had delivered if his mate woke up soon enough, which would probably happen because Esme had given the brute a hard slap to get him started toward that end before she'd slipped beneath Marcus Stanwick's arm to help hasten their departure from the alleyway.

They'd changed hansom cabs three times on their journey to her residence, so she could make sure no one else was following them and to make it difficult for anyone who might be asking questions in the days to come to chart a direct path to her. Marcus Stanwick hadn't asked why she was taking the precautions. As a matter of fact, he hadn't said a single word after she'd made her declaration. She didn't know if the profound silence was an indication that he believed her or that he didn't. Not that it mattered.

Having removed his coat, waistcoat, and neckcloth, he was now unbuttoning his blood-drenched shirt, and she fought against envisioning him divested of it. This was not the appropriate time for her to want to trail fingers over flesh nor was he the appropriate man for whom she should feel even a hint of attraction. Opening a cupboard, she pulled forth a bottle of rum that she suspected her cook used more for personal consumption than for adding flavoring to the dishes she prepared. She poured some into a tumbler, set the glass on the table within his reach, and then proceeded to help him drag the soaked shirt over his head. Taking a bit of linen, she began dabbing at the river of blood. "It's a nasty gash." From his left shoulder, it ran six inches or so down, to the steel band of his chest. "He slashed rather than stabbed but still it must be attended to if you wish to avoid infection. I can stitch it up or send for the surgeon."

With the fingers of his right hand, he took hold of several strands of her hair, rubbing them, stroking them as though mesmerized by them. "Is everything I know about you a lie?"

"My name *is* Esme." His gaze shifted to her. If she wasn't careful, she was going to fall into those intense blue depths and never find her way out. "Do you want me to stitch you up?"

"You have the skills to see the job properly done?"

"I've found no fault with my handiwork when I've had a need to apply it to my own injuries."

His eyes narrowed at her implication, that she'd stitched up herself. Which she had. He gave a brusque nod. "See to it then."

The bleeding had slowed considerably. She nudged the glass toward him. "Drink the rum. It'll help numb what's to come. I'm going to gather up what I need."

Mostly what she needed to gather was her indifference. She didn't like the manner in which her stomach had clutched when she'd realized he'd been injured. Didn't like the worry that had almost made her throw caution aside and bring him straight here. Didn't much like the way she wanted to offer him her bosom as a cushion for his head so she could stroke his hair and whisper, "You'll be all right."

He loathed her, although the gentleness with which he'd touched her locks certainly had reflected no hatred. No doubt he was not himself following their narrow escape, his loss of blood, his discomfort. Once he was put back to rights, no tenderness would echo through his voice when he spoke to her. *Is everything I know about you a lie?*

She hated wondering if he might like the truth of her.

Grabbing her box of supplies from a hallway cupboard, she made her way back to the kitchen. The glass was empty. He was holding the wadded linen against his shoulder, his tense face reflecting his pain. She set her box on the table, moved a chair nearer to him, and retrieved the rum. After pouring quite a bite into his glass, she splashed some over her hands, rubbed them together, and dried them. Before he could stop her, she lifted the bottle and spilled the rum over his wound.

He sucked in his breath through clenched teeth. "Jesus. I hadn't considered the pleasure you'd take from torturing me."

"Don't be a babe." She settled into her chair and opened her box, grateful the quivering in her stomach didn't cause her fingers to tremble. After all the harsh words he'd thrown at her, she should find some satisfaction in making him suffer—only she took none at all. "Finish off the rum I poured for you."

Glaring at her, he tossed it back. That glare did bring her pleasure. It didn't seem as hostile. Perhaps when all was said and done, they could work together—her to fulfill her mission, him to restore his good name. But that was for later contemplation. After removing a wicked-looking needle and catgut from her box, she went to work.

He didn't flinch but sat there as still as a stone statue while she dug into his flesh and began pulling it back together. He had such wide shoulders, and she imagined the pleasure to be found in skimming her hands over them when one wasn't coated in blood. Or the comfort to be found in his arms, their strength revealed by the ropy muscles that had tensed and bunched with her first poke.

He was a beautiful specimen of manhood, perfection for an artist's brush. When she was younger, when she'd fancied herself talented with oils, she would have enjoyed putting him on canvas.

"In the library, you were taking photographs."

Shaking off the memories of her youthful innocence, she concentrated on her efforts to ensure he healed properly. She could lie but saw little to be gained in doing so after everything else she'd revealed. "Yes."

"I've never seen a camera so small."

"I doubt anyone has. As you can well imagine, the Home Office has access to incredible inventors. The camera disguised as a pocket watch is a prototype." They were always trying to make useful tools look as though they were something else.

"They are responsible for your umbrella, as well, I suppose. I thought you feared yourself as sweet as sugar and in danger of dissolving should you get rained upon."

"It does have the practical application of keeping me dry."

She could feel his gaze boring into her. She didn't want him to like her, didn't want to like him. It was safer that way. She couldn't risk caring about anyone or anything because it might cause her to hesitate before running headfirst into danger or, worse, put in jeopardy someone for whom she had feelings. So she lived a solitary life, although she wasn't lonely. Or at least had never before believed herself to be so. Brewster also worked for the Home Office, and they'd share late-night chats. And then she had Laddie. Her duties kept her too busy for much else.

"Did my father know the truth of you?"

She shook her head. "I don't think he suspected, even after he was arrested."

"Were you responsible for that?"

Although the words were ground out, she assumed it had more to do with her continually puncturing his skin. Even in her needlework she preferred smaller stitches, had used the same method when tending to her own wounds, pleasantly surprised when the resulting scars were not as hideous as she'd anticipated. She was nearly halfway done with the task, their conversation distracting her as much as him. "No, I'd gained very little information from your father and wasn't yet done with him. I knew a meeting was planned. Your father had let it slip when and where. He swayed between anticipating it and dreading it. I suspected he was beginning to doubt the wisdom of the plot."

"So you lied there as well. He did converse with you."

He'd chosen his words carefully, not using vulgarity as he had in the past, and she wondered if it was because he recognized the large needle that she was using could hurt worse if jabbed directly and deeply into his wound. She hadn't told him the truth of things before because she'd been angry with his insinuations, his lack of respect for her. She also hadn't wanted him to suspect her of not being what he believed. Hadn't trusted him with the truth, hadn't trusted *him*. For all she'd known, he could have been replacing his father in the group of ne'er-do-wells.

However, it was a good deal more than that. Esme Lancaster was very good at keeping secrets. She knew the secrets of dukes and duchesses, lords and ladies. She knew the secrets of commoners, the legitimate and the not so legitimate. She knew the secrets of princes and princesses, kings and queens. She quite literally knew where the bodies were buried—she knew because very often she was the one who buried them.

And so habit had her holding the truth close, squeezing it until it was nearly painful, so minuscule as to almost not exist. But the ones surrounding his father she was weary of keeping because they made this devilishly handsome man think the worst of her, this man who in her opinion had been wronged, had been made to pay for the sins of his father. His name and honor shredded. There he was putting himself in danger, striving to discover exactly what she sought as well. In the alleyway, he'd told her to run while he intended to stay and face the ruffians. He'd stood at her side and battled with her.

They could be allies—if she divulged the truth sparsely and carefully. If she revealed no secrets that would see her deemed a traitor, nothing that would result in her standing upon a scaffold.

"I followed him that night, keeping to the shadows. He went to an empty and derelict tavern at the edge of Spitalfields. I was as surprised as he was that he was arrested. It appeared Scotland Yard was waiting. They knew he'd be there."

"Someone betrayed him?"

"It would seem."

"Did you lie about being arrested?"

"No."

"I find it hard to believe an agent of the Crown would be interrogated and sent to Newgate to rot for a while."

"The success I achieve in my endeavors is dependent upon people not knowing what my position is. I shouldn't have told you."

"Why did you?"

She pulled the last stitch taut, knotted it, snipped the needle free. "I couldn't think of a lie that would make what you witnessed of my actions tonight believable."

Using a damp cloth, she gently wiped away the blood lingering around the angry, red, swollen flesh. He'd been incredibly stoic, not flinching, not moving as she'd worked. He was no stranger to pain, she was certain of it, wondered what other scars she might uncover if she gave his body a thorough going-over. Then cursed herself for wanting to do exactly that, especially when what she truly wanted to discover had little to do with marred skin and more to do with muscle, sinew, and brawn. It had been a good long while since she'd been drawn to a man, had yearned to explore every facet of him. Inside and out. Top to bottom. She never should have allowed his mouth to meld with hers, but having done so, she was struggling not to become lost once more in the forbidden temptation that was Marcus Stanwick. Yet the tenseness in his shoulders told her he was still in pain, and there was little she could do about that. She had no laudanum on hand. The amount of rum needed to dull the pain would leave his head with regrets come morning.

Before she could think better of it, could convince herself of the stupidity of it, she leaned forward and pressed her lips to the stitched wound, acutely aware of his sharp intake of breath, his muscles bunching and flexing before holding remarkably still. She was relatively certain she hadn't caused him further pain. No, his response had more to do with awareness. A wolf that had caught scent of its mate. Lord help her, but she was having fanciful thoughts. Perhaps because the realization of how close they'd come to losing their lives in that alleyway was finally striking home. Or maybe because she'd tended to him. It had been far too long since she'd given care to anyone other than herself.

Feeling her cheeks scalding with embarrassment, she pulled back and forced her traitorous eyes that enjoyed the sight of him far too much to meet his suspicious gaze. "My mother always swore that a kiss would hurry the healing along." As a child, Esme had intentionally scraped her knees, elbows, limbs, and hands just for that brief moment of tenderness from a woman who had always made Esme feel as though she'd ruined her mother's life, having been conceived before her parents were married, forcing the unwed youth to marry a soldier who couldn't give her the glamorous existence she'd craved. "I apologize. My action was merely habit." Even though she'd never once done such a thing before.

He narrowed those incredibly blue eyes, and she knew a cutting comment was hovering on the edge of his tongue, one that revolved around her promiscuity, no doubt centering on her interactions with his father. "My parting words to you at the Mermaid . . . they were uncalled-for."

His admission, the very last thing she'd expected, took her aback. He was thinking of the harsh sentiment that had stung her, that had somehow managed to slip into the cracks in her heart to wound her in a more devastating manner than a knife to the flesh. She arched a brow. "Are you attempting to apologize because you've just realized that I have the power to call for the Queen's guards and have you carted off in chains to some dark and dank dungeon, perhaps to never again be seen or heard from?"

She thought she might have detected a glimmer of amusement, perhaps even admiration, in his eyes before they went flat, effectively concealing whatever emotion might have been struggling to break free. "When I suggested earlier that we go to a pub, I did so with the intention of apologizing there. But I got distracted with striving to survive. I regretted the words as soon as they were uttered. You were undeserving of them . . . as well as many of the ones that preceded them."

She considered tormenting him by insisting he reveal which ones precisely but some that he considered insult she did not want to have to acknowledge as being true. Far too often, she'd imagined the glory to be found in having him in her bed. Not that she was going to admit that weakness to him because he could use it as a weapon against her and he had quite enough in his arsenal to do her damage if she let him. Still, she did have the means to disarm him a fraction, to move a weapon from his armory to hers. They may have been comrades in arms a couple of hours earlier, but she needed to be prepared in case they didn't remain that way. She'd learned long ago to never underestimate the ability for friend or foe to annihilate her. "I fully comprehend why you harbor such a low opinion of me. Just as I formed an opinion regarding you based upon what I read in gossip sheets, so you've relied on rumor to weave a tapestry of my character. I doubt it will change your view of me, but it might assist you in your quest to know that the relationship I established with your father never extended to the bedchamber." Holding up a hand speckled with his blood, she shook her head. "You'll probably interpret that to mean we swived in the parlor, so let me be perfectly clear: we never ever engaged in any sort of fornication."

THE RELIEF THAT swept through Marcus was unnerving. He had no reason to believe her, and yet, he did.

Maybe it was because his shoulder ached like the very devil. Perhaps it was the gentleness of her fingers when it had been so very long since anyone had shown him any tenderness. Perhaps it was the press of her heated mouth to his warm flesh and the yearning it had awoken in him, the desire to have her never pull away. Perhaps it was because if he didn't hate her, if his father had never been intimate with her, Marcus was going to be bloody well tempted to kiss her again—this woman who was nothing at all what he'd presumed. "He told me and others that you were his mistress."

She arched a brow. "Are you insinuating he wasn't one to lie? That he was an honorable man?"

"That first night you told me he fucked you."

"No, I said he didn't visit me for conversation, and he didn't, but you assumed—as most men do when it comes to women—that I had only one other thing to offer."

"Then what did he gain by being with you?"

"That's the question, isn't it? I've asked it myself often enough. He brought me gifts, but he never made any overtures about wanting more from me than occasional company. I encouraged him to spend time with me, but I never had to ward off any unwanted advances. As a matter of fact, I sometimes wondered if I wasn't merely easing his loneliness. However, because he made our affiliation so public, I finally came to the conclusion that he used me as a decoy. If he wasn't in residence or at the club or at a society affair, well, he was with his mistress, with me."

"He never told you what he was up to?"

She shook her head. "Whenever he showed up at my door, he seldom stayed long. He'd have a scotch and then leave, for a rendezvous elsewhere, I think. Brewster or I would follow, but we never saw him meet with anyone. If he went into a pub, he would sit at a corner table alone. If he was communicating with someone, it wasn't apparent. On occasion he took me to the theater or to dinner. If he was passing off messages while I was with him, he was incredibly clever at it. I never detected anything suspicious."

"What else have you not been quite honest about?"

She got up, went to the sink, washed and dried her hands. Returning to the table, she picked up some fresh linens and began wrapping them around his chest, over his shoulder. "I never lied to you about anything of significance."

"But you left out certain details that led me to draw incorrect conclusions."

"It's what a good spy does: lead with as much truth as possible so you don't have to recall a false narrative." She quickly finished dressing his wound and released a slow sigh. "I'm rather certain you have many more questions, but the answers must wait. You're hurt and I'm dreadfully weary."

He'd journeyed through hell seeking the answers. What was a little pain when they were so close, but he could see that she was beginning to sag, to grow pale. While she'd certainly proven her mettle earlier, it had no doubt come at a cost, and she'd tended to him with gentle care that he'd not deserved. "Tomorrow I'll put you through the gauntlet until you'll wish you were back at Whitehall instead of facing me."

She gave him a wry smile. "I look forward to it. But for now, I can have my carriage readied, see you returned to your residence, or you're welcome to rest here until you regain your strength."

He had no residence to which to return. He slept at missions or in cheap lodgings or on the ropes—when he didn't have the coins for a mattress, a ha'penny would get him a bench shared with others, a rope stretched across it at chest level to lean over so he didn't crumple to the floor when he fell asleep. He sought nothing permanent because he didn't want to be easy to find. Not quite trusting her, he shouldn't remain here. And yet, being near to her might provide him with more insight because she had a good deal left to tell him. He had no doubt of that. "I'd welcome the bed."

And you in it. Pressing your lips to my skin again, blushing as you did so. He'd have never thought her to be a blusher and yet her cheeks had gone crimson and he'd very much like to cause her to turn scarlet from her hairline to her toes. He held those thoughts to himself because after giving him the care she had, she deserved only his respect and gentlemanly behavior. She still wore his blood on her clothing. He'd made a right mess of it, bleeding on her as she'd provided support for his weakening body while they'd made their way through a series of different hansom cabs and later into the residence.

"Very good," she said calmly, once more rising to wash and dry her hands. "Go on up, top of the stairs. My bedchamber is the first on the right. You may make use of any of the other three. I'll be following once I've tidied up the mess I made. My cook will have my head if she sees her beloved kitchen was used as a hospital for a while."

"I'll help—"

"Don't be ridiculous." She cut off his offer before he could complete it. "You're injured. Get yourself to bed for some rest. I can send up a footman with some warm water."

She'd cleaned him well enough as she'd tended to him. He shoved himself to his feet, hoping to find the strength to make his way up the stairs. "No need. You have the right of it. All I want is sleep."

"I'll see you in the morning then."

With a nod, he snatched up his shirt, waistcoat, and jacket from the edge of the table where he'd placed them earlier and strode from the room. Out of her presence, he gave in to the weariness that descended like a heavy fog. Remaining still while she'd worked when there had been times he'd wanted to grunt and groan at the constant prick, poke, and pull on his skin had taken a toll, not to mention the loss of blood. He hadn't thought the wound that bad, but her frock told a different story.

He reached the stairs, put a foot on the first step, and froze. His wound was on the left. Her frock was bloodied on the right where her arm had come around him, providing support, but there was a swath of scarlet across the left that resembled the result of a child's fingers dipped in paint and swiped across canvas. Why was the fabric stained with crimson on her left side? Why was there so much more blood where he hadn't leaned against her?

Abruptly, his heart pounding, threatening to seize up on him, he headed back the way he'd come and stormed into the kitchen, his feet pounding on the stone floor. At the table, she spun around, that loosely flowing frock bunched at her waist, revealing plump, beautiful breasts that he was a beast to notice, because one was smeared with blood. In one hand, she held that ghastly huge needle, threaded, ready to begin its work.

"Stanwick, get the hell out!"

"Not bloody likely." He advanced, tossed his clothing on the table beside her corset. "Why didn't you tell me you were injured as well?"

At this point, most women would have covered themselves, but she merely stood there bold and brazen, not an ounce of modesty to be seen, as she jerked up her chin, her eyes blazing with fury. "I can see to it."

"But why inflict pain upon yourself when it'll bring me unbridled joy to do so in your stead?"

Her gaze dropped to his extended hand, and for a heartbeat, he saw relief course over her features, relief that someone else would see to the unpleasant task. She lifted her eyes to his. "Skilled with a needle, are you?"

"I've found no fault with my handiwork when I've had a need to apply it to my own injuries."

Her lips twitched. "You use my own words against me."

"I use them for you, to reassure you." He didn't know why it suddenly mattered that she trusted him completely, but it did.

She angled her head slightly, a bit of teasing in her eyes that also reflected pain. "We're not about to become friends, are we?"

"Don't be absurd."

"All right then." With a small nod, she handed him the needle before settling into the chair she'd occupied while seeing to his wound. He dropped into the other, reached back for his shirt, and held it out to her. "You might wish to cover yourself somewhat."

She smirked. "Are you modest, Stanwick?"

"Your lovely breasts are incredibly distracting. I'd think you would prefer my entire focus remain on your sliced flesh rather than how much I'd enjoy running my tongue around your nipple."

Blushing, she snatched his shirt, clutched it in one hand, and pressed it to her right collarbone so the linen draped over the uninjured breast. He rather regretted that he'd asked her to hide a portion of herself away. He trailed a finger over a ragged scar that ran along her upper arm. "Another knife wound?"

"Glass. When I made my escape through a window without opening it first. No time to mess with latches, you see? Only the few seconds needed to throw something through it so I could clamber out."

Gently, he nudged her arm aside, giving him easier access to the gaping wound that marred the side of her breast. Christ, he wished he hadn't volunteered to do this. Suddenly he hated the thought of hurting her.

"Go on, Stanwick. I've had enough rum that I doubt I'll feel it."

With a nod, he went to work, her strangled groan telling him that she did indeed feel it.

"Smaller stitches, more closely bound together, if you please," she ground out. "They leave a less hideous scar."

"This one won't be seen when you're properly attired. Even the lowest cut bodices won't reveal it."

"My lovers will see it."

His stomach knotted at the thought of all the men who might have known her in a Biblical sense, and again he was damned grateful his father hadn't been one of them. "How many have you?"

"Presently, none."

He didn't know why the words brought him stark relief. "You have had lovers, though."

"Yes."

"But never my father."

"No, never your father."

He cleared his throat. "He *never* tried to get you into bed, not even with subtle insinuations?"

"No, not that he would have had any success at it. I have no objections to using my womanly wiles and flirtatious skills to get information from a man, but I don't spread my legs for it."

He jerked his gaze up to her. "I don't know if I've ever known a woman so blunt."

"I play enough games in my profession. I don't do it in my personal life. How many lovers have you?"

Like nearly every word she uttered, her question could be etched in stone. He released a low scoff. "None. Not in a good long while. The son of a traitor hardly has women falling at his feet."

"You did before Wolfford was deemed a traitor."

"How would you know that?"

"'Tis my business to know everything. You are quite good at this, and swift. Where did you apply the skill to yourself?"

"Knife wound on my thigh. You?"

"Same. Then a bullet grazed my hip once, took a chunk with it."

"Bullet tore through my calf. A rather ravenous dog attacked me once. Tore into the back of my shoulder. Couldn't reach it to properly tend it. It's an unsightly mess."

"I haven't had the privilege of viewing your back yet. I wasn't looking when you left the room. You're a finer specimen than your father."

He didn't want to be compared to his father in any fashion.

"Ouch!" She glared.

"Apologies." In his frustration, he'd dug a little deeper than he'd meant to.

"I shouldn't have brought him up. I don't want to discuss him any further tonight."

"Nor do I." He reached the end of the gash, tied off the catgut, and snipped it free of the needle. If she had made a move to leave, if she'd moved at all, he wouldn't have done what he did next. But she was as still as a statue—but not like the cold marble ones Griff had referenced—no, he was beginning to think there was very little cold about her. He captured her gaze, where heat flared, before lowering his head and touching his lips just above where the blighter had taken the knife to her. Rage bubbled within him. If he'd known she'd been hurt, he wasn't certain he'd have let the last two ruffians walk out of that alley. Slowly, slowly, he eased back. "Just to ensure it heals more quickly," he said quietly.

"Something I'm seldom able to do for myself. Thank you."

Her hair was a tangled mess. She still clutched his shirt, shielding a portion of herself from his sight. Her face was smudged with dirt and a bruise or two. He didn't know if he'd ever seen anyone more beautiful. Damn her for becoming more attractive the more he came to know her. "I have a feeling your cook isn't going to be the least bit bothered to find her kitchen a mess in the morning."

That tiny smile. "No. That was merely a lie to get you to go on up without me. But you should retire now. I can bandage myself easily enough."

Only he didn't want to retire, didn't want to leave her, but where was the good in staying? Wrapping linen around her chest would only serve to have his fingers, his knuckles, occasionally glancing over her skin, something he wanted entirely too much, in spite of his shoulder throbbing with discomfort. Her wound was no doubt providing its own agony. "I shall leave you to it then."

And his shirt. He left that with her as well, taking only his jacket and waistcoat with him. He chose the room next to hers, in hopes he'd hear her arrival, that the echo of her movements would reverberate through the wall. As he settled into the bed, he was determined to remain awake until she was ensconced in her bedchamber, preparing to retire.

But his determination betrayed him, and he succumbed to the lure of sleep, where she came to him, her sultry eyes offering promises he willingly accepted in his dreams.

CHAPTER 7

$\mathcal{M}$ARCUS AWOKE TO sunlight filtering in through a narrow slit where the draperies had not been brought completely together. Considering the ache in his shoulder, he was surprised he'd slept at all and yet, it had been the sleep of the dead. He supposed all the events of the night had caught up with him.

Gingerly, he worked his way out of the bed and glanced at the corner where he'd discarded his trousers. They'd been marred with blood, so he hadn't wanted to leave them on any furniture or carpeting, opting instead for the wood of the floor. But they were nowhere to be seen.

He spotted some folded clothing on a chair near the fireplace. On top was a note, written in delicate yet demanding script. *Yank the bellpull and a bath will be brought up to you.* Beneath the foolscap, his trousers rested, cleaned. They must have been washed and placed before a fire to dry. His shirt, waistcoat, and coat, absent of blood and either washed or brushed free of any evidence he'd been involved in a scuffle, had been mended, the stitches tiny and neat, like the ones in his shoulder. She'd done the handiwork, he'd wager—

He had nothing at all with which to wager but if he did, he'd risk it all on the chance she'd seen to everything herself. Had snuck in as silent as fog to retrieve his clothing and done the same to return it. He'd been exhausted and she'd carried on. Was she sleeping now? He very much doubted it.

The clock on the mantel revealed the time as a little past ten. He couldn't recall the last occasion that he'd slept so late. Following her written orders, he yanked the bellpull before wrapping a sheet around his naked form. *Are you modest, Stanwick?*

He smiled at the memory of her words, then warmed at the memory of what had brought them on. Her facing him as though they shared an intimacy, as though he were familiar with every inch of her. Damn his lustful longings because he wished he was.

A rap sounded on the door. "Come."

Brewster marched in, carrying a bucket, followed by two footmen who placed the copper tub before the fireplace. The butler dumped the steaming water into it and remained after ordering the others to fetch more. "I'm to shave you."

Marcus scoffed. "I wouldn't trust you with a razor anywhere near my person."

Brewster smirked. "She said you were a smart one. When you're done, breakfast will be waiting for you in the dining room."

He didn't sound as though he'd enjoyed saying that, was studying Marcus as though he didn't trust him any farther than he could toss him. "Is she awake?"

Brewster's eyes narrowed, his mouth moving like a cow chewing its cud. "Has been for a while."

"Where will I find her?" Her butler's chest and shoulders swelled up like some ancient warrior preparing to rush into battle. He was incredibly protective of his mistress, Marcus would give him that. "I can simply meander through the residence until I run across her."

"Not if I lock you in."

"You don't think I'd break down the door? Pit yourself against me, Brewster, and you'll discover you'll always lose."

"Don't be so sure. But you'll find her in the library."

"There. That wasn't so hard, was it?"

What was hard was maintaining his patience while more water was brought up. He quickly bathed, took a razor to his face, and dressed in attire that smelled of her. The terrace house was good-sized, but its layout was simple, and he had no trouble at all locating the library. He'd approached quietly, his stealth paying off as he stood in the doorway, studying her standing partially bent behind the desk, her hands resting on it, as she examined an array of what appeared to be papers spread out over it. Her dark green frock buttoned to her chin, down to her wrists. It wasn't as provocatively designed as the first night's red or last night's gold attire, and yet it was far more enticing because he thought of the pleasure he'd take in slowly setting each of those buttons free, touching a finger and then his tongue to each bit of skin revealed. To uncover the whole of her and feast.

"It's rude to stare, Stanwick."

He deflated. "How long have you known I was here?"

She lifted her gaze from the items she was scrutinizing and skewered him with her golden-brown eyes. "From the moment you arrived. How is your shoulder this morning?"

He began walking toward her. "Aches like the very devil." He stopped before the desk. "How is your—" *Breast.* He fought not to clear his throat. "—wound?"

One side of her mouth quirked up. "I find it rather charming that you blush. I'd have not expected it of you."

"I'm not blushing." He was rather certain he was, damn her. "I've just come from a rather warm bath."

She gave the tiniest of nods. "As you wish. My breast aches as well. At least your clothing isn't designed to hug you like a lover. I dispensed with the corset this morning."

Yet, still, she was so well toned that not one

aspect of her sagged or drooped out of place. "I daresay you don't require one."

"A compliment. I shall be the one blushing next."

He bit back another scathing rebuttal that he was *not* blushing. "Are those the photographs you took last night?"

"They are indeed. A list of names. Come around and look at them."

He did so, standing near enough to her to inhale the clean fragrance of her, as well as the light scent of a recently unfurled rose. She'd also bathed, and he fought against envisioning her in that tub with dewdrops rolling along her flesh. He concentrated instead on the captured images. A list of words: *Duck. Cannon. March.* "I'm not certain what I'm looking at."

"It's supposed to be the names of those involved in the plot. Apparently, they've been given alternative designations, perhaps in an effort to make them more difficult to identify. Although I'm not certain they're quite as clever as they think. Look here." Moving so her arm pressed against his, she rested a perfectly manicured finger beneath a word. "Wolf. You or your father?"

"Obviously my father. Otherwise, I wouldn't be here. In addition, it's scratched through, no doubt symbolizing he's no longer a party to their shenanigans."

"A couple of other names are scratched through as well."

"There must be close to two dozen names here. I'd not expected so many to be involved."

"I don't believe there are that many. I think some are false names, a means to trip us up, to have us searching for ghosts. Or else the entire document is designed to have us chasing our tails. It was too easy to find."

He wondered if her use of *us* referred to the two of them or to whomever she worked with before he came along. She and Brewster, perhaps. He didn't much like being excluded from her little group. Moving away from him, much to his disappointment, she lowered herself to the chair she'd no doubt shoved away from the desk earlier to give herself room to stand. He settled a hip on the edge of the desk. "How did you even know where to look?"

She shrugged. "The one to whom I report suggested I might find something in the study, that perhaps Podmore is involved. Hiding places in desks are not uncommon. But they are not usually so easy to locate. I suspect it would take you at least an hour to ferret out the one in my desk."

"Is that a challenge?"

"If you want it to be."

He was tempted, might have even taken on the task if his stomach hadn't decided at that precise moment to growl like a ravenous wolf.

She lifted a finely arched brow. "Have you not eaten?"

"I wanted to see what you were up to first." And he'd wanted to reassure himself that her wound hadn't laid her low, that she was recovering. He'd needed to know she was well, even as it irritated him that she dominated his thoughts.

"We should see you fed before you leave."

He shouldn't be bothered that she was ready to toss him out, but he was. "I'm not fully healed yet."

"You don't seem the worse for wear."

"If we're going to work together, it seems beneficial for me to stay within easy reach. Besides, I have questions yet." He sighed. "And I've nowhere else to go."

"Your brother. Or your sister. She's a countess, for God's sake. I daresay there is plenty of room in her dwelling."

"I don't want to risk placing either of them in danger, although I did leave my clothing with Griff." He spread his arms slightly, his shoulder limiting his movements. "I'm wearing his evening attire."

She gave him a hard look. "Just so you understand, I am not the scarlet woman you've assumed me to be. If you remain here, our relationship is purely business and nothing more."

He gave a curt nod. "I would expect no less." Which was a lie. He'd been hoping for more. He returned his attention to the items on her desk. "What are you going to do with these?"

"Take them to O—"

"O?"

"My contact, to see if he can determine what they mean."

"I'll go with you then, shall I?"

"If I said no, would you follow me?"

"Absolutely."

Her smile of pleasure was stunning. "I'd have expected no less of you."

Not if the titles and lands passed down through generations of his ancestors had been entrusted to his care would he have been more pleased than he was by her words. It occurred to him that she was far more dangerous than he'd originally realized because he was beginning to truly like her.

SHE HAD SURELY gone mad, to have Marcus Stanwick with torch held aloft following her as she guided him through the narrow network of tunnels beneath the city while off in the distance Big Ben tolled the hour of midnight. That afternoon, rather than fetching the once-destined-to-be-duke's clothing, they'd visited a tailor with ready-made apparel that required the minimum of adjustments. While he'd originally balked at the idea of her paying for the purchases, she'd used the tack of reminding him that his father had presented her with several expensive gifts, so she was simply returning the favor. Although no longer attired in evening clothes, he somehow seemed all the more handsome, drat him!

She hadn't much liked the relief that had washed through her with his admittance that he had nowhere to lay his head, and, therefore, staying in her residence would suit him. It suited her as well, much to her chagrin. She enjoyed sparring with him, teasing him. Enjoyed even more the way he looked at her as though he was considering gobbling her up.

And his blush. Dear Lord, but it did the most peculiar things to her chest, caused it to grow warm and tighten, even as it felt like it was expanding. It was incredibly strange to feel, to feel anything at all, especially something that had the edge of wondrousness about it. Not that anything between them would go beyond the physical, not once he knew the entire truth of her. Although perhaps she could avoid revealing it if they fornicated in the dark. However, as she envisioned it, she didn't know how anything with him would be without passion, would be only motions, the scratch to an itch.

She'd very much like for him to do more than fuck her. She'd like for him to make love to her. Perhaps to even love her. She had most definitely gone mad.

"How the devil did you even find this place? It's practically medieval," he grumbled behind her, his voice echoing alongside the constant drips of the Thames as it made its way through ancient cracks and crevices.

"I was given a map. It's not that difficult to navigate when you know the path to your destination. Although I have done some exploring on my own from time to time."

"Of course you have. Curiosity killed the cat, you know?"

"Lack of curiosity has killed a good many more." Stopping, she faced him. "You're one to talk, striving to uncover the truth of your father. I believe that would fall under the heading of curiosity."

"Redemption, retribution, restoring of honor. Not curiosity."

"O is not likely to be pleased that I brought you. He's an eccentric fellow, tends to stay in the shadows during most of our meetings, so don't take offense if he doesn't make you feel welcome."

"Trivial matters no longer offend me."

"Did they when you were an earl on the cusp of becoming a duke?"

"Much to my shame, I must admit I was quite the arrogant sod."

"You're still arrogant." But his arrogance was tempered by more than a year of struggle, humiliation, and betrayal. The flames of the torch captured the hint of amusement in his eyes, and she'd dearly love to hear him laughing out loud and to see him joyous without cares. His father's activities had aged him, and she cursed the previous duke for that, for the actions he'd taken that had led to the destruction of his own family. Before Stanwick could detect her blossoming guilt for her role in bringing about his misfortune, she spun on her heel and carried on.

The passageway narrowed, then widened, opening into an alcove, already ablaze with torches perched in sconces, but the light was orchestrated in such a way that darkness reigned at the edges where she knew other corridors emptied into this nook. Before Stanwick could lift and wave the torch about to reveal what she knew O wanted to remain hidden, she took the flaming object and seated it into a sconce just inside the portal through which they'd entered. "Don't move beyond here," she ordered quietly.

"No exploring?"

"None whatsoever."

"The eeriness of the place is like something in a novel Benedict Trewlove would pen."

"Except a dead body would have greeted us."

"Do you read my sister's husband then?"

Trewlove had become a novelist long before he'd learned he was nobility. Looking over, she offered Stanwick a small smile, wondering what other pleasures they might share, striving not to think about the greatest and most pleasurable of all. "I have his latest novel if you'd like to read it."

He gave the most subtle of nods. It shouldn't please her so much to provide him with something he desired, even if it was no doubt only a minuscule desire. She turned her attention back to the room. "I know you're here, O." Mingled with the musty scent of these caverns was the lingering stink of the acrid tobacco he used in his pipe. "This gentleman is Marcus Stanwick. We've joined forces."

The clicking of rats scurrying about, the occasional squeal, the moans and groans of the earth settling in might have unnerved some, but she ignored it because it was theater for O's attempt at skullduggery. She held up a packet. "I found the document you thought I might. Here are the photographs. Not nearly as helpful as we'd hoped."

"Perhaps you don't know what you're looking for."

"What precisely would that be?"

"Names of traitors. Like his father." She heard the absolute disgust and hatred shimmering through his voice.

Stanwick took a step forward. "My father's treachery is the reason I'm here. By working with Miss Lancaster, it's possible something innocuous the duke said might cause one of us to view his words—or even his actions—in a different light and lead us to deciphering who the devil was pulling my sire's strings because I know damned well that he wasn't the puppet master but rather the puppet."

"Who do you suspect?" came the disembodied question.

"I'm certainly not going to reveal any of my suspicions to someone who cowers in shadows."

The laughter echoing out was harsh and brittle. "I'm not going to reveal myself to someone I don't trust. Leave the photographs. You've taken a huge risk, Lancaster, bringing him here. Makes me question our trust in you. If you continue to work with him, I'll share no further information with you. You'll be on your own."

For all of a heartbeat, she considered defending her actions but had learned years ago that defending herself did nothing more than increase the suspicions and break her heart. No one listened, no one wanted to listen. Changing minds required deeds, not words, even when those efforts put one's life in grave danger. "That is your prerogative, O. My assignment is to assist you, and I shall continue in that endeavor. If we discover anything of significance, I'll let you know."

With that, she marched over to the familiar rickety table, tossed the packet on it, and spun about, heading back the way they'd come. She snatched the torch from the sconce—

Froze as Stanwick's hand, half covering hers, closed around the handle and gave a little tug. She released her hold, relinquishing the torch to his keeping. With no sign of mocking her in his expression—instead she thought she detected a bit of respect, although perhaps that was merely wishful thinking on her part—he gave a small bow, indicating she should lead them out.

She hurried forward, wondering if it was possible to outpace her racing heart, her wild thoughts screaming inside her head, begging her to explain what the devil she was doing, trusting a man she barely knew, a man who made her long for things she was never destined to possess.

"HE SEEMED LIKE a bit of an arse to me," Marcus said wryly.

She'd had her coach waiting for them a few streets away, and sitting across from her now, he wondered if anyone knew the entirety of her.

"He didn't appear to find you much to his liking."

"The feeling is mutual. Who is he exactly?"

"As you can imagine in this line of work, the less you know about your colleagues, the better. We're a mysterious lot, even to each other for the most part. So when I was given this assignment, the Home Secretary introduced him only as Oglethorpe. I've heard some refer to him as Ogre—no doubt because of his uncompromising temperament and, unkindly, because of his appearance. Had he stepped out of the shadows, you'd have seen that he is somewhat hunchbacked."

Based on Marcus's encounter with the man, he found Ogre fitting based on his personality alone but considered it very telling that she referred to him as O rather than a moniker that better suited him. Apparently, she didn't engage in any bully-like tendencies although last night had proven she had the skills to torment whomever she wanted. "He gave the impression he considered himself your superior."

"Ours is a strange coupling. The responsibility for ensuring this plot fails rests on his shoulders. I am to assist, but I also go my own way, search for my own clues. Investigate what I find suspicious. I'm surprised that my association with you angered him to such a degree that he would cut me loose, but he may have only been looking for an excuse. We often butt heads."

"I think perhaps you're underestimating your

worth. I'd wager he's jealous of your abilities, fears you'll upstage him."

"A compliment? Careful there. You're going to make me blush."

He would certainly like to, from the top of her head to the tips of her toes, blush with heated passion. She wasn't nearly as icy as she'd been in the beginning. Still, he felt she possessed more fire to be unleashed. "Will you let your superiors at the Home Office know what transpired between you and O tonight?"

"No. They may agree with him and decide to remove me from the case. I've devoted too much time to it. I want to see it through to its end."

"So what is your plan now?"

"To get drunk."

His bark of laughter echoed around him. Her flash of a smile captured in the passing streetlamps gave him a sense of near euphoria. How long had it been since he'd been . . . happy? Since the anger he'd clung to for so long swung beyond reach? "I'm serious."

"As am I. It's after midnight, too late to do hunting of any consequence with no goal in mind. My wound throbs—"

"Shall I kiss it again?"

"Behave yourself, Marcus Stanwick." Her stern tone caused him to imagine her with a ruler on the verge of rapping his knuckles. "Your wound was more extensive. It has to be bothering you."

"I've learned to ignore the aches and pains that now intrude upon my life."

"Based upon what I read of you in the gossip rags, you have turned out to be not at all the carefree and somewhat fragile creature I expected."

"I was given no choice in the matter."

"On the contrary. As I've mentioned before, you could have taken your life in a different direction, found gainful employment somewhere."

"I was raised to believe work was beneath me."

"But skulking about in the shadows isn't?"

He had come to prefer them to the light that always had shone upon him. "I have found I'm more at home in the shadows."

"They are good for hiding in."

"What are you hiding from?"

"The same as you: my past."

If he asked, would she tell him the truth of hers? He doubted that she trusted him to that degree, probably didn't trust him at all. It bothered him how easily he confessed things to her, how she made him long for a future, one that didn't include the gloominess. One where he again walked among the *ton*, not as a lord, but still respected enough to be welcomed. That was the reason he was now enveloped in darkness, hoping for the light.

Looking out the window, he was grateful to see the familiar surroundings, to know they were nearing her residence. The carriage rolled to a stop. Brewster opened the door and, in silence, handed her down. His glare at Marcus, however, spoke volumes. The butler, or whatever the devil he was, didn't like him, didn't trust him, and wanted him gone. The feeling was mutual.

Marcus followed Esme into the residence, into the parlor, where she went straight to the sideboard and filled two glasses with scotch. She extended one to him before lowering herself into the chair she'd occupied that first night. After he was seated, she lifted her glass. "Cheers."

Their eyes on each other, they each took a healthy swallow, and the tension that had been rising in him abated somewhat. She took another sip, then set her glass on the small table beside her and lifted the lid on a wooden box. "Would you care for a cigar?"

"I've never had a woman offer me one before."

She lifted one out, placed it between her lips, struck a match, and held it to the tip, puffing until it was alight. Removing it, she blew small circles of smoke into the air. "Is that a yes?"

"Yes."

Rising gracefully, she crossed the short distance to him. When he reached for the cigar, she quickly moved it beyond his grasp, her golden-brown eyes filled with challenge. Not until he lowered his hand did she bring the cigar closer, closer, closer until it was a hairsbreadth from his mouth. He parted his lips, and she slid it home. As he inhaled deeply, he tried not to contemplate how her lips had been where his now were.

After pivoting about, she returned to her chair and prepared a cigar for herself.

"I've never known a woman to smoke."

"You have quite a list of things you've *never*, Marcus Stanwick."

It was odd, how much he liked when she teased.

She studied the glowing tip, then looked toward the empty hearth. "I was twelve the first time I smoked, not a woman yet, of course. I'd stolen it from my father's study. When my mother discovered me behind the stables, no doubt turning green, that genteel lady made me stand in the corner, holding my father's heavy cigar box for—well, she said it was only an hour, but it felt like days." She turned her attention back to him. "She thought the punishment would make me docile, obedient. All it did was make me rebel all the more and desire the forbidden."

As though needing to wash the bitter taste of the tale from her tongue, she tossed back her remaining scotch like a sailor just in from sea, got up, refilled her glass, and with bottle in hand, stopped to replenish the contents of his glass, before returning to her chair for another puff and then a sip. She'd set the bottle at the far edge of the table, within easy reach, indicating she did indeed intend to get drunk. If he was patient and gave the scotch the time it needed to loosen her tongue, he'd be able to pry the answer from her luscious lips for every question about her that plagued him. Taking a slow swallow of his own liquor, he relished the burn, determined to wait her out—

And yet, he was tempted to join her in the escape, to perhaps eventually move beyond booze and cigars to silken flesh and soft valleys, to hidden treasures where a man could truly become lost. "Was your father really the village drunkard?"

"No. Nor, as I'm certain you've already sur-
mised, was the pocket watch ever his." Her eyes
had softened until they reflected a deep fondness.
"He was an officer in Her Majesty's army. He
wasn't often home, but when he was, he would sit
me upon his lap and reassure me that his job was
to deal with monsters so I would always be safe.
When I was twelve, he received orders to go to the
Crimea. Mother and I saw him off at the railway
station. I didn't want him to leave. I clung to him
and wept, terrified he wouldn't come back. He
knelt before me and told me he had to go in order
to protect his family, countrymen, and homeland.
That he had to go for the Queen. That if good people did nothing, bad people would win. A year
later he died in battle. But at least his actions are
immortalized in poetry."

His gut clenched at the deep sorrow reflected
in her voice. "Not 'The Charge of the Light Bri-
gade' surely?"

Her nod was slight, almost imperceptible. "I
suspect he knew they were doomed, that a mistake had been made and they were being sent to
their deaths, but he followed the orders anyway.
Which might be why I don't always, not when
I disagree with them, as I often do with O. But
more importantly I always regretted that my father's last memory of me was sniveling. I've only
ever cried once since. The day we received word
that he'd been killed."

Her gaze had drifted to the empty hearth, and
he wondered if the images of that final farewell

were flickering through her mind. "Is he the reason you work for the Home Office?"

Bringing her attention back to him, she rolled a shoulder. "Partly, I suppose. For a while, I wished I was a son and could join the army to avenge him. But in the end, we have to travel our own path rather than the one our fathers tread."

Which brought them back to the matter at hand. "Why didn't Brewster accompany us tonight into the tunnels? I have the impression he's your protector."

It was almost a physical shifting, the manner in which she shrugged off the past and the memories of a vulnerable young girl, like changing out of a sturdy winter frock into a lighter one for summer. "I protect myself, although he has his uses, and he does also work for the Home Office. We've been a team for a while. O, however, prefers to meet with only me. Like many of us who have witnessed how easily people betray confidences, he trusts few, you see. And Brewster doesn't need to know everything, only what is essential for him to carry out his orders. The thing is, your safety is better secured when you suspect everyone of being against you."

He'd learned that lesson the hard way, but it bothered him that she'd attended the same harsh school of reality. Once the darkness had inhabited your soul, you could never rid yourself of it completely. He often wondered what sort of man he'd find himself to be at the end of this journey. "How did you become protector of a queen?"

She took another puff on her cigar. He liked far too much the manner in which she blew out the smoke, tilting up her chin to expose the ivory expanse of her throat, a throat he would like to nibble his way along until he reached the delicate shell of her ear so he could whisper in a hoarse voice precisely what he'd like to do with her. She wouldn't be shocked by his crude suggestions. She'd find them alluring, erotic, would no doubt return the favor with vulgar propositions of her own.

"She believed me when no one else would." He swore he heard a measure of hurt laced through her tone. "The disadvantage to being disobedient is that people expect the worst and are less likely to give you the benefit of the doubt. Her belief in me quite literally saved my life, and so now I seek to return the favor."

Another inhale of the cigar, another exhale. A twist of her lips formed a mockery of a smile. "And what of you, Marcus Stanwick? Why is restoring your family name so important when those you seek to impress are unlikely to ever again welcome you into their parlors?"

Clenching his jaw at the reminder that he could never be what he once was, of all he'd lost, he glowered at her.

With amusement in her eyes, she angled her head slightly. "Did you think I would allow you to be the only one asking questions? Do you not think that, like you, I have been biding my time waiting for the scotch to loosen your inhibitions, so you'll speak freely?"

"I very much doubt those are the inhibitions you are hoping to be loosened. You are beautiful and cunning, and flirt without thought. You were made to seduce and be seduced. But I'm not here for games, Esme. How did you come to be associated with my father? Why him?"

ᴸORD HELP HER, but she was so tempted to prove they were both made for seduction, seduction of each other. Everything about him called to the woman in her. The way his fingers held his glass. The way his lips secured the cigar. The slow way he sipped his scotch. He would savor a woman's mouth in the same manner, leisurely, provocatively. He would graze his hands over her, pressing where she needed pressure, soothing with long, tender strokes what required gentleness. How tempted she'd been to take his mouth rather than deliver the cigar to it. He made her want. Desperately. He made her glad to be feminine to his masculinity. But she also knew that taking him to her bed would be a mistake for them both. She'd had a few lovers, men she'd enjoyed being with for a short time, but they hadn't been associated with her work. It was best to set boundaries and to hold to them, respect them, honor them. Crossing a line could result in a tangled mess. "I met him at one of Podmore's affairs."

If the deep furrowing in his brow was any indication, she'd flummoxed him. "Based on your questions at the Mermaid, I didn't think you knew Podmore."

She arched a brow. "If I'd admitted to knowing him, you'd have been suspicious of my questions, and I was striving to determine what you knew."

He sighed, when she imagined he really wanted to growl. "You're still striving to manipulate me."

"I will do so as long as you're striving to manipulate me. But I'll also answer honestly. You wanted to know how I came to know your father. It was at one of Podmore's affairs."

He studied her for a full minute before asking, "Like the one last night?"

"Yes."

"My mother wasn't in attendance, surely."

"No. If it's any consolation, I'm not sure your father was there for the sex that was being offered. Rather, O suspected more was afoot. It's quite complicated."

He released an impatient sigh.

"I know. You can comprehend complicated. Allow me to start at the beginning."

"By all means." His frustration with her was evident as he crushed the end of his cigar onto the glass dish that rested on the table for precisely that purpose. She rather regretted no longer being able to watch his fingers play over the tightly wound tobacco leaves. Then he picked up his glass, and she enjoyed the elegant movement of his hand. She shouldn't find every aspect of him so intriguing. Years ago, after experiencing a great deal of hurt, she'd developed the habit of keeping her emotions, her feelings, on a tight leash, seldom allowed to wander. When she entertained in this room, she was seeking information. Certainly, she never divulged it. He made her want to confess all. Or perhaps she'd merely imbibed more scotch than she'd realized.

Moving slowly, provocatively, she refilled her glass, then his, liking the way his eyes heated with her movements, his gaze never wandering from her. By the time she returned to her chair, she felt as though her blood had become molten lava coursing through her veins. She shouldn't continue to drink, but then she'd never been content to do only what she should. She took a sip, licked her lips, knowing she was unwise to taunt and tease him, but it had been so very long since she'd had the attentions of a man, especially one as sensual and virile as this one. "How is your shoulder?"

"The scotch is doing its job. The story, Princess."

It did not escape her notice that he'd eliminated the *Ice* mention from his moniker for her. Still, his address was not a warm term of endearment but she rather suspected was used to keep her at a distance. An awareness hovered between them that they'd be fools to acknowledge, that might serve to distract them from their goal. She could tell from his steady and penetrating gaze that he had refocused on the task at hand. He had a right to know how her involvement with his father had come about. Without it, perhaps things might have been different for him. "In the fall of 1872, rumors began to surface that a plot to assassinate the Queen was taking shape. Before that, there had been seven attempts on Victoria's life carried out by lone gunmen. The first was declared insane. The last—only two years ago—did it for political reasons in a bid to see Irish prisoners released. The others were simply unhappy with life. So any hint of an assassination scheme is taken seriously by Scotland Yard and the Home Office. However, these whisperings were more alarming because they insinuated at an organized effort by more than a solitary man. More concerning was that these reports indicated the *ton* was involved and the name Lucifer was often referenced."

He'd been lounging and now sat bolt upright. "So you lied about that as well."

She was offended. "I did not lie. You asked if your father mentioned him. He did not."

He narrowed his eyes as though still feeling that she'd tricked him. "Who is he then? This Lucifer."

She lifted a shoulder. "Haven't the foggiest. Or if it is even a person. It could be a designated name for the plot. O had been placed in charge of discovering what was afoot but was having very little success in ferreting out the details or determining who was involved. Therefore, the following spring the Home Office dispatched me to join him in his efforts. O had come to believe that Podmore's residence was serving as a meeting place for those up to no good, the viscount's frequent unconventional soirees providing an excuse for the traitors to gather without raising suspicions since those in attendance paid no attention to anything other than their own pleasures. And the guests are always masked. I was rather skeptical, but he suggested I infiltrate one of the parties to see what I could learn. He thought I'd have better hunting than he. Hence my visit to Podmore's that led to my eventual encounter with your father in April of 1873." She smiled. "He does not hold his liquor as well as you."

"Nor as well as you, it would seem."

"Have you been hoping to get me foxed?"

He settled back into the plush chair. "What about my father convinced you he was worth latching onto?"

Even with his ignoring her question, she knew that he had indeed hoped she'd get sozzled. He trusted her no more than she did him. What strange bedfellows they would make—but she also suspected it would be quite glorious. He was not a man to do things in half measures. His current quest revealed that much about him. "I was walking through the garden, far into it, where there was no light, only shadows, and I heard a man say, 'If we're to kill the Queen, we'd best not get caught.' It was your father's voice."

CHAPTER 8

MARCUS SHOT UP out of the chair, crossed over to the fireplace, and slammed his fist against the mantel. Then he grabbed it with both hands and pressed his forehead to it until it was digging into him and became painful. He hadn't realized until that moment he'd been striving to prove that his father had been innocent, had not been involved, had been mistakenly found guilty and hanged. *Damn you, Father. Damn you to hell.*

Swinging around, he glared at the woman sitting there so serenely, like the cold marble Griff had accused her of being. "I don't believe you."

She never averted her gaze, never blinked. "Yes, you do."

"Where's your Bible? I'll have you swear on it."

"I haven't one. My mother beat Satan out of me and in so doing managed to beat God out as well. So you'll have to take me at my word."

"To whom was he speaking?"

"I don't know. The shrubbery was thick. I tried to work my way through, to give the appearance of being well in my cups and innocently stumbling upon them, but by the time I made it to the area where I thought the voice might have come from, only your father was there. What I remember most was his silhouette, head bent, shoulders slumped as though he carried a great weight. But I continued on as though inebriated, weaving and giggling and acting like a ninny until I fell against him, and he caught me. Believing me sloshed, he kindly escorted me back to Podmore's residence and then to his carriage so he could provide me with a ride home. I took advantage of the journey to begin to establish a rapport. By the time we arrived here, he seemed quite smitten and asked if he could take me to the opera. As I mentioned last night, he never made any sexual overtures that I had to fend off, but then we had only a little over two months together before he was arrested and subsequently hanged."

"You could have misheard. It might have been someone else speaking behind those bushes. You could have been wrong about him."

"I wasn't wrong. It was your father whom I overheard discussing murdering his sovereign. Was I to ignore it and hope he didn't have the wherewithal to succeed in his endeavors? Short of inviting him to my bed, I was determined to endear myself to him so he might take me into his confidence and confess more."

He loathed her at that moment for her certainty, and despised his father for his actions that had ruined so many lives. "Go to the devil."

With a purpose in his stride, he marched across the room.

"Where are you going?" she called out after him.

He ignored her, fought to ignore the pain tearing through his soul, shredding it until he feared it might disappear completely. He stormed out through the front door, slamming it in his wake. He had to get away from her, away from the truth of his father.

He walked and walked and walked. In spite of the late hour and the miscreants about, no one bothered him. He suspected he had the look of a man on a rampage, ready to do bodily harm. He had a strong urge to strike something. If he still had a membership in a club, he'd go to one with a boxing ring and pummel someone, be pummeled. Give blows. Take blows. He wanted to punish, be punished. What a fool he'd been, all this time holding out hope that he was on a gallant mission to save his family's honor when there was no honor to be saved.

He reached the Fair and Spare, closed up for the night, except for a dim glow coming from a solitary window. His brother's office. Searching the ground, Marcus found a couple of pebbles and tossed them at the glass. Soon after Griff, haloed by lamplight, looked out, then disappeared. A few minutes later, he opened the door and stepped onto the stoop. "What's wrong?"

"He was involved. Father. In the plot to kill Victoria."

"You doubted it?"

"Did you not?"

"I was the spare, not his favorite son. He never liked me, and I never liked him. That he might be involved in something so atrocious did not surprise me. I thought you wanted to find the others responsible, see them pay."

"I was hoping in discovering them, I would determine he wasn't truly part of it." More fool he. Even as his hopes regarding his father's innocence had begun to dim under the onslaught of information, he'd held on to the tiniest shred of belief.

"You look like you could use a drink. Come on up."

"I shouldn't."

"No one is going to see you this time of night or learn that we've been in contact."

"I suppose one glass wouldn't hurt. If your wife's not waiting for you."

"She's at the cottage. I'll be heading off to be with her once I'm done here." Griff had ensured Kathryn acquired her grandmother's cottage by the sea in Kent, and they spent a good bit of their time there.

"One drink." He followed his brother inside and up the stairs to his apartment. Griff had made something of himself and something for himself. He had a fulfilling life and a woman who loved him. Marcus was glad Griff had found happiness.

As had Althea. He suspected it was a state that would always elude him.

He took the glass Griff offered and settled into a chair near the window while his brother took the one opposite and studied him thoroughly before asking, "So how did you confirm he was involved?"

"She overheard Father talking with someone about the plot."

"She?"

"Esme. The one who left me the missive."

Griff arched a brow. "You mean Father's—"

"She wasn't his mistress," Marcus interrupted because he didn't want to hear his brother associating a crude word with Esme. Strange how he suddenly felt an overriding need to protect her reputation. "Yes, he kept company with her, but they were never intimate."

"Then why did he say she was his mistress?"

"We can only speculate but assume it was to keep others off the scent of what he was truly doing. If he wasn't about, where did you think he was?"

Griff clenched his jaw. "With *her*. Do you think Mother knew the truth of it?"

Marcus shook his head. "Their relationship was never particularly warm. She wasn't happy about his gallivanting around London with another woman, but I suspect she was grateful it kept him from her bed. It was her embarrassment and the disgrace at his being found out to be a traitor that did her in."

Griff scrutinized him as though Marcus had hidden away a wooden puzzle piece that his brother needed in order to complete the puzzle. "If she wasn't his mistress then what did she gain by associating with him? She struck me as a woman who required more than baubles, trinkets, and jewelry to remain loyal."

Marcus knew whatever was spoken within this room would go no farther, that Esme's secret would be safe. "She's"—an incredibly intriguing woman and already he regretted his display of temper that he'd cast her way—"an agent of the Crown."

Griff sputtered on the scotch he'd been sipping. "Pardon?"

"I was as surprised as you to learn she works for the Home Office."

"I've never heard of a woman employed in such a capacity."

"I suppose that's one of the reasons she's so effective at it. No one suspects her of holding that sort of position. Apparently, she was striving to earn Father's trust so he would confide his plans to her."

"Does she have any idea why he chose this route?"

"No. He may have taken his reasons to the grave with him."

"Are you going to share your findings with Althea?"

Their sister had a right to know but too many questions remained. "Not until I have more answers. Have you seen her recently?"

"We had dinner together last week. She and Trewlove had just returned from another trip to Scotland to visit his parents." He shook his head. "I know his surname is Campbell now, but I'll always think of him as Trewlove. It had to be an odd thing to learn his parents had been searching for him all those years when he was in Ettie Trewlove's keeping."

His mother had given him over to the baby farmer as a way to keep him safe. It was only recently that he'd been united with his parents and taken his rightful place as his father's heir, according to Scottish law.

"At least they found him, and Althea is a lady once more, as she deserves."

"Lady Tewksbury. Christ, all the various names associated with the nobility can certainly cause some confusion. Maybe the Crown did us a favor by simplifying things for us. Mr. Griffith Stanwick. Mr. Marcus Stanwick. It's perfectly clear how we should be addressed, even to the most uneducated."

But Marcus had spent his entire life preparing to be the duke, to be addressed as His Grace. It had resulted in him feeling a little more lost than the others, of having to search a little more deeply to discover exactly who he was when it had become clear he would not become who he was meant to be. He wondered about the path Esme may have traveled to arrive where she was.

"Is this Esme going to assist you in your quest?" Griff asked, as though he'd detected the direction in which Marcus's thoughts had turned.

"It's her quest as well. The plan is still afoot apparently, and the Home Office is no closer to determining who is behind it."

"If you need me—"

"I won't." He could tell his terse response didn't sit well with Griff. "You have a wife now. And a business to oversee. I'm not going to ask you to put it all at risk."

"Is she going to watch your back the way I did?"

"She already has."

Which was the only reason that as the sun broke through the early morning mist, Marcus was knocking on her door. Or so he'd convinced himself that was his solitary reason for standing there impatiently waiting to be granted entry. It had nothing at all to do with the regret and restlessness he'd endured after storming out on her.

Griff's business had several bedchambers for members who needed privacy, and Marcus had made use of one of them. Not that he'd slept a wink. He'd simply stared at the ceiling, occasionally glancing toward the window, all the while haunted by thoughts of her. As a grown woman, so daring and bold. As a child being beaten by her mother to such an extent that she would lose all faith. Not that his was particularly strong of late, but his father, despite all his faults, being a harsh taskmaster, and expecting perfection of his heir, had never lifted a hand to his son. Most certainly Marcus's mother had never entertained the notion of harming a soul with so much as a swat.

Then there was the loss of Esme's father, and he couldn't help but believe that it had shaped her above all else. That while the army might not have had her, she'd found a way to carry on her father's work, a man that if the warmth in her voice when she spoke of him was any indication, she had loved as deeply as it was possible for a child to love a parent. Who had regretted that his last memory of her was in tears. Perhaps that was the reason he had yet to see her shed a single teardrop—because she wanted it to be no one else's last memory of her.

The door opened and to his bitter disappointment, it was the damned butler, who had the gall to arch a thick, dark eyebrow and smirk. "I don't think she was expecting you to return."

He didn't relish the thought that after he'd left, this irritating fellow might have joined her in the parlor to enjoy her company. He was taken aback with the realization that he did relish her company, even when they traveled the harshest of paths, the ones he wished they could avoid. "Is she awake?"

"With the sun, always."

Marcus edged his way past the man. "Where will I find her?"

"I'll announce you."

He grabbed the butler's upper arm, surprised by the firmness of the muscles he found there. This man was definitely prepared to do battle for her. "I don't need to be announced. Where is she?"

Brewster studied him for a heartbeat, two, his

jaw tense with displeasure. "She's in her chamber of solitude. Down the hallway, descend the stairs at the end. But I'd approach cautiously if I were you. She doesn't take kindly to being disturbed."

He resented that this fellow knew intimate details of her that Marcus didn't. He wondered if they were lovers or had ever been. How free was she with her affections? If not for his need to see punished those who'd lured his father to destruction, he'd walk back out the door, leave the two of them to their work and whatever else they shared. Instead, he followed the directions given, quietening his steps on the stairs when he heard the grunts and harsh breathing. Was she with a man now, taking him into her body? Would that fellow kiss the wound on her breast? Plow his tongue into her mouth, know the flavor of her?

Marcus knew he should pause, head back up, and wait for her in the parlor. But some perverse part of him wanted—needed—the reminder that her favors might be easily given, that the camaraderie he'd begun to experience with her would never be more than two people sharing a single purpose, even if their pursuit of it stemmed from different reasons.

When he did finally catch sight of her, relief washed through him, followed by a quick, forceful tightening of his gut. She was alone, her back to him, her derriere outlined in exquisite detail because of the taut trousers hugging her form like a second skin. Her shirt, similar to what he wore, was snug, billowing only slightly with her movements. Secured by a wide ribbon, her hair had been pulled back and up, so the long strands dangled very much like a horse's tail, swinging to and fro as she dashed forward and back, side to side. Bouncing on bare feet, she darted in with a tightly balled fist to hit a padded square attached to a metal bar secured to a stand that allowed her target to swing around when she struck it. When it nearly completed its arc, she belted it again, sending it back the other way. The contraption reminded him of a jousting quintain used by a knight to perfect his aim at delivering blows with his lance. She was sparing her mark no quarter.

Exhibiting grace, strength, power, and determination, she stole his breath, and he feared she'd pocket it and never give it back. He wanted to take hold of that tail of her hair, wrap it around his knuckles to secure her in place—against his chest so he could tip her head back and claim that mouth presently set in concentration. He'd never wanted anything more in his life, not even the dukedom. "Imagining that's my nose?"

CHAPTER 9

$\mathcal{E}$SME JUMPED BACK, out of reach of the oscillating arm, and swung around. He'd come back. She'd worried all night that he wouldn't, that he'd roam the streets and seek shelter in a doorway somewhere. But he looked clean and tidy. Had recently taken a razor to that magnificent jaw of his. She wondered if he'd gone to his brother, stayed in his company through the night. Standing before her now, he made it impossible to think clearly, to do anything other than stare and take in every aspect of his presence. Christ, he was naught but trouble for her. She should command he leave immediately. Instead, she took a step forward. "Don't flatter yourself that I give you any thought at all."

Flatter yourself that I think about you constantly, that I could not sleep for thinking about you.

One corner of his mouth lifted slightly as

though he'd detected her lie, and then it dropped, and a deep somberness settled over him. "I apologize for my rudeness and abrupt departure last night."

"All this time you thought he was innocent." The first hour after he'd stormed out, she'd sat in her chair, contemplating his expression and the agony she'd seen reflected in his eyes until she'd finally realized what she'd witnessed. If she'd not had so much scotch coursing through her veins, if she'd not been so saddened by the sorrow that she might never see him again, she'd have figured it all out sooner.

He gave a slight nod. "More fool I."

"It's only natural not to want to believe the worst of those we love."

"If he was capable of such a heinous act, who is to say I am not as well?"

"You are the one to say it, make it so. You are not your father, just as I am not my mother. I would never in a thousand years strike a child, especially for something as trivial as mud on her frock because she wanted to see where the toad got off to."

With his jaw clenched, he nodded toward the quintain. "So perhaps she was the one you were imagining there."

"No, you had the right of it. It was you."

Dropping his head back, he laughed, the sound big, bold, and beautiful, one that could capture hearts, was threatening to thaw hers. He was far more dangerous than the men in the alleyway—he could make her yearn again for things she could never hold. A man who would stay at her side no matter how difficult it might be, who would look beyond her flaws to find aspects of her worthy of love.

"I deserved that," he said when his laughter was no longer echoing between the walls.

"Yes, you did."

"I don't know if I'll ever get used to your blunt honesty."

She very much doubted he would be in her presence long enough to get used to anything about her. Once his quest ended, he'd have no reason to stay.

He glanced around the room, at the swords and rapiers on one wall, the pistols in the glass case, the sandbag hanging from the ceiling, and the small boxing ring with its padded floor. "Brewster called this your chamber of solitude."

"He knows not to bother me when I'm here— without an invitation."

"You'd hone your defensive skills better if you had an opponent."

"Brewster sparred with me until I broke his nose. He did not take it well."

"After my behavior last night, I suspect you'd very much like to break mine."

To break his would be an unforgivable sin, to ruin the perfection of his features. Nature had taken great care when lining up his bone structure, the edge of his nose a sharp blade, his jaw strong, his brow broad, and his mouth full, enticing. It promised wickedness.

She'd been concentrating so much on his fine features that she nearly missed that he had shrugged out of his coat and tossed it aside, onto a nearby bench. "What are you doing?"

The waistcoat joined the coat, and he began undoing the buttons on his shirt. "Providing you with a sparring partner. I could use the practice and need to loosen my shoulder." Reaching over his back, he grabbed the cloth, pulled it over his head, and flung it onto his coat. He dropped down onto the bench and removed his boots and stockings. Even the man's enormous feet were attractive. Was there any aspect of him that was flawed? It was deuced irritating.

After getting up, he began ambling toward the ring. "Coming?"

"With your wound, I'm not certain this is a good idea."

"Scared?"

She bristled. "Absolutely not. I'm simply striving to spare you another encounter with the needle."

"Don't worry about me, Princess. How's your breast?"

His frankness regarding the human body coming at last heated her to her core. Few people actually spoke *that* word aloud. It was relegated to erotic novels. She wondered if he whispered it in his lovers' ears. "You tell me."

"From what I observed, quite perfect."

Warmth suffused her at the compliment. She'd never been vain, but she couldn't help but be flattered by his observation. He slipped between the ropes and into the ring. Shaking out those long sinewy arms, he arched a brow and waited.

Drat him! He'd given her no choice because she refused to *not* accept the challenge and be judged a coward. She marched forward. "Don't say I didn't warn you."

MARCUS COULDN'T REMEMBER the last time he'd felt so alive, anticipating an encounter, a moment, a woman's nearness. Given the manner in which his body was tightening, she might as well be approaching completely naked. It was absolute madness—the relief that came over him when she didn't immediately toss him out on his arse but had accepted his apology. More than that, she'd deciphered the reason for his upset the night before, which meant she'd been thinking about him at least some. Probably not as much as he thought about her, but then he seemed to be a man of obsessions, whether it was his father, his need to find the others responsible, or her. How was it, when was it, that she had become an obsession?

"We're wrestling, I take it," she said, having joined him, standing only a couple of feet away. "Not boxing."

"You're welcome to hit, use whatever means at your disposal to overpower me."

She smiled, somewhat evilly, actually. "You don't strike me as someone who would punch a woman."

"So you'll have a slight advantage."

She rolled her shoulders and neck before bending forward slightly in a pose anticipating an attack. She bounced on those tiny bare toes of hers, toes he wondered if anyone had ever kissed. He'd like to run his tongue along the arch of her foot. He shook his head. He was on the verge of battle, not lovemaking. Based on the outcome that night in the alleyway, he knew she'd be a formidable foe. He welcomed the challenge of her.

Then she was running toward him. As he prepared to fend off the blow by capturing her in his arms, she suddenly leapt in the air and those feet he'd been contemplating were digging into his gut, doubling him over, sending him staggering back. By the time he'd regained his balance, she'd retreated, bouncing on the balls of her feet, her hair swinging back and forth. Her triumphant smile made him want to kiss her, damn it. "Impressive, but you'll not catch me unawares again. You should have taken advantage of the moment and brought me down."

"Brewster never complained when I took pity on him."

"I'm not Brewster, and I don't require pity. You're going to regret not finishing me off when you had the chance."

"You're going to regret underestimating me."

Crouching slightly, he began circling her. The

ring was smaller than what he was accustomed to using at his gentlemen's clubs. It forced proximity, close fighting, which he decided was by design. In an alleyway, a mews, or a street, he had an opportunity to distance himself from his adversary in order to gain a little time to reestablish his footing. But in close quarters, adjustments had to be made when he was in the thick of things.

He feinted darting in; she rapidly backed off. She was as quick as a fox, he'd give her that. He feigned an attack three more times, before finally swooping in to catch her off guard, spin her about, and clamp his arms around her, pressing her back to his chest. In spite of her earlier efforts at the quintain, she smelled intoxicating and he lowered his head for a deeper breath. "I think it only fair that I interrogate my captive. How old are you?"

She went lax in surrender. "Three-and-thirty. You?"

"Thirty. How many lovers have you taken?"

Suddenly her foot was behind his calf, pulling him off balance. He landed hard on his backside, and she pounced, straddling his midsection, grabbing his wrists, and pinning them on either side of his head, levering her weight to hold him in place. He deserved it for misjudging her surrender as a ploy for preparation. He'd never found an opponent's triumphant smile so incredibly sexy. He wanted to wipe it off her face with a kiss that lasted for days.

"None of your business," she said levelly. "How many lovers have you taken?"

"Hundreds." It was a lie, but the astonishment in her eyes gave him an advantage. Bending his knee and planting his foot to give him the ability to push off, he levered himself and rolled her onto her back, reversing their positions so she was trapped beneath him. "Based on the manner in which you speak and carry yourself, you've been tutored by the very finest, I'd wager."

She arched a brow. "Is there a question, thou-who-has-imprisoned-me?"

He liked this lighter, teasing side to her, imagined her younger, more carefree, before she was charged with protecting a queen, and thus guarding an empire. "Was it part of your training for the Home Office?"

"No. My mother sent me to a finishing school. She had high hopes that I might land myself a gentleman."

"And did you?"

"No. You're hurting me."

He loosened his hold. "My apolo—"

She slithered up until she was able to wrap her legs around his waist. She squeezed. Damn, but the woman had powerful thighs, and he imagined her holding on to him just like this as he pounded into her, rode her hard, fast, and with purpose. "You little trickster."

"That was far too easy."

Releasing his hold on her wrists, he lowered his elbows to the floor, bringing his chest in contact with hers—or at least her bosom. She had an awfully fine bosom. He cradled her face between his hands. "You beguiled me. So have you never married?"

"Never."

"That's unusual for a woman of your years."

"Have you not yet realized I'm an unusual woman?"

Oh, he'd realized it, was intrigued by it. "Come close?"

"No. Your name was bandied about as a potential suitor for several ladies. Did you ever set your cap on one?"

He had narrowed his selection down to one but hadn't yet begun his courtship in earnest when his life fell apart. At the time he'd been grateful that he'd not brought disgrace to her. On occasion, he wondered if she might have cast him aside as Althea's betrothed had done to her. He realized too late that he'd become distracted, lost in the memories. Sacrificed his advantage.

Esme clenched her jaw and squeezed her legs into a viselike grip that had him cursing while triumph glittered in her eyes, brightening the gold, giving the shade of her eyes an unholy gleam. He shouldn't be mesmerized by her, but damn, he was. Levering himself up, he reached back with one arm and grabbed her calf, striving to break free of her hold. She gave no quarter. He didn't know if he'd ever had such an impressive challenger.

He rocked, rolling to the side, back, then forward. She clung on tenaciously.

"Give up," she ground out through clamped

teeth, her head lifting from the mat with her efforts to keep him secured.

"The devil I will." No rules in this sort of an encounter. He decided to take advantage of the lack of them. Grabbing the swinging tail of her hair, he twisted his hand until the long strands curled around his fist. Holding her in place, he latched his mouth onto hers and plundered.

God help her. Never in her life had Esme ever surrendered so swiftly, so absolutely, without remorse or regret, although she was fairly certain both would visit her later. When she could think clearly.

At the moment, however, thought was beyond her capabilities. All she could do was feel. The sweep of his tongue across hers. The hunger, the yearning, the desire. The heat of his mouth as it consumed hers. This was no prelude to battle. It was complete conquest.

She'd allowed it to happen because she'd desperately wanted it to. From the moment he'd tossed his shirt aside and provided her with a view of the expanse of his chest and bared shoulders, she'd wanted to touch, to stroke, to rub. Just as she had the night when she'd tended his wound. She'd known it was unwise to step into the ring, that her resistance to the lure of him was not as it should be. Even now, with her legs sprawled on either side of him and the hard evidence of his desire nudging against her mound,

she'd never known such power in surrender—
because he hadn't won. If the groans vibrating
within his throat and through his chest were any
indication, he was as helpless as she was to this attraction that had been simmering between them,
probably since the moment she'd first glided into
her parlor and they'd set eyes upon each other.

Based on their encounter at Podmore's, she'd
known he was a man who would give no quarter,
that he would always throw himself into a kiss
with the same determination and enthusiasm he
exhibited when searching for traitors, when confronting ruffians in an alleyway, when struggling
with the truth of his father.

With her hair bound around one hand, he held
her in place while he rolled to his back, bringing
her with him. His other hand skimmed along her
spine, pressing her to his magnificent chest. Bringing her own hands up, she cradled his jaw, taking the kiss deeper, exploring his mouth with the
same care and attention to detail she gave any new
source of information, searching for the hidden
gems that would bring satisfaction.

Growling low, he cupped the curve of her bum
with a large, powerful hand, his fingers digging
in, then soothing. She was grateful for the trousers that provided only a thin layer of material
between his skin and hers.

Pulling gently on her hair, he lifted her mouth
from his and nibbled his way along the underside
of her jaw. "I'll grant you the victory," he rasped.

"It was mine, rightfully earned."

Releasing his hold on the long strands, he cradled her face and held her gaze. She didn't like how easy it was to fall into the blue depths of his eyes or how badly she wanted his mouth ravishing hers again. There was such passion in his actions that she could almost believe he found her desirable beyond the limits of lust. Certainly she'd had her share of men wanting to bed her, but she suspected she was quickly forgotten after they left her—whether she'd succumbed to their charms or not. She didn't want Marcus Stanwick to forget her.

Gathering herself up, she slid off him, nearly mournful at the absence of his heat, his body, against hers. Needing more distance between them, she scooted away until her back hit the ropes. "Will you give up your pursuit now that you know for certain that your father was involved?"

He shoved himself to a sitting position, folded his legs before him, and rested his elbows on his thighs. "I'm more determined than ever to get to the truth."

Relief swamped her because their association would continue for a while longer, and she fought very hard not to let her gladness reveal itself. Reaching up casually as though every nerve ending wasn't joyous, she untied the ribbon holding her hair in place and shook out the strands. "Your shoulder is bleeding."

He glanced down at the trail of blood that had seeped out between the stitches. "Easily stanched."

She shoved herself to her feet. "Why don't you see to it? I need a bath. We'll meet in the library in an hour to determine where we go from here, shall we?"

"After what transpired between us a little while ago, it might be a wiser course to go our separate ways."

"What transpired was all part of the game to win at any cost. You hoped to unsettle me with an unexpected move, I played along and sought to reciprocate. Temptation, desire, yearning had no part in any of it. I'm still an ice princess, Marcus Stanwick. You'll not thaw me." That last bit was most certainly a lie, tossed in to help her retain her pride. The moment he'd touched her, she'd melted completely and utterly.

"Is that all it was?" he asked silkily.

She bestowed upon him a cold, arrogant glare. "Do you want to stay and work together or not?"

"I want to stay."

"Then there's to be no more foolishness in trying to get the better of me. We're equal partners in this. Agreed?"

"Agreed."

"Good. The library. In an hour." It would take her that long to shore back up her defenses in order to resist the lure of him.

CHAPTER 10

$\mathcal{I}$F SHE HADN'T been affected by that kiss, then she was indeed made of ice. If Marcus had been wearing his boots, the power of it would have knocked them clear off. He'd never had a woman meet him on such equal terms, give in equal measure what she was receiving. Women welcomed him, but few had been able to match his passions—even if only for a kiss. But Esme Lancaster was formidable in every way imaginable.

As Marcus lifted away the scrap of linen he'd pressed to his shoulder, he was grateful to see the bleeding had stopped. He'd felt no discomfort or pain as they'd tumbled about. He'd been too focused on her, on striving to get the upper hand. Then when he'd kissed her—

She was no ice princess. She was all heat and fire. Once he'd taken the plunge, he'd felt he was swirling about in a vortex of flames that served to only increase the pleasure. That she hadn't experienced the same—

How could she have not?

After splashing water on his face, he washed up, striving not to imagine her on the other side of the wall, lounging in a tub of steaming water, with droplets rolling along her skin, between her breasts. If he hadn't been worried about bringing her discomfort because of her wound, he might have indulged and given her breast a squeeze when he was kissing her but folding his hand over her derriere had certainly been satisfying. She was firm everywhere. Her arse, her legs, her arms. She moved with such purpose. And he needed to do the same now.

Swiping his shirt from the bed, he donned it and then his waistcoat, neckcloth, and coat before heading down to the library.

Her hands braced on the desk, she leaned over it, studying something before her. She now wore a frock the shade of golden-orange autumn leaves. It brought out the red hints in her mahogany hair. He closed and opened his hand, recalling the soft texture of the strands. It had been a mistake to touch her so intimately because now he wanted only to touch again. Even if she'd burned him, he'd yearn to touch again.

She glanced up and offered him the smallest of smiles. "Good. You're here. I'd like you to look this over. It's a list of the nobility. I've scratched through the names of those Brewster and I have been able to eliminate as potential conspirators."

Only then did he notice Brewster standing off to the side, arms crossed, his eyes as hard as flint. Marcus saw him in a different light now: her assistant, her confidant, her trusted ally.

"Let us know if there are any you feel can be eliminated," she said, drawing his attention back to her.

"Since I would have removed my father from the list, I don't know that I'm the best judge. It seems to me it would be someone we least suspect, someone whose name we would immediately remove as being an improbable traitor."

She smiled fully then. "You see, Brewster, I told you he was a clever chap."

Brewster seemed not at all happy, and Marcus suspected he'd just passed some sort of test. "I have a better idea. Let's pay Podmore a visit this evening and find out exactly what that list of seemingly random words represents and why he keeps it hidden."

"We risk his learning we suspect him of being involved in this plot—and that we are aware it is still being planned and coordinated."

"You don't think they're aware we're in pursuit? Is that not the reason that they've yet to strike against the Queen—because they don't know what we know? Is that not the reason you were pursued when you left Podmore's?"

"I suppose you have a point." She sighed. "All

this waiting around is deuced irritating. O doesn't want us upsetting the applecart but perhaps it's time we did."

NEAR MIDNIGHT, ESME and Marcus took up positions within the shadows of Podmore's garden to wait until the last of his guests departed. The once heir to a dukedom was as still as death but stood near enough to her that she could feel the warmth emanating from his body. He very much reminded her of a predator that had stalked its prey and was now anticipating the perfect moment to strike. She could sense that every aspect of him was on alert. She'd never wanted to wrap herself around a man more.

They'd debated whether to inform O of their plans, but in the end had decided against it. Somehow, that decision made being here with him all the more intimate, as though this was their mission and theirs alone. As though they were sharing something unique to the two of them.

Brewster had remained with the carriage, parked in a mews a few streets over. She was left with the sense that the two men didn't quite trust each other. They were like two roosters, puffing out their chests and crowing, strutting about, striving to dominate the henhouse. Brewster wasn't accustomed to sharing her on a daily—or nightly—basis. In the evenings, when they had no threads to pull or avenues to pursue in their mission to ensure the Queen's safety, he and she would play chess or read before the fire. They seldom shared any personal details of their lives, but a camaraderie existed between them that she found comforting. She viewed him as she might a brother or dear friend. She'd assumed he'd felt similarly, but the tension in the household, between these two men, made her wonder if she'd misread Brewster's feelings toward her. If she had, what else had she gotten wrong? Was she a fool to trust the man standing beside her, to be so intrigued by him, to even now remember the flavor of his mouth upon hers and to want to experience that taste again?

He turned his head toward her, and she did hope he hadn't somehow managed to detect her thoughts. "Podmore doesn't seem to be entertaining tonight."

"If he's even home." They could see light emerging from only one window, conveniently, the library.

"Shall we explore the possibility?"

"By all means."

To her surprise, he wrapped his bare hand around hers and led her out of the thicket toward the stately manor. She'd been a child the last time someone had taken her hand in such a protective manner, as though he wanted to ensure she wasn't separated from him. It gave a strange tug to her heart as she kept in step with him. She was not one to get sentimental, and yet where he was concerned, she seemed to have rather emotional thoughts. What if he'd been older or she younger and they'd known each other when everything in her world had gone awry? Would he have stood as her champion or would he have believed—as everyone else did—the worst of her? She didn't fault him for believing it during the past year, but now that he knew her better . . . it was silly to even speculate.

During tonight's excursion she had no plans to identify herself to Podmore. The few times she'd attended his affairs, she'd done so incognito. It was the reason she now sported a hairpiece of wheat-colored strands, had stuffed linen scraps into the oversized bodice of her corset so her figure took on a different shape, and wore the hood of her pelisse drawn over her head so it shadowed her face. But strands of the wig trailed over her ridiculously large and altered bosom. Like most men, Podmore would remember only the blond hair and the bosom.

Marcus had decided he was in no need of a disguise. He'd made no secret of his objective and thought it to his advantage for word to spread that he was getting closer to discovering who had been involved in the conspiracy. No one would associate her with him because he'd also made perfectly clear—before his father was arrested—how much he loathed the duke's mistress.

Esme was accustomed to being despised, and yet for the first time since she was a young impressionable girl, she imagined the joy of being loved. Not by this man, of course. There was too much past between them, even though they'd only recently met. He'd formed his opinions of her, and while she may have altered them some, she suspected that remnants of his disgust remained, like dying embers easily sparked back to life, to flame.

The trail he took avoided light spilling out of the library, ensured they wouldn't be seen until they were ready to be. He skirted around to the edge of the window and peered in.

"Is he about?" she asked.

"I can see a leg stretched out from the chair facing away from us, near the fireplace. I assume he's lounging there, drinking, reading—or maybe contemplating strategy and his next move."

"Shall we go in through the terrace doorway?"

"No, it's a deuced large library, and he's bound to detect us rattling the latch or if necessary picking the lock. If he's going to run, I'd rather chase him into the garden than through corridors he knows better than I do. This way."

He led them to the servants' door. He tried it, found it locked, released her hand, and crouched. In the darkness, she saw more than heard the tap of the picks he'd taken from his coat. Not a skill normally acquired by a future duke. She had to admire how he'd adjusted to his new circumstance. She knew a good many lords who would have lamented, pouted, and sulked at the unfairness of the life they'd envisioned being stripped away from them. But he'd made the best of it, learning new skills, finding ways to survive, to make something of himself. He might never return to the higher echelons of Society but wherever he landed when all this was behind them, she had no doubt he would remain a man to be reckoned with.

She thought she might covertly seek him out, simply to reassure herself that he was a gentleman of accomplishment because a part of her couldn't help but believe that he was where he was because of actions she'd taken regarding his father. What if instead of using the duke to try to uncover who the others were, she'd spent her time convincing him to change his allegiances, to assist in her undertaking, to become ally rather than foe. He might have retained his ability to breathe and his titles.

But O had wanted her spying, not cajoling. He was rumored to be the best at ferreting out information. While she'd been working for the Home Office for ten years now, they'd never before worked together. She'd known him by reputation only and had looked forward to partnering with him, to learning from him. Thus far, she'd been disappointed in the lessons because they'd added little to her repertoire of skills.

She heard the resounding *click* as Marcus slowly, gently pushed the door just before he was pulling her through the narrow opening. Silence greeted them. It was after midnight, servants were abed. He located a lamp and lit it. Once more he took her hand, and they crept through corridors, making their way to the library where they'd first kissed.

Not what she needed to be remembering at that moment.

Why couldn't his kisses be like every other one

she'd ever received: pleasant and easily forgotten? Why did his have to brand her skin, her memories, her dreams?

At the library he paused and set the lamp on a nearby table before opening the door and striding quickly into the chamber to halt Podmore's escape. Following, she reached Marcus where he'd staggered to a stop.

Podmore wasn't going to be running . . . ever again. His blood-drenched shirt and vacant stare ensured it.

As THE CARRIAGE rumbled through the streets, Marcus contemplated that any other woman might have gasped, screamed, or swooned at the grisly sight of a murdered man. But not Esme Lancaster. He'd seen the sorrow of a life taken reflected in her eyes before she'd shored herself up to face what needed to be done. She'd very calmly gone to the desk and crouched to better reach the hidey hole. When she'd finally stood, she'd announced, "The document is gone."

A few minutes later, so were they.

"Only three people knew we were going there tonight," he said quietly.

"I trust Brewster with my life."

The spark of jealousy that flared at her utter conviction toward another man irritated him, although he took perverse pleasure in the fact that Brewster had been relegated to riding topside with the coachman.

"Or perhaps you suspect me of slipping out of the residence earlier and killing him," she said.

"I don't think one of us killed him. I think one of us said something—perhaps innocently, perhaps not—to someone who then took the matter in hand to see him done in."

"I have another theory, actually. One I don't like much more. Whoever O turned the photographs over to sometime today understood that the documents had been discovered and saw Podmore as an unreliable partner in this mess, and thus decided to eliminate him." She looked out the window. "I feel despair for whichever servant discovers him in the morning. I grieve for the loss of him. He always struck me as more interested in play than politics. Even tonight, to die with a deck of cards in hand."

Not quite in hand. His fingers had been lax, the cards scattered over his lap, except for one, an eight of diamonds that had been resting on the table.

"Was he playing patience or was he playing with someone, unaware that person would strike him down?" she asked.

"I don't think he was playing cards at all."

Within the confines of the dark carriage, she was merely a silhouette, but he was aware of her turning her attention back to him. It struck him like a bolt of lightning. Why did he have to be so aware of her, every movement, every sigh, every silent moment of concentration when she was working things out.

"Why did you pick up the card that was resting on the table?" she asked contemplatively.

It was presently residing within his coat pocket. "Because it tells us who killed him."

"How so?"

"In Whitechapel, there's a gang known as the Devil's Hand."

Her skirts rustled as she moved up to the edge of her seat. "As in Lucifer's hand? Could their leader be the Lucifer whose name is bandied about in relation to this plot against the Queen?"

"I wondered the same thing when I first heard mention of Lucifer, but their leader's name is Willie."

Her sweet laughter circled around him, drew him toward her, and he imagined her as a young girl, carefree and innocent frolicking through a park. He had an urge to see her without cares, racing over the moors at the ducal estate, her laughter sending birds into flight. Without even trying, she filled his head with such fanciful thoughts. When the hilarity had her falling back against the squabs, it took everything within him not to cross over and take possession of that tempting mouth, not to lay her down and ravish her, alter the sound into something more erotic, more sensual, more . . . simply more.

"Willie," she repeated, catching her breath. "That's hardly the name of someone prone to inducing fear. Why do you suspect he's behind tonight's happening?"

"Most of his crew can neither read nor write.

And he strives to protect their names from being associated with the gang so when someone is recruited, he is given a card." He withdrew the one from his pocket, held it up so the glow from the passing streetlamps reflected off it. "When they've done a job, they leave the card behind as proof of their action."

"Why would someone confess?"

"It's not necessarily a confession. Its greater purpose is to serve as a warning as well as a signature of sorts to ensure Willie learns the deed was done by their hand. Only Willie knows who carries which card."

"Do you think they were expecting us?"

"Possibly. I am certain it was either a warning or a message to someone."

"How can you be so certain of all this?"

"Because I once was a member of the gang."

CHAPTER 11

$\mathcal{A}$ SILENCE FOLLOWED HIS pronouncement. Marcus was grateful that before she could fill it with questions that he wasn't ready to answer, the carriage came to a stop. He shoved open the door, leapt out, and reached back to hand her down—a small courtesy that a week ago, he couldn't have imagined himself doing for her. A week ago, he'd despised her. Now all he wanted was to bed her. To become so lost in her that he forgot the harsh realities of his past, the dark path he'd trod in search of answers, not only about his father but about himself.

Once inside the residence, he headed into the parlor and straight for the scotch. He refused to acknowledge the disappointment because she didn't follow, because the fading patter of her footsteps suggested her destination was elsewhere. He detected her ascending the stairs, no doubt heading toward her bedchamber. He wondered if she needed some time alone to deal with the gruesome sight that had greeted them earlier. Just because she didn't swoon, it didn't mean that her feminine sensibilities hadn't been battered. Any other woman he would have immediately comforted. Her, he judged to be so strong as to be insulted if he offered any sort of solace.

He tossed back a scotch, refilled the glass, and dropped into the chair that he'd begun to consider his. Strange how he felt more at home here than he had in any grand residence in which he'd lived. She was not the homely sort and yet she did have a way about her of making a man feel welcome. Perhaps his father had associated with her because she comforted, and he didn't feel judged for actions that most would never forgive.

Marcus was nearly finished with the amber contents of his glass when he heard her footfalls nearing. The gratitude he felt at her returning was cumbersome. Since his father's betrayal he'd lived a life of needing no one. And yet he had the absurd thought that perhaps he needed Esme.

She glided in, having changed into some loose garment that flowed around her. In her arms was a black-and-white ball of fur.

"You have a dog?"

"Aren't you a clever spy? This is Laddie." She abruptly dropped the dog in his lap and took his glass. "He's certain to brighten your mood."

"My mood doesn't need brightening." Yet, he couldn't hold back his smile as the spaniel stretched up on his hind legs, rested his front paws on Marcus's shoulder, and licked the underside of his jaw.

Returning, she set a full glass on the table beside his chair and swept the dog back into her arms, retreating to her chair. Her chair. His chair. The next thing he knew he'd be thinking of them as a couple.

"This time of night, Laddie is usually asleep, but I needed a cuddle and he's ever so good at providing them." She went quiet briefly, before saying, "Podmore didn't deserve the ending he received. I think it's possible that because of the chaos that happened at his residence, perhaps it was merely a meeting place, unbeknownst to him. I can't see him being serious enough to be involved in a plot. The document found in his desk baffled me. I truly had not expected to find anything."

"He might have known something without knowing what he knew. Or perhaps someone else was using his desk without his knowledge."

"That makes more sense. Perhaps they came to retrieve the document, and he was unexpectedly at home, someone who could identify them. Although he'd obviously welcomed them because there was no blood anywhere else. What a ghastly way to go. I shall add seeing him avenged to my list of duties."

"You have a list of people to be avenged?"

"I can't stand injustice of any kind. Bullies are not to be tolerated. And we seem to be dealing with quite the bully here." She buried her fingers in Laddie's silken strands. He watched her hand circling, longed for her to stroke his chest. "Tell me about your involvement with this gang."

His sigh could have toppled trees. "It's not one of my prouder accomplishments." He hadn't had enough scotch to reveal everything, didn't want to reveal anything, but she sat there, petting her dog, patiently waiting, her gaze steady and unblinking. She wouldn't sit in judgment, no matter what he confessed. He was certain of that. In only a few days, his opinion of her had altered dramatically. She was someone his sister would enjoy spending time with, someone his brother would realize was not cold marble. He could imagine his father bringing his traitorous thoughts here because he hadn't invested his life with Esme, because he wouldn't consider his actions a betrayal to her. Whereas he had to know he was betraying his wife and children. Perhaps he'd become scarce around his family because of the guilt surrounding his plans. But here, he could drink his scotch and find some measure of peace. Never knowing the woman with whom he felt safe, the one he proudly escorted about town and made no qualms about introducing as his mistress, might very well lead to his downfall. She was so easy to trust. Marcus could hope only that he wasn't falling into the same trap.

"As you're well aware, before they hanged him, the Crown stripped my father of his titles—a dukedom and an earldom—and properties, everything entailed. They even managed to take a good bit that wasn't. The price of being a traitor. I'd never considered myself to be anything other than the heir, the future duke. I discovered later that Griff had his dreams for a business—"

"The Fair Ladies' and Spare Gentlemen's Club."

"He hated being the spare. Doesn't admit into his club any firstborn son who will inherit a title." Hence, the spare gentlemen. "He thinks we get enough attention from among the ladies of the aristocracy."

"I'm rather certain you did—if the gossip sheets are to be believed."

"I didn't fare too poorly but was rather glad I hadn't taken a wife who'd have been forced to endure the mortification and censure when our lives went to hell. We were all unprepared. I'd not pursued any personal financial endeavors as I had access to the family funds and was spending my days learning all that was involved in managing the estates—my responsibilities and duties there. I had a bit set aside from wagers made, but for the most part I was invested in ensuring I did right by everything and everyone who would one day be entrusted to my care."

"Then it was all taken away. Your future, your plans. All that you envisioned your life would be."

He heard true empathy in her tone and wondered again what path she had traveled to be where she presently was. What had been torn from her grasp?

"The little I did have I used to ensure Griff and Althea at least had a roof over their heads. But I was consumed with anger, not fit company for man nor beast. For a while I became lost in the murkier aspects of London. I believed my father had to have been associated with the vilest of creatures. And so I hunted there. Eventually I crossed paths with the Devil's Hand gang and was recruited by Willie. I learned to pick locks, break fingers, and frighten those who owed him money. For a while I found the violence cathartic. I welcomed getting embroiled in fisticuffs, striking out, causing hurt, being hurt. I'm ashamed of that now, to know that I have it within me to be barbaric, that there is a darker aspect to my character."

"At heart, I suspect a bit of barbarian lurks inside all of us. You've obviously regained control of yourself. Perhaps you felt you were deserving of some punishment for your father's actions."

He shook his head, even though he was in complete agreement with her. "How could I have not known what he was about? I was determined to use my association with the Devil's Hand to my advantage. I began to ask around—if I wanted a member of Parliament, a prime minister, or even a queen killed, who would I hire? I was a bit more subtle, but you get the gist of it. Now and again, the name Lucifer surfaced. A night came when one of Willie's henchmen, knife in hand, attacked me. Griff had begun watching my back and he did the blighter in. He had no choice, but it ate at him. Soon after, we parted ways and he opened his club. I left Willie and his gang behind and struck out on my own. A few more attempts on my life convinced me I was close to learning something. So I came to you hoping you might have the missing information I sought and here we are."

HERE WE ARE.

Where exactly were they?

In her entire life, Esme had never felt quite so unsure of her place. If he were a mark, someone from whom she'd been ordered to gather information, she'd be striving to seduce him with kisses and promises for more intimate encounters, which she would never keep. But they were willingly sharing their knowledge, were uncovering much of it together, so seduction wasn't necessary. And yet, she found herself wanting to seduce, to be seduced, to hold fast to those promises that would lead him into her bed. He'd certainly kissed her as though drawn to her, but he'd been prudently keeping his distance ever since she'd left him in the ring.

She was struck with the realization that even though Marcus had associated with the worst of what London had to offer, he was a decent man. Lost for a while but clawing his way back to civility. Even when blinded by anger at his father's betrayal, he'd ensured his siblings were provided for as best he could.

From infancy, he'd been walking a path, a single destination ahead and always in sight—when suddenly the road beneath his feet had crumbled into an abyss. She'd had a similar experience in her youth but had decided to travel the new road upon which she'd landed. It held no surprises until him. He was a surprise. "So who is this eight of diamonds?"

"I haven't a clue. That's the beauty of this system. Everyone is anonymous."

"What card was associated with you?"

"I refused to take one. I wanted people to know who I was, so I simply went by Wolf."

As he'd explained earlier, an homage to the title he would have inherited. "What will you do when all this is behind you?"

"Short of the Queen returning the titles to me, which I'm fairly certain won't happen, I've considered hiring out as a private detective. If I'm—we're—successful here, hopefully my name will no longer be associated with treason but some sort of heroics, and my reputation as a man of honor will be restored. People, especially those among the *ton*, will feel they can trust me again. There's always some daughter who has run off, a son engaged in mischief that needs to be confirmed, or an unfaithful spouse who needs to be caught in the act if a divorce is to take place. In some ways, during the past year, I've felt more alive than I ever had before. The cloak-and-dagger aspect appeals to me. Tonight, creeping through Podmore's hallways"—he shook his head—"I'd have rather not found him dead, but I relish that edge of danger."

He was holding her gaze, delving into her soul, waiting, she was certain, for her to confess the same. And so she did. "I have found something about the danger to be quite addictive. I think perhaps it's the never knowing what I'll find. Or that moment of uncertainty, when I don't know if I'll be triumphant. Sometimes I feel that much of my life is simply holding my breath, waiting for the singular second that snatches it away completely."

"Precisely."

She couldn't tear her eyes from him. Never in her life had she been so mesmerized, had she felt so *understood*.

"How long have you been doing this?" he asked quietly.

"A decade." A puff of laughter escaped from her. "I can't believe it's been that long. I was twenty-three when I went to work for the Home Office."

"That bodes well for me then when it comes to a lifetime of satisfaction if you've not yet grown weary with the task."

"I can't imagine doing anything else, of being content to pour tea for friends in the garden in the afternoon. Although at one point that was what I saw as my future."

"What happened to change it—your future?"

Within her lap, Laddie began to squirm. Thank goodness. The intensity with which Marcus was studying her made her want to tell him everything—but the memories, even after all these years, were painful and she didn't want to travel through them. Not tonight. Not with him. She never wanted him to pity her, and he would. She wouldn't be able to stand for him to know of her weakness. "I have to take Laddie out into the garden."

She rose and so did he. "I won't be but a moment," she said.

"I'll escort you."

She was a fool to hope it was because he enjoyed her company. More likely, he didn't trust her and suspected she was going to do something more than let her dog out for a wee. "As you wish."

After setting Laddie on the floor, Esme began strolling through the residence; Laddie led the way, his paws clicking over the parquet, periodically muffled by a rug they crossed, until they reached the kitchen. The cocker hurried to the door, began scratching at it and whining. Esme detoured to the large wooden table where an unlit lamp rested. She struck a match. "Will you open the door to let him out?" A wooden fence that separated her property from her neighbors' properties on either side would prevent him from running off.

She lifted the glass globe and lit the wick, vaguely aware of the door opening and Laddie dashing out. Loud, chaotic barking ensued.

"Something has him in a dither," Marcus said.

With lamp in hand, she walked to the door. "Probably just a squirrel. He'll tire of it soon enough."

Edging past him, she stepped outside, aware of his following near enough that she could feel the warmth of his body. How she wanted to rest against him, have his arm circle her. What fanciful thoughts she was having. It had been so very long since she'd taken a lover, and it would certainly complicate things between them if they became intimate. Although he would probably tell her he could handle complicated. Fighting to tamp down any desire, she held the lamp aloft, but it didn't provide sufficient light for her to see far enough in order to determine why her dog was engaged in frenzied barking. "He doesn't usually put up such a fuss. Laddie! Hush!" She glided in the direction that the barking and growling seemed to be coming from.

"Bloody 'ell! Dog bit me!" a rough voice yelled, a voice she didn't recognize.

A yelp quickly followed, and Laddie went quiet. Panic surged through her. Marcus was already running toward the rustling coming from one side of the garden.

"Run!" Another voice. Deeper, gruffer.

Two shadows broke free of the darkness, quickly followed by a third silhouette. She was relatively certain the last one was Marcus, giving chase. Who were the men and what the deuce were they doing here? But more importantly, where was Laddie? Holding up the lamp, dashing carefully through the gloom, she called out for him, even as her gut, her heart, her very soul told her it was pointless. No other sounds filled the garden. No sniffing, no growling, no rustling of foliage as Laddie explored the surroundings to find the perfect spot to lift a leg.

Then the lamplight captured a speck of white. White mixed with black. An unmoving mound on the ground. Her heart lurched and her chest tightened as she slowly lowered herself to examine the inert form of her beloved Laddie.

DAMNATION! THE BUGGERS got away!

The scotch had slowed Marcus's reflexes and by the time he'd arrived in the alleyway, the blighters were nowhere to be seen. They'd either had transport waiting for them or they'd scrambled over a wall into another property. He crept up and down the darkened path, listening intently for any movement, but all was silent. He cursed soundly before heading back into Esme's garden.

He was only a few steps in when he spied her kneeling in a halo of light provided by the lamp resting on the ground near her hip. She reminded him of a painting of the Madonna he'd once seen: serene and angelic. And beautiful. So damned beautiful, making it difficult to breathe, as though he was still chasing after those damned scapegraces. But then another sight caught his eye, white strands reflecting the glow from the lamp. "Bloody hell."

Without further thought he was running for all he was worth toward her. When he was near enough, he skidded to a stop on the dew-coated grass and dropped to his knees. Her hand resting on the dog's chest, Esme didn't look at him but said quietly, "He's breathing, but he's not moving."

In her voice, he heard a depth of sadness so profound that it awoke within him the sympathy for another that he'd buried long ago, when his life took its drastic turn toward unfairness for him and his family. "One of them probably struck him." Maybe the one who'd been bitten, in fury or fear, had delivered a blow or kick. "Knocked him out. My hands are larger. Let me carry him inside for you."

She barely nodded before easing back, lifting the lamp, and standing. Shifting toward the cocker, he gently slipped his hands beneath its body and cradled it in his arms. The dog made no sound, didn't twitch a single muscle.

Marcus followed Esme into the kitchen and tenderly laid Laddie on the table, stepping aside so she could once again bury her fingers in her pet's fur. Here within this room, where walls served to contain the lamplight, so it brightened the space, he saw the track of tears, the dampness on her cheeks. She wept for an injured dog. How was it possible, with the exception of her beauty, that he had managed to misjudge every other aspect of her? Tenderly, with his thumb, he reached out and gathered up some of the glistening dew.

She lifted her gaze to his, the desolation in her golden-brown eyes causing a painful tightening in his chest. "For five years now, Laddie has

served as my companion, my most trusted, devoted, and stalwart friend. If he dies—"

"He won't." He couldn't remember the last time
he'd sounded so sure about anything, and it was
reckless of him to give her hope. He was neither
a veterinarian—did they even treat dogs?—nor a
physician. What did he know about canine injuries? What he did know was swooning women.
"Have you any smelling salts?"

"What need have I for smelling salts? I don't
faint."

"Spices then." Moving away from her, he began opening drawers and cabinets until he found
some jars and cloth sacks labeled with the names
of spices. He sniffed the contents until he located
something particularly pungent. Pouring some
into his cupped palm, he returned to the table
and placed his hand right beneath Laddie's nose.
The dog's face twitched slightly. "That's it. Come
on. Be a good lad and wake up."

Moving his hand nearer, he waited while the
dog took a couple more breaths and finally his
eyes fluttered open.

"Oh, Laddie!" Esme cried, swooping the cocker
up into her arms. Marcus couldn't remember
ever seeing her so animated, so joyful, so . . . like
women who weren't weighted down with bur-
dens.

"I'd be careful with him," he said gently. "I had
a friend who fell from his horse and conked his
head. He had something the physician called a

concussion. He was confused for a while, walked like a drunk."

"Do dogs get concussions?" she asked him earnestly as though he were an expert on the creature, and he wished he was just so he could reassure her. He didn't know why he suddenly had this strong need to soothe her worries.

"I don't know. I don't know if anyone knows, if they've been studied. As far as I'm aware, veterinarians only tend to horses and cattle. Perhaps set him down and see what happens."

She placed her pet on the floor, and Laddie merely lowered himself to his belly and placed his chin on his paws. Esme lifted him back to the table where he resumed the same pose. "That tin there." She nodded toward a coppery container on the counter with *Laddie* painted in block letters on it. "Cook bakes special biscuits for him. Will you get him one?"

He dusted off his hands over the sink first before retrieving the treat that smelled suspiciously like liver and kidneys, neither of which had ever truly appealed to him. He handed it to her, watching with interest as she offered it to her dog. Her smile as Laddie gobbled it down was the sort about which poets mused. Marcus wanted it captured in oils, along with the delight in her eyes. Along with the single teardrop that still clung tenaciously to her lashes, a reminder of her warm, caring heart.

"Well, he might not want to frolic about, but his

appetite doesn't seem to be suffering." She looked at Marcus. "I don't suppose you were able to get a look at the intruders."

"No. They were quite adept at making their escape."

"Who do you think they were? What did they want? Do you think they followed us from Podmore's?"

All questions he'd been asking himself. "If they meant no harm, they'd have not run off."

She gave a quick nod, walked into the hallway, and disappeared around the corner. He heard a knock, then her voice. "Some ruffians were prowling about in the garden. When Laddie discovered them, they made a hasty exit after hurting him. Have a couple of footmen patrol the gardens until dawn."

"Righto," Brewster replied. "Laddie?"

"I think he'll be fine. Stanwick tended him."

"I don't trust him."

"Laddie?"

Marcus heard the grunt, took pleasure in imagining Brewster scowling. "Stanwick."

"He's given us no reason not to trust him."

"Which is exactly what someone we shouldn't trust would do."

Silence greeted that pronouncement, and Marcus was a tad disappointed she didn't defend him again, but more vigorously. Then he heard her slippers brushing over the floor, and she was soon back in his company. "Brewster is going to have a couple of footmen keep watch."

"So I gathered from the conversation."

Her cheeks turned a rosy hue, the only indication she might be embarrassed or regret that he was aware of a discussion she'd no doubt wished he hadn't overheard. "Would you mind carrying Laddie upstairs? He sleeps in my chamber."

Marcus was actually grateful for that tidbit of information. Based on what he'd witnessed tonight, the cocker would defend his mistress to the death if anyone entered her room with malicious intent. Marcus had always believed canines instinctually knew good people from bad. Perhaps evil gave off a rancid smell.

Laddie didn't object when Marcus gingerly cradled him in his arms again and carted him up the stairs in Esme's wake. He couldn't decide if he liked what she was wearing. It flowed so much that it camouflaged the shape of her body, but because of the silky-smooth way it floated around her, he was relatively certain she wore very little, if anything, beneath it. He imagined it sliding along her length and pooling on the floor, her stepping out of it and into his arms to thank him for returning animation to her dog.

At the landing, he followed her into her bedchamber and staggered to a stop. He'd envisioned her sprawled over red satin sheets, surrounded by red-and-purple pillows. He'd expected decadence. Nude statues and paintings.

Not the white-trimmed-in-pink duvet. Not the two wingback plush chairs with the pink-and-white brocade cushions. Not the large painting of a shoreline with a little girl, pail in hand, bent over examining a seashell. The pastel pink-and-orange sky with just a trace of blue and only a few wispy clouds indicating dawn or sunset. And certainly not the porcelain doll sitting on her vanity. *Great Expectations* rested on the bedside table.

"You can set him on the right side of the bed," she said. "That's where he sleeps. Or where he starts out, I should say. Eventually he'll curl against me."

For the first time in his life, Marcus was jealous of a dog. When he stepped away, he was surprised Esme remained standing by the window, as though his proximity to the bed was a danger to her—or perhaps a temptation she wouldn't be able to resist. He couldn't deny that tossing her on it had certainly crossed his mind. He could still feel her tears on his thumb, wanted to plumb her hidden depths, wanted to discover if she was as passionate between the sheets as he anticipated.

"I think I'll have a physician examine Laddie once it's daylight," she said softly, her gaze homing in on Marcus.

"If you can find one willing to look at an animal."

"I'll pay him enough that he will do anything I ask."

He had the disturbing thought that even without payment, Marcus would do anything she asked. How had he come to this point? It was more than the earlier tears, the softness of her heart. It was her strength, her courage, her belief in her righteous endeavors. He was incredibly tempted to cross over to her and take that luscious mouth of hers. But because the temptation was so great, he said, "I should abed."

"Thank you for seeing to Laddie, for bringing him back around. I'd have never thought to try spices."

He shrugged. "I suspect he'd have eventually woken up on his own."

"Still, it was reassuring not to have too long a wait." She trailed a hand over the silky white curtain with its pink trim. The entire room seemed far too delicate for her. Too innocent.

His bedchamber was darker hues, hunter green and burgundy. Too masculine for her. He'd thought she resided somewhere in between the décor of his room and hers. She was a conundrum, an enigma. How much of her was real? How much pretense? If he were to seduce her, which woman would he find in his arms? The devil of it was that everything about her intrigued him. "Good night, Esme."

"Sleep well, Marcus."

As he strode from the room, he doubted he was going to sleep at all. She was going to haunt his dreams, driving him mad with desire.

CHAPTER 12

$\mathcal{B}$Y THE TIME the sun chased away the fog, Laddie was his usual perky self, so Esme dispensed with the notion of fetching a physician. After breakfast, she and Marcus scanned the gardens, searching for any clues that might assist in discovering the identity of the men or what they'd been seeking. They found only trampled flowers and foliage. And one large rock near where Laddie had lay crumpled. She assumed it to be the weapon used to silence him or get him to stop attacking. She'd never known the cocker to be so fierce, but then until last night, he'd never had reason to be.

"You should probably continue to have someone keep watch through the night," Marcus suggested as they strolled back toward the residence.

"They could have just been burglars," she said.

"You don't believe that any more than I do."

"I wish Laddie had bitten that one fellow hard enough that he'd not been able to run. Then we could have gotten some answers." They were sorely lacking of late.

In her library, she removed from her desk drawer the photographs of the document. Before handing a set over to O, she'd printed a set for herself. Marcus sat with one butt cheek on the edge of the desk. She refused to acknowledge how much she liked the way the fabric of his trousers hugged that firm backside and the thigh nearest to her. She wondered if he'd always been so perfectly sculpted or if his recent endeavors had shaped his muscles to a mouthwatering firmness.

"Do you think those are suddenly going to reveal information they hadn't before?" he asked.

"I like having them as a reference, in case something might jump out at us." Crossing her arms beneath her breasts to ensure her hands didn't reach out to stroke that beguiling thigh, she turned slightly and pressed her hip against her desk. "If I were going to plot to assassinate a queen, I would want at my side someone I trusted implicitly. Your father might have felt the same and the culprits are closer to home than we realize."

"Such as myself?"

"I thought we'd established that I don't believe you were involved, and you don't believe I was."

"Brewster thinks I am."

"He doesn't like that you're young and handsome. He thinks you might turn my head, cause me to lose focus."

He grinned. "Could I turn your head?"

With one more kiss, with a stroke of that large hand along her back, with an endearment whispered in her ear. "I'm not so foolish as all that. I'm well aware that men prefer their women to be younger than they themselves are."

"You're three years older than I. That hardly makes you an ancient crone. Besides, I prefer my women seasoned."

"Hmm." She arched a brow. "With salt or pepper?"

"A little of both. I've never favored the innocent. I can't believe you have either."

She doubted she'd ever been with anyone who had traveled the dark paths he had. He was the very opposite of innocent, and she found it incredibly appealing. He was probably more her equal than anyone she'd ever been with. Oh, she was tempted, so very tempted. But if they got involved, would it cloud their judgment? She couldn't quite dismiss Brewster's concerns, even though she didn't harbor them. But had she already been blinded by what Marcus had suffered? Was she seeing him as clearly as she ought?

"I believe we've strayed from my original train of thought." One corner of his mouth hitched up, and she was rather certain that he was fully aware that she was striving to distract herself from images of him in her bed. "He was closest to the Marquess

of Fotheringham. Or Hammy, as he called him."
Reaching down, she picked up one of the photographs. "There's a Piggy listed here. Scratched through. I wonder if that was the marquess."

Taking the photograph from her, Marcus studied it as though it might reveal more to his eye than hers. "He died a little over a month before Father was arrested."

"Yes, I'm aware. A riding accident at his estate, apparently. Fell and broke his neck, although no one witnessed it."

"I thought nothing of it at the time. It wasn't unusual for him to start his day with a solitary ride. But now . . . after Podmore . . ." His voice trailed off as he seemed to drift into speculation. He shook the photo as though by doing so he might cause something hidden to shoot to the fore and become visible.

"I made discreet inquiries of his heir," she confided.

His hand went still, and he arched a brow, amusement dancing in his eyes. "How did that go?"

She offered him a wry grin. "Not so well. I managed to cross paths with him at a museum, a lady lost looking for a particular exhibit, which he offered to help me find. From there, we spent about an hour together."

"As I recall Walter was all of sixteen at the time his father died. I imagine the lad became immediately lovestruck with the attentions of a much older woman directed his way."

"He did seem to appreciate having a sympathetic

ear as we strolled through the exhibits. But he provided no useful information."

"Fotheringham married rather late, nearing
forty before he finally took a wife."

"She wasn't much help either except to confirm
he spent most of his evenings away from home.
She seemed a silly chit, more upset that she had
to wear black than that her husband had passed."

"She was at the museum as well?"

"No, she was having a dress fitting—entirely
inappropriate for a new widow—but I arranged
to have a fitting at the same time—a recent widow
as well—and so we commiserated."

"She didn't recognize you as Father's companion?"

"No. Few aristocrats actually saw me with him,
and he never introduced me to anyone. Besides, I
was gray-haired and dowdy. Part of my training
included learning tricks mastered in the theater
to make someone not look like themselves. Man-
nerisms play a large role in that." Perhaps she
shouldn't have admitted the latter. He might begin to wonder how much of her aloofness toward
him, the distance she maintained between them,
was an act of self-preservation.

"Did Father provide you with any information
about Fotheringham to make you believe he was
involved?"

"It was his lack of wanting to talk about him that
made me suspicious. Immediately after Fotheringham's death, the duke became extremely melan-

choly. He would sit in front of the fire in my parlor and toss back scotch as though it were water. A couple of times he passed out. One night he wept uncontrollably. When I tried to console him and encouraged him to talk about his upset, he would say that he couldn't."

"Father never was good at voicing his emotions."

"I was under the impression that it was more than that. Rather he was holding a secret. One night he did mutter that it was his fault, and I wondered then if he was referring to the accident. I comforted him as best I could, hoping he would reveal more. But he never did. Do you believe Fotheringham could have been involved?"

IT WAS WRONG to resent his father for coming here to draw comfort from Esme—and yet resent him he did. Even if he'd never bedded her, he'd known her gentle touch, her concern, her worry. He'd been comfortable enough with her to break down in her presence. A man Marcus had never seen shed a tear, a man who ridiculed anyone who didn't appear strong at all times.

Marcus tossed the photograph onto the desk, got up, and strode to the window that looked out on the garden where last night two men had been skulking about. He'd originally suspected that other lords might be involved but not as many as those photographs hinted at. Four hundred years ago, perhaps. But today they were civilized. Although at the moment he felt anything but. "I'd just be guessing, and I don't really see that it makes any difference now."

"I would like to confirm that this list has some authenticity to it."

Slowly he turned to face her. "Do you know if a search of our residence, in particular my father's study, took place? Was anything uncovered there?" Although if it had been, surely they'd shared it with her and they wouldn't presently be so uninformed.

"Nothing of any significance was found."

"Did you go through the residence?"

"No."

"Considering the luck that you had in finding Podmore's cubbyhole, perhaps you should have. Maybe we should take a look now. As of last week, it was still uninhabited and locked up." The Crown had taken possession of it, and he suspected it would remain idle for a while, until Victoria created a new title and gave the entailed properties to the new holder. No one would want to be associated with Wolfford any longer. Or perhaps the Crown would sell everything off or distribute it among the Queen's favorites.

Esme grinned mischievously, and he could see that she very much liked the idea of sleuthing. "And we both have the skills to enter without a key. When do you think would be the best time to go lurking?"

"Now, when we can see without a lamp. Otherwise, someone might catch sight of the light and send for a constable or Scotland Yard."

She backed off, taking her rose scent with her. "I'll have the carriage brought 'round."

After she wandered out of the room, he turned back toward the window. He'd returned to the residence only once since his family had been kicked out of it, with few possessions to their name. He'd gone at night, stealthily creeping through with only the dim light of a single lamp to guide him, desperate to avoid detection. He'd not found anything to help him—and any small item of value that he might have carried with him had been removed—but perhaps he'd missed something, something that Esme with her clever ways might notice. Still, it was with a measure of dread that he prepared himself for a journey into his past.

CHAPTER 13

THE HONOR OF picking the lock at the servant's entrance fell to Marcus, and as Esme watched him, she couldn't help thinking that he would have had the job done in a tick if he weren't breaking into what had once been his family's residence but now belonged to the Crown. She'd considered suggesting that she come alone, to spare him what she feared might be a bombardment of memories, but suspected he wouldn't appreciate knowing that she realized how difficult coming here might be for him. At one time, he would have inherited the grand residence upon his father's death. It had to be infuriating to face what had been taken from him, not through any fault of his own. Neither he nor his siblings had done anything to deserve the punishment and yet it had been visited upon them because they carried their father's blood and among royalty and nobility blood was everything.

After they'd arrived in the mews, she'd sent her driver on an errand, certain he'd return before they were done exploring the place, although she was beginning to think he might return before they'd even entered the dwelling. Then she heard the tiniest of clicks and Marcus's sigh. Straightening, he released the latch, shoved the door open, and bent slightly, motioning with his hand that she should precede him.

It was eerie to walk into a residence that was absent of sound, the life of it hollowed out. It felt different somehow from an empty residence that one was viewing with the possibility of purchasing or letting. These walls seemed haunted, as though they knew they'd been betrayed. A shiver raced up her spine as she carried on down the hallway, aware of the door behind her closing and snicking into place and the echo of Marcus's boots as he followed her.

Glancing in the kitchen, she envisioned all the staff who had once worked there. She reached the butler's office and stopped. The furniture, draped in white, remained. "Do you think your father might have hidden something in there?"

Marcus had come up behind her and she was aware of the tension radiating from him. "I'm not even certain my father was aware the downstairs existed."

She peered at him over her shoulder. "I find that difficult to believe."

"He was a duke who yanked on bellpulls and people magically appeared to do his bidding." He sighed. "Although I suppose there's no harm in looking."

No harm and no joy as it turned out. Although she did get a sense from all the ledgers and notices from shops that an inordinate number of spirits was purchased for this household. They searched the housekeeper's room, the wine store, the laundry . . . every room used by staff. Since the servants had taken their personal items with them when they were let go, very often there was little to look through.

"I hope the staff found good employment elsewhere," he said quietly as they trudged up the stairs. "That they weren't penalized for having been employed by a traitor."

"Having served a duke, they were no doubt able to land on their feet. I can't imagine anyone would have held them accountable for their employer's bad judgment."

"It is astounding how the actions of one can affect so many."

They reached the top and an antechamber where the footmen prepared to serve dinner. He shoved on the door and walked through, holding the portal as she followed. The dining hall was nearly as large as the main floor of her residence. Again, everything was draped in white: the long table, chairs, cabinets that no doubt held china or heirlooms. She was tempted to strip away all the cloths so she could feast upon what she was certain would put her own mother's furniture to shame.

He came to a set of double doors, pushed them open, and strode into the cavernous chamber. As she stepped through the portal, the fragrance of books swept over her, even though all the shelves and tomes were hidden behind white linen, transporting her to a time when she had devoured books because they'd carried her away from an unforgiving mother and a stepfather who couldn't quite decide what to make of her, who'd wanted to marry her off young, so she'd no longer be their problem.

While she'd ceased movement in order to take in the grandeur that was still visible—the dark mahogany walls, the heavy golden drapes, the large chandelier—Marcus had continued on until he reached the massive fireplace. Reaching up, he yanked down the covering to reveal a large portrait of his family. She recognized each member because she'd made it her business to be able to know them on sight, in case their paths should have crossed, or an opportunity presented itself for her to make discreet inquiries of them. The older woman sitting on the settee was his mother, the young lady beside her his sister. The duke stood behind the only piece of furniture in the painting, his two sons flanking him, the settee narrow enough that the full length of Marcus and his brother was visible.

Marcus had been slenderer when those oils had been brushed over that canvas. And softer. Not in a feminine way, but he was without cares. His brow harbored none of the lines in it that it did now. His eyes didn't look at the world with cynicism. His mouth wasn't set in a hard line as though daring one and all to come at him. His jaw wasn't taut as though he yearned to pound his fist into something. She rather wished she'd known him then, but only for a minute. He wouldn't have appealed to her as he did now. He'd have been far too innocent, too naive, too trusting. The man standing there gazing up at the portrait tempted her far more than he should, more than was safe or wise.

As though she were the tide and it were the moon, the portrait gently drew her toward it, her feet making no sound as they traversed over the thick Aubusson carpet until she was standing beside the man she'd once considered her nemesis.

"That was painted the Christmas before all went to hell," he said quietly.

1872, then. After the rumors of an assassination plot had begun surfacing. Had the duke been strategizing even as he posed there with his family gathered around him? Or had he yet to become an accomplice? "I'd not thought it done so recently. You all look remarkably young."

"I wonder how long he'd been involved in the planning of the betrayal. I see no deception in those eyes. I thought if I looked at the portrait more closely, I would see that I should have known what he was about." He shook his head. "How could I have not known?" He scoffed. "But look at me. I appear to be a young man who cares about only his own pleasures. I remember being a bit cross because the artist was taking so damned long with it. I wanted to go skiing in the Alps with some mates. I left as soon as the last drop of paint touched the canvas. The thing is, even if I'd known it was to be our last Christmas together as a family, I don't know if I'd have stayed. We were never close."

She had a strong urge to pull his head down and cradle it against her bosom, to murmur words of comfort. But she'd been the heartless harlot for so long that any softening at all was a bit terrifying.

"Well"—he released a long exhale—"staring at that isn't going to get us anywhere, is it?" Spinning around, he yanked the cloth off the massive rosewood desk. "Put your talents to work. I'll look elsewhere within the room."

As he marched away and began tugging other cloths from their mooring to be carelessly tossed on the floor, she had a feeling he had a need to put some distance between them. Perhaps he was embarrassed to have revealed so much, for giving her that small glimpse inside of him. The young Marcus in the portrait would not have been bothered by it. But then he had yet to have been effectively destroyed. Had not been forced to re-create himself.

The desk was a monstrosity, three solid walls, the fourth side containing an opening between two towers of drawers that revealed themselves to be empty when she opened each one. No doubt they'd been gone through when the duke was arrested. Whatever had been contained within had not been shared with her, so it was either useless or something deemed for particular eyes alone to gaze upon. She was considered a foot soldier, told only what was necessary to get the job done.

Glancing over at Marcus, she watched for a minute as he examined drawers in delicate tables. She could so easily envision him sitting at this desk, lord of his domain, managing estates, seeing to the well-being of those under his care. All of this should have been his. It was wrong for it to have been taken away. But if he'd merely stepped into the role of duke, would he now move so smoothly, like a wolf on the prowl, throughout the room? Such purpose in his strides, such concentration in his gaze. He considered and explored thoroughly each object he approached. She shouldn't be enthralled by something as simple as the wave of a hand over a figurine, the stroke of a chair that might have something hidden beneath the fabric, the riffling of pages through a book before gently setting it aside—respecting the treasures that would go to someone else not of his blood because eventually the Crown would gift this residence to someone or sell it. He should lay claim to the non-entailed possessions. Perhaps he would once some honor was restored to his family name. She wanted him to have all this.

For that to happen, they needed information.

Kneeling, she began running her fingers over the smooth wood, occasionally pressing, searching for something that might trigger the opening of a concealed compartment. A *click* sounded, on the side, near the front of the desk. "I've found something!"

His fragrance of spice and man was suddenly surrounding her within the close confines, causing an unexpected dizziness to assail her as she breathed him in more deeply. What an absolute fool she was.

"What is it?" he asked, a tightness and eagerness in his voice.

"A small door has sprung open, revealing a cubby." She reached inside and her finger was pricked. Odd. "There's something—"

Taking a bit more care, she grasped it and brought it out. He scooted back, placed his hands on her waist, and dragged her from the cavernous opening. Crouching before her, he asked, "What did you find?"

She unfurled her fingers to reveal an intricately carved wooden soldier in a red coat, sword at the ready, the tip of which had probably caused the pinprick of pain in her finger.

"Bastard," he ground out in a low growl, gently taking it from her, dropping from his haunches to his backside, and pressing his spine against the desk. "I was eight years old, in this room, striving to gain my father's attention, playing with this fellow, pretending I was him, battling Napoleon's army, racing around when I knocked over a porcelain figurine of a woman herding lambs. He snatched my soldier from me, declared me too old for such nonsense. I awoke the next morning to find all my armies gone from my bedchamber. I mourned the loss of my favorite fellow." He scoffed and looked at her. "He went to the bother of hiding it in his cubby? Was there nothing else in there?"

She shook her head. "But there might be another secretive compartment. I'll keep looking."

He turned his attention back to the swordsman. Was he reliving his childhood?

"He shouldn't have taken it from you," she said softly. "But then there is a lot that shouldn't have been denied you."

He gave her an ironic smile. "Perhaps that's the reason I'm on this quest. I was too young to do anything when this little warrior and I were forced to part ways. Why the devil did he save it and not toss it out with the others, and in a place where I was unlikely to ever find it?"

"I fear there's a lot about your father we'll never understand. Maybe he regretted that he'd not let you keep it."

"But to hide it. It makes no sense. However, though we were forbidden to remove anything from the residence, I believe I will hold on to this." He slipped it in the pocket of his coat.

"I won't tell." She didn't know why the words came out sounding like a vow she would die to fulfill.

They worked together to finish searching the desk, but it held no more secrets. They spent the next three hours going through every room in the residence, and in each one, he revealed something about himself. Not with words, but with his facial expressions. He was not usually so easy to read, and she suspected he'd be appalled to know that his emotions here were too great and close to the surface. In his father's bedchamber, anger ruled. In his mother's, sorrow. Remorse in his sister's. Admiration in his brother's. In his own . . . in his own, she detected him struggling to come to terms with the enormity of what he'd lost. Her heart ached for him as he hunted for answers to a past that would lead him to a better future. But they found nothing.

As they wandered back along the hallways, preparing to take their leave, she said, "I know this journey must have been hard. You grew up here."

"No. I don't think I grew up until I found myself on the streets."

MARCUS FELT RAW and exposed, haunted by the memories that had bombarded him as he strode through the various rooms. The lack of love, the unkindness, his father's oppressive nature. He'd thought when it all became his, he would shape a different destiny for himself and his descendants. Instead, his father had shaped it for him, and it wasn't one he much liked.

Although he certainly found no fault with his life at the moment. Somehow, Esme had known what a trial the search through the residence would be for him, and she'd arranged for them to have a picnic. While they'd been occupied, her driver had picked up a hamper at Fortnum & Mason, a company that prided itself on providing the best of fare for those who wanted any easy means of carting food around with them. She'd brought him to a park in an area of London that had been renovated by Mick Trewlove, a man known for rebuilding decrepit neighborhoods. Surrounding the park were homes that ranged from simple terrace houses to more elaborate residences with lawns surrounding them. People from all walks of life, except the nobility, lived here so it was unlikely anyone would recognize either Esme or himself.

He was stretched out on a blanket, raised on an elbow, sipping the red wine she'd poured for him. After what the past few hours had entailed, he shouldn't feel content to simply be here with her as she scrounged around in the hamper.

"How about a Scotch egg?" She held up a hard-boiled egg encased in sausage and crumbs.

"Absolutely." She extended it toward him, but he merely arched a brow.

With a wicked smile and a murmured, "You devil," she delivered the delicacy to his mouth, her fingers lingering as he closed his lips around them. He'd probably eaten a hundred of Fortnum & Mason's famous Scotch eggs over the years, but he couldn't recall a single one that tasted better than this one, with the saltiness of her fingers as

she withdrew them lingering on his lips. Closing
his eyes, he nearly groaned at the simple savoring
of so delicious a morsel.

Opening his eyes, he discovered her studying
him intently, her cheeks pinkening, just before
she returned to her task of setting out the offer-
ings. "It's been well over a year since I've had a
Fortnum & Mason hamper," he confessed.

"Who was the lady with whom you enjoyed it?"

Since the establishment was known for providing delicious picnic fare, he wasn't surprised by
her question. "I'm not one to kiss and tell."

"So kissing was involved."

"It would have been a waste of an expensive
basket of goodies if not."

She laughed, the sweet trill echoing around
him and piercing his heart as effectively as Cu-
pid's arrow. He suddenly found her to be more
dangerous on a sunny hillside in a park than in
a darkened alleyway because she made him long
for what he'd once had, made him believe it might
all be his to hold again. "I imagine you've been on
your share of picnics with gents."

With everything set out before them, she
picked up her own glass of wine. "Actually, this
is my first. I do hope I'm doing it correctly."

He couldn't imagine that she'd not gone on
picnics aplenty, with young swains who would
be vying for her hand. Taking a sip of her wine,
she gazed off into the distance where children
frolicked about, and he wondered if she regret-

ted the confession. "How did you come to be where you are today?"

"The same as you. I came in a carriage to the park."

"That's not what I'm asking, and you damned well know it. I suspect you noted a good many of my vulnerabilities when we were traipsing through corridors earlier. Tell me how you happened to become a protector of royalty."

She took another sip, licked her lips, and studied him. He wanted to reassure her that she could trust him, but words shouldn't be needed. He was willing to trust her with everything. He wanted her willing to do the same.

"Shortly after my father perished, my mother received a letter of condolence from the Queen"— the relief that swept through him with the realization that she was going to share her story, that she trusted him enough to do so, was astonishing— "in which Her Majesty mentioned that she was aware my father had a daughter. I later found out that Victoria had spoken with him when he served at the palace. Anyway, in the letter, she wrote that when I was old enough, she would find a position for me in the royal household. Mother was beside herself with the notion that I might meet someone of import and marry well. Hence the reason she sent me to the finishing school. As for herself, not six months after my father died, during her period of mourning, she married the parish vicar who was somewhat of a drunk, but as strict in his ways as she was. They kept me on such a tight leash, I couldn't wait to leave home. As I had no means for supporting myself, the opportunity to be elsewhere didn't happen until I was nineteen and went to work as one of the Queen's two wardrobe maids. Are you familiar with the position?"

"I can't say as I am."

"It allowed for a good deal of intimacy to develop between the Queen and myself. Not as much as if I'd been the Queen's dresser, who was Marianne Skerrett at the time and was my superior, but I had a chamber down the hall from the Queen's. I tended to her wardrobe and her personal items and remained near should she require anything at all. I had great ambitions of one day advancing to the position of queen's dresser. Quite a bit of prestige comes with it as well as a rather good salary. I'd been a year in my post when Prince Albert passed, and the Queen and I became closer because she knew I'd suffered a devastating loss as well and so even though it had been years since my father's death, still I commiserated with her and was more understanding of her overwhelming grief than most."

As she took a moment to gaze in the distance, he could envision her bringing comfort to her monarch. He also had the sense that what was coming next was not so easy for her to share. She released a long sigh that contained the tiniest of shudders as though she was steeling herself for facing the past.

"I shared my duties with the other wardrobe

maid. Her name was Beatrix. She was half a dozen years older than I was and we were the firmest of friends—or so I thought. I told her everything. I even confided that I fancied one of the palace guards. His name was Richard, and he was so incredibly handsome in his uniform. I was quite smitten. Near the end of my second year as a wardrobe maid, I began to experience pains and noticed some swelling. Here." She flattened a palm to her abdomen. "I shared my worries with Beatrix—in the strictest of confidence—and soon after I noticed staff looking at me rather strangely. People who were talking would go quiet when I neared. Eventually I discovered rumors were circulating that I'd had an affair with a palace guard and was with child. Beatrix had to have started them because the change in my shape wasn't noticeable when I wore clothing."

"Did you confront her?"

She gave him a wry smile. "I did, but I wasn't then who I am now, and was rather meek in my confrontation. She admitted that she'd told people, but also that she did, in fact, believe I was with child. After all, I'd told her about my infatuation with Richard, and also unfortunately about all the times my mother got after me for my disobedience. Why would I not flout society's rules by lying with a man."

"She betrayed your confidence. Something must have driven her to do that."

"Later I learned she was jealous that the Queen seemed to favor me because Beatrix also wanted the position of queen's dresser. I was mortified by the gossip and devastated that my trust had been misplaced. Naturally someone associated with such scandal, a young woman who would bear a child out of wedlock, can't be in the proximity of the Queen. Miss Skerrett told me that I was to be dismissed. My mother was sent for. She was furious that I'd brought her and her husband shame. I told them I'd lain with no man. Miss Skerrett suggested I be examined by a physician, but my mother would not allow it, fearing the rumors being bandied wildly about would be proven true and cause further embarrassment. I was sent home, where I was locked in my room for refusing to divulge the identity of the man with whom I'd fornicated. Fortunately, Beatrix had kept the name of the palace guard to herself, no doubt because he could have confirmed that she was lying. My mother and stepfather were contemplating my future. Should I be sent to a nunnery or workhouse? Should I be turned out? I think they were leaning toward the last, just have me pack my bags and make my own way. I was so frightened. Whenever my father spoke about bad people in the world, I envisioned them with swords and rifles. But words can be effective weapons. They nearly destroyed me."

He thought of the harsh words he'd used against her in the beginning, before he'd truly known her, and he felt as though his heart was being flayed. "Esme, the unkind things I said, directed your way—they were born out of an anger with my father, not with you."

He wished her soft smile wasn't so tranquil and reflected such understanding. "I'm not such a delicate creature now, Marcus."

The pain he was experiencing intensified. She'd suffered through a scandal not of her making and had come through stronger on the other side. How had she managed it? "You told me once that Queen Victoria believed you when no one else would."

She nodded. "Yes. I hadn't told her about the rumors or the strange happenings in my body because you don't bother a monarch with trivial matters—"

"They weren't trivial. You were being treated unjustly." Which he happened to know a little something about.

"As it turns out she agreed with you. I suppose when I was no longer about Miss Skerrett had been forced to explain my absence and told her that I'd been dismissed, and the Queen wanted to know the reason for it. I'd been home only a few days when she showed up at our door. She demanded the truth and so I told her that I didn't know why my belly was swelling or I felt poorly. She insisted I be examined by one of her physicians. And well, you certainly don't deny the Queen's command."

As she took several more sips of her wine, he waited, desperate to know the whole of the tale, yet dreading where it might go. Placing the glass in her lap, she intertwined her fingers and folded them around the stem. He wished he'd taken hold of them before she'd given them a purpose, and yet perhaps the telling required she maintain some distance. She cleared her throat. "She has several physicians. Dr. Graves was the one who saw to me. A kinder, gentler man I've never known. He deduced I was not in fact with child, but there was a growth. It had to be cut out, and in the removing of it . . . well, part of me had to go as well. The part that would have borne children."

Feeling as though he'd taken a punch to the gut, he sat up abruptly. "Esme—"

"It's all right," she said, although her smile revealed the lie. "Don't look so devastated. It was a while ago. I've accepted my limitations. It took me a little over a year to recover. My mother lamented that no man would have me now that I could no longer bear children. The Queen wanted me back in her household, offered me my choice of positions." She shook her head. "But I had no desire to go back there, to be among those servants who'd believed the worst of me. My condition was not something to be spoken about because we don't discuss our bodies, do we? We act as though they are something about which to be ashamed rather than celebrated. We certainly don't mention surgeries that involve such a personal part of our anatomy. Even if I dared do such a thing, people were unlikely to believe me. No, Beatrix had ensured they'd believe the worst, and they'd continue to do so. They'd be convinced I'd either lost the child or birthed him and given him up.

Scandal is so much more titillating than truth. So I couldn't bring myself to return to a place with memories of such ugliness.

"However, neither could I abandon Victoria, the one woman who believed me and saw me spared a slow and horrendous death from disease. While I was at the palace, serving her, I had an occasion to meet the Home Secretary, quite by accident. We crossed paths in the hallway, and he introduced himself. I paid him a visit, told him I wanted to follow in my father's footsteps and be of service to the Crown. The army wouldn't have me. Perhaps he would. I explained that I would have great success at gathering information that might be needed because men don't see women as a threat and thus would trust me more easily. I could use my womanly wiles to coerce confidences because men like nothing better than to boast about their exploits to a woman who can do them no harm. He was rather intrigued by the notion. We spent two days talking about the possibilities and how I would operate. And then he hired me."

"To seduce men."

"To be honest, I gather most of my information from women."

"You seduce women?" He'd like to watch that.

As though she'd read his thoughts, she gave him a small teasing smile. "Not in the manner that you're no doubt imagining. I simply befriend them. As Beatrix taught me, people are not good at keeping secrets. They like for others to know that they have information they don't. Men tend to boast to their wives or the women they're stepping out with when they're on the verge of doing something they believe makes them appear interesting or bold or not like the others. Often I'm tasked with determining who they might have told and then lending a sympathetic ear.

"A few years ago, a moneybox being transported by railway was stolen. All evidence pointed to Peter Anderson. But when they arrested him, he denied it, naturally. And he most certainly wouldn't tell them where he'd hidden the money. But he might have told his wife. I took a room at a boardinghouse near their home and ensured our paths crossed often. She had few friends, especially after her husband was accused of theft. But I was incredibly compassionate toward her plight, myself being the wife of a convicted forger, after all."

He grinned. "You're like an actress, taking on different roles."

"Quite. The key is to be relatable to their circumstances. If they're lonely, I offer them friendship. Sad, I offer them comfort. Mortified, I offer them understanding. I've always been where they are. Eventually they trust me and tell me what I need to know." She released a quick burst of air. "At which point usually they're arrested and convicted as an accomplice."

"Do you feel guilty about turning on them?"

"I'm a heartless harlot." She shook her head. "Oh, I might have felt a twinge of regret, especially if I really came to like the person, but they've broken the law. Who is to say they won't do it again or something worse? Deep down they aren't good people. The situation with your father is the first time I've taken on the role of mistress, and that's only because he identified me as such. As I've told you, our relationship never went that far. I draw the line at my bed-chamber door."

"Always?"

"Always. To do otherwise would compromise me and the information I gather."

"Not all your assignments are as docile as the one involving Mrs. Anderson or you'd not have those scars."

"No, but the Home Secretary ensured I was pre-pared for difficulties. He sent me to the instruc-tors who trained his other agents. I was taught how to fight and use various weapons. I was pro-vided with all sorts of gadgets. They found I was well suited to the tasks given me. Except for this last one, I've always had success and achieved my goal quickly. And I rather enjoy it. It's much more exciting than ensuring the Queen's wardrobe is in order or rubbing liniment on her knees when they're aching. I should be grateful to Beatrix, I suppose, for showing me there is an ugliness in some people that is easily masked. So now I'm al-ways trying to peer beneath the mask."

"And what do you see when you peer beneath mine?"

"Someone I like far more than I expected. I wish fate had been kinder to you."

He was beginning to resent his journey less. If not for his father's actions, he'd never have come to spend time in the company of this remarkable woman. Reaching out, grateful when she didn't move back but simply held still, he cupped her chin in the palm of his hand and stroked his thumb along the soft skin below her jaw. "I'm terribly sorry you experienced all that hellaciousness at court, the betrayal and what followed. But Britain is lucky to have you. Your father would be proud, I think."

A light pink tinged her cheeks. "Thank you for that."

He considered kissing her, here on this little knoll, and he might have if she hadn't moved back slightly so he no longer touched her. She lifted the bottle of wine. "We should finish this off and then head back to the residence. After baring my soul, I could use some time in my chamber of solitude. Perhaps you'd do me the service of going a round or two with me in the ring."

"Don't expect any mercy."

"I wouldn't dare."

He might battle her for all he was worth inside the ring, but outside of it, he wanted to protect her. However, until the culprits were found and apprehended, Esme would continue to place her life at risk, and he realized that keeping her safe mattered much more to him than his own family honor.

CHAPTER 14

$\mathcal{I}$T WAS A strange thing to be so incredibly aware of a man that Esme could sense his presence in the residence, even when they were not in the same room. She knew when Marcus was on the verge of entering the dining room just before he crossed the threshold. She looked up from her desk just before he strode into the library. She knew when he was wandering about his bedchamber unable to sleep, knew when he took his wanderings farther afield into other rooms. Somehow, she felt when he was exiting the residence.

Within her bedchamber, she'd been lounging in a chair by the window reading, with a fully recovered Laddie in her lap, when she became aware of Marcus engaging in the latter and taking his leave. She stood up so quickly as to send her cherished dog scrambling down her skirt to the floor. Parting the draperies, she saw Marcus striding up the street. Cursing him soundly for not informing her that he intended to go out to-night, she grabbed her reticule and drew on her pelisse even as she darted from her room, down the stairs, and out into the night in pursuit.

Perhaps he was on a personal mission—to visit his brother or a brothel or—

Her thoughts staggered to a stop at the possibility that he was seeking female companionship, that he might bestow those wondrous kisses of his upon another woman. She was more than willing to be the receiver, had been disappointed that when they'd returned home from the park and gone to her chamber of solitude for a bit of wrestling, he hadn't taken advantage of the numerous opportunities afforded him to kiss her. He'd certainly looked as though he'd wanted to, several times. Perhaps she should be forthright in letting him know she yearned for further intimacy. Even if there could never be more between them than an affair. He would wish to have children, surely, and the sort of wife who tended to a home, not the sort who skulked about. Therefore, if she had him at all, it would be for only a short time, but it was better than not at all.

Although if she didn't pay attention, she was going to lose him entirely.

He was walking about as bold as he pleased while she was hugging the depths of darkness provided by trees or buildings where light couldn't reach. Why hadn't he told her of his plans? Did he not trust her? Was she a fool to trust him? Had she been duped by his good looks, his charm, and the harsh life he now lived but didn't deserve?

He hailed a hansom cab. With a curse, she quickened her pace. This hour of the night she was unlikely to find one in time to see where he went, but the fates were on her side because another appeared straightaway. "Follow that cab at a discreet distance," she called up before climbing in.

He wasn't merely stretching his legs then. He had a destination in mind, one a good distance away, and she was determined to discover precisely where it was and his purpose in going there.

THE HANSOM DRIVER let him out in one of the dodgier parts of London, an area he'd haunted for several months where he'd acquired the sort of skills that if caught exercising saw most men sent to prison. Breaking into dwellings, picking pockets, engaging in fisticuffs with no rules whatsoever. Threatening, bullying, even on occasion terrorizing.

He'd learned to hide in shadows, to watch and judge the dangers in his surroundings. He'd learned patience and how to bide his time.

But this afternoon, wrestling with Esme, all he'd longed to do was pounce. To take her mouth that smiled with triumph and to own it. To take her harsh breaths from her exertions and turn them into moans of pleasure. To shed her of the garments that clung to her curves and give his hands the freedom to journey over the dips and swells that made his mouth water. Where she was concerned, his patience was on a short leash. And if he gave in to his desires, he would lose sight of the goal that had consumed him for more than a year. His focus would turn to her exclusively, and what did he have to offer her but a broken man? A man with no future until he resolved the past.

His harsh laughter echoed down the darkened alleyway through which he now trod. As though she would want anything to do with a man who had yet to find his way through the quagmire of his life. More than ever, he needed to discover who had lured his father to his downfall. And recent events had clarified some things, had provided a clue that might assist him in getting back on the correct path.

He came to a stop opposite a building that more closely resembled a warehouse than a residence, but the owner viewed it as his castle, his fortress. It even had a bloody throne room. That was where Marcus would begin because it was where Willie felt most powerful. As it was after midnight, when the darkest deeds were done, the Devil's Hand gang leader was no doubt waiting for his minions to report in on any missions he may have sent them on.

Slowly, Marcus glanced around, intently he listened. Other than the scurrying of the rats, nothing else was happening around him. After crossing the street, he hugged the side of the building as he made his way to the back corner, where he paused and inhaled the strong odor of acrid tobacco.

Marcus peered around the edge of the building. The watcher had a forearm placed across his midsection serving as a resting place for his other elbow as he clenched his pipe between his teeth and puffed, one ankle casually crossed over the other. Apparently, they weren't expecting trouble tonight, merely keeping a lookout, waiting for the others to return. Marcus dashed around the corner and, before the guard's eyes could fully widen, he'd delivered an uppercut to the blighter's jaw that closed those eyes and had the bugger hitting the ground in an unmoving lump. Digging a thin rope out of his pocket, Marcus made short work of tying the man's hands behind his back and then binding his feet. After gagging him, Marcus dragged him away from the tiniest speck of light so he wouldn't be seen. Then he took a moment to glance around and ensure the disturbance had attracted no attention. Quickly he returned to the door, not surprised to discover it wasn't locked. After all, a guard had been in place.

Like a wraith, he silently slipped inside and made his way along empty corridors until he neared the large room he sought. Pale light spilled out into the hallway. Pressing his back to the wall, he listened. All he heard was glass being set against wood. With any luck, Willie would be well in his cups with a loose tongue that might finally garner Marcus the answers he sought.

Peeking around the doorjamb, he saw no others in the chamber, only the gang leader sprawled on his huge wooden throne with its garish display of colored glass, which Marcus assumed represented jewels, embedded along its edges. An ignorant man's rendition of what a throne should look like. Sauntering in, Marcus took some delight in Willie coming to attention and straightening slightly.

"Wolf, I 'eard ye was dead."

"Not for your lack of trying. I worked for you and still you sent men to do me in."

Willie shrugged. "There was a five-'undred quid bounty on yer 'ead, lad. I'm a businessman first. I couldn't pass that up."

"Who was going to pay the bounty?"

"Lucifer."

Marcus narrowed his eyes. "You're not Lucifer?"

The gang boss chuckled darkly. "No."

"Who is he then?"

"I 'aven't a clue. Never seen the blighter, but 'e's skilled at gettin' messages to me."

"You work for him then."

"That would imply I was doin' things for 'im willingly. 'E's not the sort of man ye refuse to do favors for—if ye want to keep breathin'."

Marcus glanced around again, to ensure no one was lurking in shadows. He hadn't expected

Willie to be so forthcoming in his responses, had thought he might have to persuade him. The room was barren except for the throne and the table beside it that held a glass and a bottle of gin. So why was the man being so cooperative? "Where will I find the eight of diamonds?"

"In the morgue, sadly."

Had Marcus gotten things wrong? He took two steps forward and removed the card from his jacket. "A man was murdered last night, and this was found near his person."

Willie nodded. "I sent 'im out to do Lucifer's biddin', but Eight was found this mornin' dancin' on the wind beneath Blackfriars Bridge."

Hanged? Suicide or murder? If Marcus had money to wager, he'd wager on the latter. "Did you know that was how his night would end?"

A slow shake of his head. "I'd 'ave sent someone else. I liked Eight. 'E was a good man."

Obviously, he and Willie had a different definition of the attributes that constituted a *good man*. "What else do you know about Lucifer?"

"'E suspected ye'd come 'ere tonight"—he slowly rose to his feet like a phoenix rising from the ashes and spread his arms wide—"and I've been charged with sending ye to 'ell."

Reaching back, Marcus took hold of his knives, drew them forth, and held them at the ready. His first thought was that he was grateful Esme wasn't with him, that he hadn't told her that he'd planned to confront his old nemesis, that she wasn't in harm's way. His second thought was

that it felt strange to be going into battle without her at his side. He recalled the night in the
alleyway when she'd taken him by surprise. He
adjusted his stance and said, "Give it your best."

Willie cackled, very much reminding Marcus of a crow. "The advantage of sittin' upon the
throne is that I don't 'ave to fight. I's got others for
that." He dropped his head back. "Let's play the
devil's 'and!"

The gang boss had always had a flair for the
dramatic. Marcus swung around to meet the onslaught of attackers, with clubs and knives held
at the ready, barging through the doorway. Six.
Devil take him. He should have realized finding
Willie alone had been far too easy a chore. He'd
thought the men he and Esme had encountered
in the alleyway had been following her from Podmore's, that stopping her had been their objective.
But recognizing one of the blighters from the alley,
he realized he'd been their intended target, they'd
been chasing him. He'd been certain no one was
on his trail. So how had they found him?

Those questions were to be answered at another
time, if he survived his current predicament, if he
somehow managed to evade the circle of brutes
surrounding him. They were an ugly, odorous lot
with greasy hair and whiskered faces. Blackened
teeth. Pockmarks. Grime beneath their finger-
nails, visible because of the holes in their gloves
through which poked their fingers, the alteration
of the hand coverings often deliberately made because it allowed for a firmer grip on knife handles.

He knew a moment's regret that he hadn't kissed Esme one more time, that he hadn't taken her to his bed, had never brought her pleasure. That he didn't have the memory of her sighs and moans and cries as ecstasy shimmered through her to take with him into hell. He was fairly certain heaven wasn't his destination. At least he'd encounter his father and could ask him what the devil he'd been thinking.

Yelling like a banshee, a wildly enthusiastic lout came for him. Raising a leg, Marcus kicked him in the gut, sending him backward with enough force that he managed to take the fellow coming up behind him to the floor. Spinning around, Marcus wielded the knives with expert precision, slicing an upper arm and a cheek, bending down to get the thigh of another bloke. But they were coming too fast, too many. As he struck out at one man, out of the corner of his eye, he saw the glistening blade coming for his throat, threw up an arm to deflect it, leaving his belly unprotected as another knife swiftly came in—

Thunder roared throughout the cavernous room. A high-pitched scream followed. The knife went flying. Blood sprayed in an arc as the attacker cradled his bleeding hand close against his midsection and backed away, sobbing. Everyone else had gone as still as stone statues.

Marcus turned his attention to the doorway, where a lone woman stood. Tall and glorious and confident. Holding what he recognized as a Beaumont-Adams revolver, a gun with a chamber that held five bullets. He shouldn't be surprised she had access to a weapon used by the army. He absurdly wondered if it had been disguised as a pearl comb for her hair or a flamboyant piece of jewelry. Or if, perhaps, it had even belonged to her father.

"I have four bullets remaining, and I'm a dead shot," she said with unnerving cold disdain. "I would suggest—"

Letting loose a murderous howl, a ruffian raced toward her. She quickly leveled the gun and fired. The assailant screeched and clutched his shoulder as his knife clattered to the floor. "What portion of 'I'm a dead shot' was unclear?"

"Now, ye've got only three bullets," Willie said.

"But I've evened the odds somewhat and one of them has your name on it—"

"'Ow'd ye do that?" the fellow from the alley asked. "'Ow'd ye write 'is name on it?"

She didn't take her gaze off Willie. "It's merely an expression. Call off your minions and tell them to drop their weapons."

"Or wot?"

"You'll die. And if not you, it'll be the next man at whom I aim. I've been generous thus far, but my patience is wearing thin."

"Who the devil are ye?" Willie barked.

"Satan's mistress," Esme stated calmly. "I'm known to make grown men weep." She waved the barrel of the gun at him. "Order your men to disarm."

"Drop yer weapons," Willie grumbled.

Without her asking, Marcus holstered his own knives, gathered up those from the floor, and strode to her side. Lord help him but he'd never wanted to kiss a woman more.

"Did you get what you came for?" she asked, with an undercurrent of pique in her tone.

"He doesn't know anything."

"We're going to leave now," she announced, "and you're not going to give chase."

"Lucifer will 'ave me 'ead if I let Wolf go."

"Don't give chase and you'll find five hundred pounds sitting on your doorstep come dawn."

"A thousand."

"Eight hundred."

Willie nodded.

But once Marcus and Esme were in the hallway, they ran, out of the building and down the street. As they passed an alley, he threw the confiscated knives into it. A few yards away was a waiting hansom. They'd barely climbed in before it took off, and he had a feeling she'd generously paid the driver to ensure he wouldn't leave before she returned. The woman left nothing to chance. Her revolver and reticule were resting in her lap. She wasn't going to shoot him, but even if she was contemplating it, he didn't bloody well care. He'd come close to dying and the thrill of still being alive was racing through him.

"Christ, you were magnificent back there." He cradled her cheek, plowing his fingers up into the loosened strands of her hair to give him purchase, and turned her face toward him, taken aback by the anger and hurt he saw there.

"You didn't think I needed to know what you were up to?" she spat out.

Her fury with him should have doused any flames of desire, but it only served to increase the smoldering within him. "I didn't want to place you in harm's way."

"So you placed yourself instead. Alone. With no reinforcements whatsoever. What an utter fool you are."

He was most certainly that, because the more cross she became the more he wanted her. He'd grown up in a family where emotions were never shown. Highs and lows were never revealed. Dreams and disappointments were never shared. His parents had never let on if they worried about him, not even when he'd fallen from a horse at the age of nine and broken his arm. During the past year, he and Griff had grown closer, but Marcus had yet to connect in any meaningful way with Althea. To have this woman *worried* about him . . . he didn't quite know what to make of it. To be so vexed, she had to *care*, at least a bit. When was the last time any woman had?

Dear Lord, were those tears glistening in her eyes, captured by the passing streetlamps? "Esme—"

She smashed a fist into his unwounded shoulder. "How the devil will you restore your family honor if you're dead? You're so damned reckless."

"You're so glorious in your fury." And he knew then that no matter how terrifying those first few moments had been when Willie's minions had surrounded him, he'd have moved heaven and earth to lay eyes on her again. "Nothing would have kept me from returning to you."

"You idiot man. You . . . you . . ."

He watched as a tear rolled along her cheek. Without thought, he swooped in and captured it with his tongue. "Don't weep, Esme. Don't—"

He covered her mouth with his own because he could think of no words to reassure her and it hurt, deep down, where a small part of his heart had not rotted, to see this courageous woman, this warrior, distressed at the thought of his demise. He couldn't voice the depth to which her arrival had terrified him more than being surrounded by thugs with knives. If she'd perished, he'd be the one weeping, inconsolable. How was it even possible that she could mean so much to him in so short a time? Was it because they journeyed on the same quest? Because of the battles they'd fought, the confidences they'd shared? What he felt was so much larger than a common goal—

Lust. It was just lust. It had to be because the thought of it being anything more . . . she wasn't going to fall for a man who thrived in the darkness, who had considered once striving to dethrone the leader of the Devil's Hand, of taking his place in order to control those who paid homage to him.

The salt of her tears on his lips unmanned him. Her eagerness drew him in. Perhaps it wasn't lust but merely a need to reaffirm that they were both alive, that air filled their lungs, and their skin was warm. Hers so soft. Her cheeks anyway. Her chin. Her throat. His fingers skimmed over her face as the kiss deepened.

In spite of the small confines, she was agile enough to climb into his lap. He dropped his head back and she followed, eagerly taking possession of his mouth as though she owned it. Perhaps she did. Somehow it had become hers. He couldn't imagine another woman's lips upon his, couldn't imagine ever wanting the taste of another woman. She consumed him. Caused him to burn like an eternal flame. This passion for her would never be doused. Even if he took complete possession of her, already he knew he'd want her again. She would have been a formidable wife for any man but fate had dealt her a devastating blow. Yet instead of wallowing in her misfortune, she'd become guardian of a queen. Had become a queen herself, of fire and brimstone, courage and strength.

As the carriage slowed, they broke away from each other and she scrambled off his lap to face forward, leaving him only her profile to gaze upon and an inability to determine her mood from that alone. "Esme—"

"I reacted to being alive. Don't make more of it than that."

The hansom stopped, the doors sprang open, and she made a hasty departure. Climbing out, he looked up at the driver. "You've been paid, I assume."

"A fortune, mate." Then he set the horse into motion and disappeared into the encroaching fog.

Marcus strode up the steps and into the residence. She was standing near the table of decanters, already downing something as he approached.

"Esme." She set the glass down with a soft clink but didn't turn to look at him. He wished she would. "Thank you for rescuing me. I'll find a way to pay you back those eight hundred pounds."

"I'll send word and the Home Office will provide the funds, although I suspect Willie—honestly, he needs a more ferocious name—will find himself in the clutches of Scotland Yard before he has a chance to spend any of it." Slowly she faced him. "I do wish you'd trusted me with your plans."

"It wasn't a matter of trust. I was afraid it might go bad, and I didn't want you there if it did. I have no desire to see you hurt."

"If that maggot of a gang boss had succeeded, I might have never known what became of you, might have always wondered why you just . . . left. I have few people in this world about whom I care. Unfortunately, Marcus Stanwick, you've become one of them. Please have the decency to at least leave me a note."

"What makes you think I didn't?"

She blinked, studied him, blinked again. "Did you?"

The hope in her voice made him wish he could provide her with a different answer. "No." And he would have regretted it with his last breath. To have left her wondering, when he knew what it was to have no answers to another's actions.

"Well, at least you're honest."

"And you, Esme, are you honest, honest with me? Did you kiss me in order to feel alive?"

"I kissed you because I couldn't not."

"Then kiss me again." Wrapping his hand gently around her upper arm, he drew her nearer, grateful she came willingly. "Kiss me again," he rasped, pleaded.

Her mouth was on his before he had a chance to drop to his knees and beg. For this woman, he would have. As she entwined her arms around his neck, he enfolded her in his embrace, pressing her body against his, aware of her softness against his hardness. She did nothing in half measures. With fiery passion, she swept her tongue through his mouth, as he took the opportunity to explore hers. She tasted of dark scotch and wicked intentions, and he knew their night was not going to end here with this kiss. He'd wanted her from the first moment he'd seen her stride into this room, so confident and cocksure. Not only had she taken ownership of this room, but somehow, against his will, she'd taken ownership of him.

She—bold and daring perfection—didn't protest when he lifted her into his arms. He broke off the kiss and held her heated gaze for all of two seconds before striding from the room.

"Your shoulder—"

"Was kissed by an angel and is healing miraculously."

She buried her face in the curve of his neck and nibbled at the sensitive skin beneath his jaw. "I'm hardly an angel."

"I'm not going to argue semantics." Reaching the stairs, he started up the steps.

"We should go to your chamber," she said quietly, almost shyly. "Laddie isn't particularly mannered when it comes to sharing me."

His low chuckle echoed between the walls. "He and I are of a like mind then, because I'm a beast when it comes to sharing."

She licked around the shell of his ear, and his knees went weak, before she whispered, "I've wanted you for a while now."

"Then tonight you shall have me."

CHAPTER 15

WHILE EXCITEMENT AND an anticipatory thrill coursed through her, Esme understood that being intimate with Marcus might be unwise and put a strain on their working together further, but she craved his kisses and touches as she did air.

When she'd entered that warehouse-like structure and seen him surrounded, terror had struck at her very heart and soul. She'd have destroyed them all to save him. Would have seen them all in hell if he'd died. The enormity of her feelings for him at that moment had nearly overwhelmed her. To think she might have lost him completely without ever having known him fully, to have never shared intimacy, to have never shown him what she felt for him . . . she'd have lived the remainder of her life with regret.

She wouldn't give voice to the words she was feeling because she was well aware their time together would be a fleeting thing. When they achieved their goal, they would part ways, with only the memories of their time together to remain. They would be enough. She would make them be enough.

He carried her into his bedchamber, kicked the door closed in his wake, and marched over to the bed where a servant had lit a solitary lamp. After setting her on her feet, he reached over and turned up the flame to increase the glow, so it washed over both of them. While she'd have preferred the darkness, she didn't want to miss the opportunity to see him in all his naked glory. Besides, he knew of her scars. They weren't likely to take him by surprise and cause revulsion.

After shrugging out of his coat and tossing it to the floor, he unfastened her pelisse and cast it aside. With his large, roughened hands, he cradled her face and held her gaze. "You are a remarkable woman, Esme Lancaster."

"Then kiss me."

His grin was the sort that caused women to completely lose their heads and tumble willingly into beds. The sort that seduced, yet she was already seduced. But still he revealed his pleasure at her words. Then his mouth captured hers with an urgency and rapaciousness that she wasn't quite certain she'd ever had any other man direct her way. Oh, certainly she'd enjoyed enthusiastic partners, but she'd never been left with the sense that she was their complete focus, a thirst they could not quench, a hunger they could not satiate.

That she and she alone was all that mattered in the world at that moment.

The residence could burn down around them, and he'd not notice. Neither would she.

She'd never felt so empowered. Good Lord, was this what it was like to be a queen, so adored, so worshipped?

Only she didn't want to be on a pedestal alone, not without him there beside her. Therefore, she kissed him back with equal zeal, single-mindedness, and attention. He was the only man in her life of any significance. She poured all of her regard for him into the kiss, taking immense satisfaction in his resounding growl and the tightening of his arms around her.

Through their clothes, she could feel the warmth of him but wanted the heat of his flesh pressed directly to her skin, branding her as his. She worked her hands between them and began freeing the buttons of his shirt, completing only half the task before he broke away, reached back, and dragged the shirt over his head. It went the way of his coat.

Then he was liberating the fastenings of her frock, and she was soon stepping out of it. He grinned. "I knew you didn't bother with petti-coats."

"They're a hindrance in a fight."

"And in lovemaking."

Her heart jumped about in her chest. She'd expected him to use a crude word to describe what they were doing, a word she'd always associated with the act because she'd never given her heart to any man and so how could it be lovemaking? And yet, she feared she might be losing her suddenly rebellious heart to him. It would hurt when he left, but now wasn't the time to ponder that or to consider how the pain of his parting would be worth the price of having known him fully.

Reaching out, she stroked the bulge of his trousers. He groaned low, almost as though he were in pain. Another stroke before cupping him. "I think I'm going to find you quite impressive."

Moving away from her, he sat on the edge of the bed and tugged off his boots, followed by his stockings. Coming to his feet, he unfastened his trousers and shucked them. Oh, yes. Her mouth went dry.

Tenderly cupping her chin, he tilted her face up until he could meet and hold her gaze. "Because of your surgery will I hurt you?"

She shook her head. The first few times she'd experienced discomfort until eventually she didn't. However, none of her partners had been as striking as Marcus was. "I don't think so."

"You're to stop me if I do."

She nodded, but the movement was a lie. She wanted him buried to the hilt, inside of her as deeply as possible, stretching and filling her.

He trailed a finger along her throat, over her collarbone to her cleavage, and down to her corset. Making short work of releasing the hooks, he was soon tossing it aside. Her shoes and the remainder of her undergarments followed suit.

His gaze, like fire raging, slowly traveled over her. She knew the moment his eyes landed on the scar that ran the length of her abdomen. When he would have touched it, she took hold of his hand and brought it to her breast. "I don't feel anything there, but I do here."

With a nod, he reclaimed her mouth with the same powerful urgency he had before and his fingers kneaded the pliant orb, pinching her nipple, then soothing it. Suddenly, his arms clamped her to him, and he tumbled them onto the bed.

HE NOTICED THE scars. Every damned one of them. The one on her thigh, the one that would form on her breast. A small one on her upper arm she'd not told him about. The one above the mound of dark springy hair between her legs. The one that had robbed her of so much, that had put her on a path that led her into his arms. He believed in neither fate nor destiny, and yet without the scars, inside and out, that they both carried, they wouldn't be here, side by side, facing each other, flesh against flesh, mouths devouring, sighs and groans echoing around them, heat building to a combustible level.

She didn't hesitate to wrap her hand boldly around his cock and stroke with such purpose that he very nearly spilled his seed then and there.

"I could do this all night," she said in a throaty purr.

He stilled her actions. "I won't last a minute. I've not had a woman since . . . the damned picnic with a hamper that summer last year." He licked along her throat. "But it's more than the drought of lovers. It's you." He journeyed up to her throat, nibbled on her lobe, relished her sweet moan. "It's all you. Every aspect of you, inside and out, causes me to burn with want, with need."

He dotted kisses over her shoulder, down to her breasts where he liberally peppered them. She hadn't released her hold on him, and he felt her fingers tighten around him. He almost groaned from the pleasure of it. "Even if I had lain with a woman last night, still, tonight, you would ignite my passions."

"I haven't been with a man in a good long while. I know men prefer their women innocent and virginal."

He lifted his head. "I find no fault with you for taking lovers."

"To do so is a sin."

"So we'll enjoy hell together." And he reclaimed her mouth.

HE WAS WRONG there. She'd never felt as close to heaven as she did at that moment, in his arms while they did deliciously wicked things to each other, stroking, kissing, nibbling, licking. She was on fire, but it generated the sort of flames that created, not destroyed. Glorious sensations. Her nerve endings danced and flickered. Her toes, nay, her entire body, wanted to furl in on itself even as it stretched along the length of his body.

He urged her onto her back and nestled himself between her thighs. With her fingers, she outlined the contours of his magnificent chest and shoulders as he reached down and positioned himself before pushing into her. Her body welcomed him, adjusted to his length and breadth. Lord, but it felt good, wonderful to have him seated firmly inside her. When he started rocking against her, the glorious sensations began to build, coursing through her body, in undulating waves like the sea greeting the shore, increasing in intensity.

Raised on his arms, he hovered above her, his beautiful blue eyes locked on hers. He withdrew, pushed forward, the powerful thrusts increasing in momentum, in force. He was magnificent in his concentration, his jaw tightened, his gaze focused as though he were memorizing every line and curve of her features. She could sense the tension in him increasing, his breaths becoming sharper, shorter. Never had a man lasted so long, moved with such determination, such exactitude, such purpose . . . not for him. For her.

She who never wept nearly did. Tenderly she cradled his face. "Don't wait on me. It feels wonderful. It's incredible. But this is as far as I go."

"Pardon?" He didn't stop his actions, but the movements were less frantic.

"I've reached the summit, but I can never . . ." She knew there was more. Occasionally she'd brought herself to climax, but it had never happened with a man. Although she'd often pretended. But she couldn't with him. With him, for some reason, she had to be honest. "I can't fly off the pinnacle. But you should go ahead—"

"Bugger that."

Suddenly, he was gone, no longer inside her, kissing his way down the length of her torso, spreading her thighs farther apart until he reached the heart of her womanhood and kissed there. No, it was more than a kiss. It was a feasting. His tongue stroking, lapping, circling.

"Oh, oh my." She couldn't stop the tiny mewls escaping her throat. When he looked at her over her mound, his eyes smoldering with passion and promise, she realized she'd not come close to reaching the pinnacle because she suddenly found herself trembling with sensations that were impossible to ignore.

"You will come for me, Esme," he growled. A lick, a suckle. "You'll scream my name until the fire I ignite within you burns out."

She'd faced murderous thugs, but never had she been more terrified. Sitting up slightly, resting on her elbows, she managed to thread the fingers of one hand between the strands of his hair. "Marcus—"

"Don't be afraid, sweetheart. You won't be alone. I'll follow with you pulsing around my cock." His eyes still on her, he intensified his ministrations.

She'd never known sensations so marvelous.

"You taste so good, better than anything that's ever come out of a wicker hamper."

A burst of laughter escaped, and she bit down

on a knuckle. A woman didn't giggle when a man's face was buried between her legs, and yet he made her happy. So gloriously happy.

Gliding his hands up, he cradled her breasts, his thumbs skimming lightly over her hardened nipples, causing them to strain toward the touch. "Oh, yes, please keep doing that, keep doing everything. I've never—"

She'd never known that her flesh could sing out in such wonder. That stars would hover at the edge of her vision, that everything within her would explode at once and that she would indeed be screaming out his name, a benediction, a triumph.

He thrust into her. "Christ, I can feel you throbbing around me. It feels so good, Esme. You feel so good. Wet, hot, and tight."

Then he bowed back, groaning her name, going still for a heartbeat, two, before collapsing on top of her, supporting his weight on his elbows so as not to crush her, when she wanted him flat against her. She skimmed her fingers lazily over his dew-coated back. Waiting as their harsh breathing subsided to confess, "I've never had a man go to such effort for me before."

He planted a kiss on her shoulder. "Then none were deserving of you."

She wrapped her arms and legs around him, holding him near, wishing she remained heartless because it was going to hurt dreadfully when their time together came to a close.

CHAPTER 16

A COUPLE OF HOURS earlier, he'd rolled off her, brought her in close, and fallen asleep with his hand cupped over her hip possessively as though claiming, "Mine." Or perhaps it was merely Esme's silly imagination conjuring such sentiments because she wanted him to *want* her. The feelings coursing through her now—she'd never before experienced them. She'd never felt so close to someone, as though he were part of her. They breathed in tandem, and she couldn't seem to stop studying him, with his long dark lashes resting on his cheeks, his sharp aquiline nose, his sturdy jaw, and that remarkable mouth that had brought her such exquisite pleasure.

His eyes fluttered open, and he smiled contentedly. "Hello."

She had the uneasy sensation that she might

be blushing, as a wave of pure pleasure swept through her. "Hello."

"My apologies for falling asleep, but you fair wore me out."

"It's all right. I liked watching you when you were unaware that I was."

He angled his head slightly. "Are you suddenly shy?"

"I made quite the spectacle of myself, coming apart as I did."

His grin widened. "I intend to have you screaming at least once more before you leave."

"You're the only one who ever has made me react with such wild abandon. I thought that perhaps the surgery had removed that womanly part of me, so I couldn't properly join with a man. On my own I can find release but—"

"I'd like to watch that."

She furrowed her brow. "What?"

"You pleasuring yourself."

"Absolutely not." It was too personal, too intimate, and yet what she'd recently done with him was equally so.

"I'll return the favor, perform for you."

"You are wicked."

"Because I want to know every aspect of you?" His fingers kneaded her hip. "As for what you said earlier, the absence of a womb makes you no less a woman."

"Some would disagree, my mother in particular."

"Devil take her then. I've never known a more womanly woman than you."

She gnawed on her lip. "But you and I, we didn't fit as we should, or you wouldn't have had to go to the extra trouble." She'd never fit properly with anyone.

"Sweetheart, we're not two perfect puzzle pieces to snap into place. Occasionally adjustments are needed. The next time you come apart for me, Esme, it will be with my cock buried deeply inside you."

She nearly came apart then with the intensity of his promise burning in his eyes.

With the hand on her hip pushing gently, he nudged her onto her back and rose up on an elbow. Slowly he glided his finger along her center from the dip at her collarbone to the scar bisecting her abdomen. She placed her hand over his, halting his journey. "Don't touch it. It's so hideous."

"It's beautiful, Esme. A mark of survival." Leaning down, he pressed a kiss to it, then peppered others along the raised welt. "My brave girl. Life has treated you unfairly."

"To be totally honest, I don't know that I wanted children. Certainly, I felt a measure of regret when the decision was taken from me, but I don't miss not having babies. I have quite the fulfilling life, and so you shouldn't feel sorry for me."

He lifted his gaze to her. "I don't pity you, not in the least. Still, I admire your tenacity in the face of adversity."

"You've had your own share of misadventures."

He chuckled low. "I suppose that's one way to refer to them. I'm having a time of it retaining my anger at having endured them when they led me here." Straightening, he kissed her thoroughly before pulling away. "To you."

Then she was no longer thinking of her scars as he once again captured her mouth and drew her nearer, so his torso half covered hers. She stroked her foot up and down his calf, dug her fingers into the taut muscles of his back. Had he been so well defined when he was a lord? Or had the dangers he'd encountered forced him to develop a body that could quickly react to attack, that had the ability to survive when others wanted to destroy him?

Holding her tightly, he rolled them both until she was straddling him. Only then did his mouth leave hers to journey over her throat. "Lift your hips," he ordered urgently.

When she did, he positioned himself at her opening, and she slowly eased down, taking him fully, bracing her hands on his chest so she was upright and holding his gaze.

"Adjust yourself in the manner needed so you feel the fire between your thighs," he said. "Then ride me, fast and hard, slow and gentle. However you prefer."

She'd never known a lover could be so unselfish. "You'll tell me if I hurt you."

He grinned. She so loved the cockiness of it. "Sweetheart, you're not going to hurt me."

She slid forward and back, rose up, came down. Then the kindling sparked, and she dropped her head back, relishing the sensations that promised ecstasy with him seated within her. His hands covered her breasts, and she sighed. "Yes."

Her breasts loved his hands, the way they kneaded and squeezed, taunted and teased. The gentleness mixed with his persistence. Never before had she been in control, been the one setting the tempo, the vigor, the potency. Strange that in this aspect of her life, she'd been passive, not the aggressor. It suited her to be in charge, to dominate, to set the pace. And he knew it, wasn't threatened by it.

Flinging her head forward so the curtain of her hair draped around them, she held his gaze, rocking against him, lifting her hips, slamming them down, watching as his eyes grew more heated, listening as his breaths became harsher, more labored. "Are you enjoying this?"

"Immensely."

"I want you to yell out my name."

Clenching his jaw, he nodded. Next time, she was going to tie his hands to the bedposts and torture him with her movements. But for now, as the pleasure built, all she wanted was to hurl herself into the abyss of unparalleled pleasure. When it rocked throughout her, the joy was increased by his grabbing her hips, thrusting deeply, and growling out her name.

This time she was the one who collapsed, sprawling over him, her face tucked into the curve where his neck met his shoulder, inhaling the musky fragrance that surrounded them, her breaths coming in satisfied gasps. "I could become addicted to this."

"Good, as I've not had my fill of you yet."

She'd always sensed that men desired her—she'd learned the many ways to ensure that they did—but with him it was different somehow, richer, more profound, more necessary. He made her feel desired not only for her physical beauty but for every inner aspect as well. With him, she could almost claim to be cherished. "A few more times and you'll grow bored with me."

"I very much doubt that."

"You're quite imaginative when it comes to bedding."

"Feel free to return the favor. Never hesitate to tell me what you want or need, Esme."

I need you. Oh, that was a dangerous way to go, fraught with heartache. From the moment the rumors had begun circulating that she was with child, she'd felt as though she was facing the world on her own. While Brewster assisted her in various ways, he'd never actually battled beside her as Marcus had. She liked having a partner who viewed her as an equal in all things. "You once asked me how many lovers I'd had."

He stroked the length of her back, tiptoeing his fingers over her spine. "I was being an arse. It's none of my business."

"Three. I thought you should know that I'm not quite the harlot I've been painted."

"Was one your palace guard?"

"Richard? No. I rather lost interest in him when I learned he believed the rumors that were being spread about me."

"Does Beatrix still work at the palace?"

"Would you challenge her to a duel for my honor?"

"I bloody well might."

She wondered if he could feel her smile against his skin. "She was let go, without a reference apparently. The last time I spotted her, she was employed as a maid-of-all-work for a tradesman and his family, which included six children, so I imagine she is kept quite busy."

She enjoyed just lying here with him, talking, feeling the rumbling in his chest whenever he spoke.

"I'm glad she paid a price for her betrayal."

"I am as well. After her, I couldn't bring myself to trust anyone, not completely. It's one of the reasons I'm viewed as heartless. I locked so much of myself away." But somehow he'd found a key or perhaps he'd merely picked the lock to her heart.

"It's difficult to trust when someone tosses that precious gift aside." He turned his head toward her and slipped a finger beneath her chin, tilting it up, until he could hold her gaze. "Your previous lovers . . . did you trust them?"

Stacking her hands beneath her chin, she

studied him. "Not for anything more than a few romps."

"Does that apply to me?"

She was taken aback by how serious he sounded, as though the answer mattered. "I haven't quite decided about you yet."

She released a squeal when he flipped her onto her back and pounced on top of her. "Then let me see what I can do about that," he said, just before claiming her mouth.

He was going to destroy her resolve, work his way permanently into her heart—a heart he'd probably have no interest in holding forever. But once his, she didn't know how it would ever belong to anyone else.

CHAPTER 17

THEY WERE LATE to breakfast. To be honest, she was surprised they'd made it at all. Every time she got up to don her clothes, he'd watch her with a predatory gleam and just when she was almost put together, he'd remove every item and take her again. It was a wonder she could walk with the touch of soreness between her legs indicating how well and often she'd been pleasured.

Finally, with a teasing laugh, she'd run naked to her own bedchamber and locked the door. She couldn't recall ever feeling so young and uninhibited. She wanted to skip through fields of flowers, twirl about in the rain.

Now he sat across from her at the small square table where they ate from the plates a footman had brought to them earlier before departing. She'd sent Brewster to fetch two copies of the *Times* so they could catch up on the latest news.

Not that Marcus was paying much heed to reading the words inked upon paper. Instead, he continually gave her come-hither looks that warmed her to her core. She suspected they'd be returning to bed once they'd had their fill of bacon, eggs, sausage, and toast.

Or as they were alone, perhaps he'd simply knock everything off the table and spread her out on it. Yes, she was rather certain that was what he was contemplating. "Behave yourself," she stated succinctly.

He grinned. "I think you prefer me when I don't."

"You're such a randy gent."

"Only because you're so becoming and incredibly difficult to resist. And you blush when I whisper naughty words in your ear."

He'd done that during their last foray in the bed, and she'd never been so titillated. "Read your newspaper."

"It's not nearly as interesting as you."

"You don't have to give me false words. You've had me already."

"They're not false. Every aspect of you fascinates me. I like discovering new things about you."

Through him she was discovering new things about herself. That she could indeed climax with a man buried deep inside her. Was it because her previous lovers hadn't gone to the bother that Marcus did to ensure she lost complete control or was it more that she hadn't trusted them enough to let herself become so uncontrolled? She'd always been a bit self-conscious about her scar and what it visibly symbolized. Perhaps she had felt a bit less of a woman, but with Marcus she found nothing lacking in herself because he found nothing lacking in her.

He'd turned his attention to the newspaper, and suddenly he went very still. "It says here that Victoria is in residence at Balmoral."

"Not unusual. She spends considerable time at her castle in Scotland. To be honest, I think she has a tender for John Brown." He'd once served as a gillie for her husband, Prince Albert, but after the prince's death had become personal assistant to the Queen.

"My sister recently married a man with an estate in Scotland."

"The Earl of Tewksbury." More widely known as the bastard Benedict Trewlove, although he'd gone by the moniker *Beast*, before his true origins were discovered. One day he would inherit the dukedom of Glasford. "What are you thinking?"

"We've been striving to determine who was involved in the plot by making inquiries and attempting to catch snippets of conversations that might reveal something useful. But what if we were able to bring the culprits to us in one place and fool them into revealing themselves?"

MARCUS STOOD WITHIN the grand foyer of the Duke of Glasford's Mayfair residence, waiting as the butler went to announce their arrival. Marcus wasn't quite comfortable coming to Althea for assistance, but he was damned tired of the hunt and was willing to do whatever was necessary to bring it to an end. Still, he was the eldest and it was his responsibility to protect the others. He'd done a rather poor job of it, leaving them to fend for themselves, but at the time, he'd thought he had no choice. How different things might have been if he'd only gone to Esme a year earlier, if he'd had her counsel and assistance.

At his side now, she circled her hand over his back reassuringly. "How long since you've seen your sister?"

"I've observed her from the shadows from time to time, simply to ensure she was well, but we've not encountered each other or spoken since just before she married Trewlove."

"You didn't attend her wedding?"

He shook his head. "All I ever wanted for her was to be safe and happy. I visited after she became betrothed, and she assured me that she was both those things. I didn't want to do anything that might risk her not obtaining what she deserved and was afraid my presence at the nuptials might possibly bring danger to her door."

"But you had no qualms about bringing it to mine."

Looking over at her he smiled. Her voice contained no heat, only a teasing sort of pique. "You can take care of yourself."

"You didn't know that at the time."

"When I first laid eyes on you from a distance, I deduced you were a woman to be reckoned with. It's simply the way you hold yourself, the way you take command of the area around you. You can be intimidating."

"You weren't intimidated."

"I had nothing to lose."

The echo of rapid footsteps had him turning his attention toward the opening of the wide corridor as his sister emerged at a swift clip with a smile wreathing her lovely face, her giant of a husband following behind her. Rushing up to him, she took hold of both his hands and squeezed. "Marcus, I'm so happy you appear to be in splendid health. I've been frightfully worried about you."

He wasn't surprised that she kept some distance between them, rather than hugging him in welcome. Affection had long been absent in his family, and he'd often felt he was living among strangers. As a result, he'd embraced any excuse to be absent of their company. He rather regretted it now, having learned a tad late how important family was, how they could—should—be relied upon when facing life's challenges. "It's good to see you, Althea."

Looking past him at Esme—who had not worn her red hairpiece and was dressed modestly in a dark green frock that didn't dip below her neckline—Althea furrowed her brow and narrowed her eyes. "You look somewhat familiar . . . and yet I can't quite . . . place . . ."

Then her features morphed into disgust, and

she jerked her attention back to him. "Why have you brought Father's doxy here?"

"Esme wasn't Father's mistress."

"I beg to differ. Once I saw her with him. She is not welcomed here. Mother suffered humiliation because of their very public affair." They'd all still been living with their parents, so it had been impossible not to see the strain the gossip had put on the marriage. But then there had always been a coldness and distance between his parents. Althea had been closest to their mother and taken it all very hard. Especially because she'd been experiencing the swirl of the Social Season and was forced to endure pitying looks and conjecture regarding her parents' relationship. She'd been giddily betrothed to the Earl of Chadbourne before their father was arrested, at which point the scapegrace lord had tossed her aside.

"Althea, it was not as it all appeared. We'll explain everything but know that I trust her with my life." *With my heart, with my very soul.* The words he'd been unable to voice aloud took him aback, and yet he understood the truth of them. Still, he wasn't certain Esme would welcome them.

His sister angled her chin defiantly before turning her attention back to the woman at his side. "I suppose, welcome then."

Esme lowered herself into a graceful curtsy, one she no doubt bestowed upon the Queen when their paths crossed. "Lady Tewksbury, it is indeed an honor to make your acquaintance."

She sighed heavily. "Althea will do. My husband

isn't quite comfortable yet with his title." She turned to the silent, assessing man standing slightly behind her. "Ben, this is my brother, Marcus, and the woman with him is Miss Esme, was it?" She arched a blond brow.

"Esme Lancaster," she and he said at the same time, and he couldn't help but form a small smile that only caused his sister to narrow her eyes at him.

"Welcome," said the man once known as Beast, who, like Marcus, had roamed the darker corners of London. "Shall we retire to the parlor? Scotch and brandy seem to be required for this visit."

"It'd be most appreciated," Marcus said.

Once they were all settled with scotch for the men and brandy for the ladies, each couple sitting on a settee facing the other, Marcus told his sister, "I'm grateful to see you looking so well."

"I'm extremely happy. You?"

Strange to realize in spite of everything a part of him was happy, the part that spent time in Esme's company—when they weren't confronting brutes who wished him harm. But even then, having her near, fighting in his corner, brought him joy because she guaranteed he wouldn't be defeated. "Anxious to put the past behind me, and that involves finding those with whom Father conspired."

"You're still searching then?"

"Yes, and that's what bring me—us—here." He glanced at Esme. "Would you like to tell them or shall I?"

"Tell us what?" Althea demanded.

Beside him, Esme scooted forward slightly. "My relationship with your father . . . was, well, actually quite platonic. I work for the Home Office, you see, and my purpose in spending time with the duke was to gather information, and I believe he kept company with me in order to provide an excuse for being away from home a good bit of the time."

She briefly explained how she'd become aware of his being involved in the plot and then consequently used her wiles to keep him near. Marcus watched as Althea's eyes widened in disbelief. It was a remarkable tale, and if necessary, he would convince his sister of the truth of it. But when Esme was finished, Althea merely slumped against the back of the settee and sat there in silence for several minutes as though absorbing everything. Finally, she looked at him. "You believe all this?"

"I have no reason to doubt it. And it makes sense. In addition, we've had encounters with ruffians and others which lead us to think we're close to ascertaining who is behind the plot. But we want to hasten the discovery. That desire has brought us to your door."

Althea sat up as though he'd yanked on strings attached to her, and he could sense an excitement about her. "You want us to help? Whatever you need, brother."

It occurred to him that her eagerness indicated she'd felt slighted by not being included before now, and while he hesitated to involve her at this point, he hoped the risk would prove to be minimal. "We want to make use of your husband's Scottish country estate—for you to host a ball there. Invite every noble. As they're no doubt still curious about the newest lord among them, a vast majority is bound to come."

Several months earlier, in March, Trewlove had been introduced to Society as the rightful Glasford heir. Shortly afterward he'd married Althea, and they'd spent some of their time in Scotland because Trewlove's parents—the Duke and Duchess of Glasford—rarely visited London or entertained and they'd all wanted the opportunity to get to know each other better since it had taken the older couple more than thirty years to find their lost son.

"How will this help you?" Althea asked.

"The Queen is in Scotland. We'll let it be known that she intends to make an appearance at the ball and will stay that night at the Glasford property." Esme shifted her attention to Trewlove. "I can't imagine a Scottish manor house that has been in your family for generations doesn't have a few secret corridors that were used long ago when the English unexpectedly came to call."

Trewlove took a sip of his scotch before replying, "My father shared a few hidden passages with me."

"It would be helpful if there was access to one in the bedchamber in which the Queen would sleep so we could quietly secrete her away before any harm befalls her."

"If like Father," Marcus said, "the others involved are noblemen, it is quite likely they'd see
this affair as the perfect opportunity to finish off
what they'd begun. We assume they'd postpone
any attempt to kill her until everyone was abed so
they could slip in, do the deed, and escape without being caught. But we'll be waiting for them."

"Will you just be hiding in the room?"

"Eventually. But we also need to be able to
roam freely about in case we hear any snippets
of conversation that could lead us to the culprits
before the Queen's arrival. No one will find my
presence strange. You'd want your family, including Griff and Kathryn, to be there. As for Esme,
she'll pretend to be a servant. She won't have
quite the freedom to move about as I will, but she
has the skills to make the most of it."

"You don't think that if she's spotted people are
going to find it odd that the woman they knew as
Father's mistress is hanging about?"

"You almost didn't recognize me," Esme said,
"and you have more reason than most to have
remembered what I look like. At the affairs I attended with your father, I was usually masked.
He did take me to the opera and theater a couple
of times, but we always arrived after the curtain
had been raised and sat at the back of his box.
And I watched the performance through rather
large opera glasses, so my face was partially concealed. While it was common knowledge he'd
taken a mistress, very few actually saw me to the
extent they could identify me. And it has been

more than a year since anyone has seen the flamboyant redhead. I'm not saying I won't be recognized but I do think the possibility of it is quite slim. I won't be wearing the red hairpiece and will be rather demure in my clothing and bearing. Unnoticeable really."

"What if all this is for naught and nothing comes of it?" Althea asked.

"Then we've enjoyed a ball and each other's company," Marcus said.

"But if the Queen is killed," Trewlove said, "it will be believed that this little affair was arranged for that purpose and any number of us will be hanged."

"What I am about to tell you," Esme said in a low voice, "very few people know, but Marcus has assured me you will hold this confidence. There is a woman who impersonates Victoria from time to time, on the rare occasion when there is perceived danger. Few can tell the two apart. She will be the one who will actually attend your affair."

"She would put her life at risk?" Althea asked incredulously.

"It is her job, as it is mine. For queen and country."

For the first time it seemed it was possible that Esme had won Althea over because his sister said not a word but merely studied the elegant and confident woman at his side. While everything within him had stiffened at the reminder that Esme wouldn't put her own safety first.

He almost stood up and announced, "Forget it.

We don't need to know who was involved in the plot. I don't give a bloody damn who Father was working with. Devil take family honor. I will restore my name in other ways."

But he knew that even if he gave up, Esme wouldn't. She was charged with protecting the Queen. She would see to the task at the expense of her own life, with or without him. He wasn't going to leave her to go it alone.

Finally, Althea looked at her husband. "What are your thoughts?"

"I don't want my parents involved. They've been through enough in this lifetime, and I will vouch for them that they have no interest in seeing the Queen harmed, so there is no need for you to suspect them or require their presence. I'll convince them to take a journey to Europe for a few weeks. Regarding the task of arranging for a ball to be held at the estate—how long would that take?"

"Three weeks or so if we don't want people suspicious that something is afoot. Invitations printed, sent out. Most are at their country estates now." Althea looked at Marcus. "We're in London because it's where Ben is most comfortable, and the Trewlove family resides here. It would be odd not to have his brothers and sisters present. I'm rather certain you can count on their support." Trewlove and five other children, bastards all, had been raised by Ettie Trewlove as though they were her own.

"Trewloves like nothing better than a good

fight. You'll be close to having an army in Scotland," Trewlove said.

"Then there's Griff," Althea said. "Does he know of your plans?"

"Not yet," Marcus admitted. "The estate in Scotland was the key. If you objected then we'd have to come up with an alternative scheme, so we began with you."

"Why don't we send for him and Kathryn, and then we could discuss the details of this daring strategy? We'll have dinner together, shall we? After so long, it would be lovely."

Lovely was not how he would have ever described dinners in the Duke of Wolfford's household. Tension always radiated around the table, their father dominating conversations, their mother timidly seldom contributing to any discussion. Yet he had missed the sense of belonging. "I look forward to it."

"Do you love her?" Althea asked.

Following dinner, Trewlove had poured each of the gentlemen a glass of scotch before taking Kathryn and Esme on a tour of his mother's gardens, leaving Marcus with his two siblings on the terrace with the last of the sunlight slowly dwindling away. A courtesy no doubt to give them a chance to talk more privately. He hardly knew how to respond to Althea's question, but he knew Griff was equally anxious for an answer. Since his arrival, he hadn't snubbed Esme. However, he hadn't been particularly warm toward her either. "She's a remarkable woman."

"That would be a yes then," Griff stated succinctly, disappointment rife in his tone.

Marcus took a sip of his scotch rather than plow a fist into his brother's handsome face. His feelings for Esme were complicated; she was complicated. "We already explained what her relationship with Father entailed. She wasn't responsible for anything that happened to us."

"I hate to admit it," Althea said, "but I rather like her. She certainly knows her own mind and seems quite capable."

"She is definitely that," Marcus concurred.

He caught sight of Trewlove and the two women walking beneath the arched arbor. While they appeared to be taking a leisurely stroll, he noticed how Esme casually glanced around constantly. He very much doubted she was taking note of the assortment of blossoms. Like him, she was keeping an eye out for any indication of imminent danger and had probably already marked a path for a hasty exit if needed. She would have identified weaknesses and strengths in those with whom they'd shared a repast. She would be able to describe in exacting detail every servant they'd encountered. He wondered if she ever took a holiday, ever completely relaxed. Even in his arms, at first, she hadn't let herself go. She needed to be in control, and so after their initial lovemaking, whenever they'd come together, he'd ensured she was in charge.

"He's certainly watching her as though he's a man in love," Griff said.

"Bugger off," Marcus growled.

"No longer heir to a dukedom might turn out to be to your advantage," his brother mused. "You certainly couldn't marry her if you were duke."

He wasn't certain she'd marry him in either case, that she would give up this perilous life for him, that he could live with the worry if she didn't.

CHAPTER 18

$\mathcal{E}$SME KNEW THAT the most efficient way to arrange what they needed to occur at the ball was to tell O of their plans because he could facilitate ensuring Victoria stayed at Balmoral until after the ball so people would believe that she might indeed attend. He could also coordinate Mary's participation. While upon close inspection, she couldn't pass for Victoria, Esme wanted her to only arrive at the residence wearing a veiled hat and declaring that a megrim required her to immediately retire to her assigned bedchamber.

But Esme didn't want to involve O. Or anyone from the Home Office, for that matter. Since the night she'd taken the photographs in Podmore's study, she couldn't help but suspect there might be someone in their midst working against them— either innocently or intentionally. She had decided not to even tell Brewster the true plans. He would accompany them, of course, but he would do it with the understanding that they were there to protect the Queen should she attend the ball. She also didn't want to inform O or the Home Office because she was quite sure they would argue with her on the merits of the plan. In all likelihood it wasn't going to work but Marcus had the right of it: they needed to try something.

This Lucifer fellow was evasive and skilled at hiding his identity. She feared he wouldn't hold on to his patience for much longer and would strike against the Crown when they were the least prepared. Why else have Podmore killed and then murder the man who had done the deed? After a year of being dormant, he was once again on the prowl. She didn't think he was tying off loose ends because he was giving up on his goal, but rather he was preparing to finish it. He was good at covering his tracks. He worried her.

However, it was crucial that one more person be aware of the scheme as her approval was crucial. Hence, Esme and Marcus were presently on a train headed for Scotland.

"A shame we don't have a private railway coach," he said from his place beside her on the compartment bench. "The motion of the train could make for an interesting experience."

"You are so terribly wicked."

"Wouldn't you like to give it a try?"

She would like to be bedded by him anytime anywhere. Not that she was going to confess all that when they weren't alone. Strangers sat nearby.

She'd caught a couple of the younger ladies eyeing Marcus, no doubt attracted to the handsome gent, and she suspected they were straining their ears to catch snatches of the conversation. "Do behave. We don't want to draw attention to ourselves."

The railway would get them to Aberdeen more quickly and time was of the essence. The Queen's and Mary's cooperation needed to be confirmed before the invitations could be designed, printed, and delivered. No point in moving forward without the collaboration of the linchpin.

"You do realize that every man seated in this car has noticed you and is probably fantasizing about bedding you even as we speak," he said.

"I should have dressed as an old woman then."

"I doubt it would have made any difference. There's just something about you that can't be ignored." Threading his fingers through hers, he placed their joined hands on his thigh. "We'll be arriving quite late at night. You're welcome to use my shoulder if you wish to sleep for a while."

"Did you have a private compartment when you were a lord?"

"No, I preferred traveling by a horse-drawn coach. But trains are faster. We should be there and back in no more than four days. What if she won't see you?"

She smiled softly. "She will. That's not my worry."

"What is?"

"That she'll think it's a ridiculous scheme or

might put too many at risk. But I'm convinced this Lucifer fellow is too cautious. He won't do anything publicly. Because she's become such a recluse, is seldom seen in public, a ball with her present will be a temptation too great to resist. We'll simply need to persuade her of that."

"I have complete faith in your ability to do so."

She smiled at him. "Flattery, Mr. Stanwick, will get you everywhere."

"When you look at me like that . . . bloody hell but I wish we were alone. I'd flatter every inch of you."

She wished they were alone as well. Rather than confirm that, however, she simply squeezed his hand. Strange how sitting there holding hands almost seemed more intimate than being naked together between the sheets. Intimacy, she was discovering, came in many different forms and degrees.

He brought his mouth nearer to her ear, and she instinctually moved closer to him. "I've been thinking of your plan to go as a servant," he said, his voice low. "It's too limiting, won't give you much access to the lords and ladies who will be in attendance. I've come up with a better idea. You should go as my wife."

HE WAS ACUTELY aware of her stiffening and withdrawing, physically by removing her hand from his grasp and emotionally by erecting an invisible but chilling barrier between them. The horror that crossed her lovely features took him aback.

"Don't be ridiculous. Marriage is not for me."

Did she never consider it? Knowing society as he did, he could well imagine her arguments: She was quite on the shelf. She couldn't bear children. Her lack of purity. He cared about none of those reasons, considered them all absurd.

But perhaps what she truly meant was that marriage to *him* was not for her. Perhaps like her previous lovers, he was fine for a romp between the sheets for a short while but once they'd attained their goal, they'd part ways. Not that he could blame her. While his brother and sister had been fortunate to find someone willing to overlook their pasts, he had been the heir and the family name and titles had been more strongly associated with him. He'd practically been bathed in them since birth.

"I wasn't proposing, Esme." Not that the notion hadn't crossed his mind a time or two. It pricked his pride to know she was so vehemently opposed. "But if you're going to pretend to be a servant, why not pretend to be my wife? It would give you the freedom to walk about among the guests, to overhear conversations, to judge attitudes and actions. It would make you more visible, make everyone else more visible to you. People wouldn't question our being seen together if we needed to share some information."

She visibly relaxed but didn't retake his hand.

"Oh. I see. Yes, that makes sense. It might be the way to proceed. We would need to come up with a story to explain our being together. How did we become acquainted?"

He glanced around at the other passengers. Most had fallen asleep. No one sat in front of them or behind them. No one could hear what they were discussing. "I was letting a room from you. Weren't you the one who advised me that it was best to keep to the truth as much as possible?"

Her smile was slight, almost regretful. "So I have a boardinghouse. That could work. As a business owner, I would be expected to be a bit more assertive. I just don't know if people would accept that you would marry a commoner. You were considered quite the catch a Season ago."

"As an aging spinster, on the shelf, desperate to marry, you threw yourself at me. Considering the position my father left me in, I decided I could do worse than you."

She scoffed. "You should be so fortunate as to have me as a wife."

Now she was changing her tune. He offered her a teasing grin. "Precisely. I think people would find my marriage to you believable."

She studied him. "Were we secretly married?"

"Not secretly, but quietly. I've not been in Society for over a year. Why would I announce my marriage?"

"When did we marry?"

"Pick a date."

"I've always liked August. The fifteenth."

He suspected she'd selected a date with some meaning to make it easier to remember. "Why is that date special?"

"It's my birthday."

"I'm sorry I missed it."

"You were busy getting married."

He chuckled, knowing he was going to miss her if they met with success and would have no further reason to remain in each other's lives. "Indeed, I was."

"Our being married *would* allow me to move about more freely. Well thought out, Marcus. Well done."

"You're not disappointed it wasn't an actual proposal of marriage?"

"Absolutely not." She looked out the window at the darkness that had settled over the land.

Pity, as he found he was a tad disappointed.

CHAPTER 19

$\mathcal{I}$T WAS LATE that evening when they arrived in Aberdeen. They made their way to a hotel where Marcus secured a room for one Mr. and Mrs. Stanwick. He didn't find it at all odd to refer to Esme as his wife. She was wearing gloves, so no one had been able to detect that she didn't house a ring on her left hand. He would need to remedy that situation before the ball.

She'd brought a small trunk and he had a satchel that contained a change of clothes, so he would look his best when meeting with Victoria.

Within their chamber, Esme stood before the low flames on the hearth as though striving to warm herself. "You sounded quite natural introducing me as your wife."

He tossed his coat onto a chair and began unbuttoning his shirt. "I thought I should begin practicing. I'll need to be convincing at the ball."

"How will you dispense with your wife when all this is over? Will we just announce that it was a farce?"

Dropping into the chair, he began tugging off his boots. "I don't know that we'll need to say anything. My association with the nobility will only happen if they're in need of my sleuthing services, and my marital status is unlikely to ever come up. It's not as though I'll be socializing with them. Among the common folk who will be neighbors and acquaintances, no one will know that I ever claimed to have a wife. If it makes you uncomfortable to be associated so closely with me or you think it will compromise your position with the Home Office, come up with another way to get yourself entrenched in the midst of these people."

"I'm certainly not ashamed to be seen with you, Marcus. And whatever assignment I'm given next will involve getting close to people who have no idea who I am. I simply want to ensure that our fake arrangement doesn't cause trouble for you later on when you begin your search for a wife in earnest."

"Marriage is not for me."

Her brow deeply furrowed, she moved away from the fire. "For God's sake, why not?"

Standing, he tugged off his shirt. "Are you going to tell me why it's not for you?"

"Too many reasons to count."

He wondered how many of those reasons might have taken hold because of words spoken by her mother. "Maybe I'll feel differently regarding marriage in a few weeks, but not to-night. At the moment, I'm dead tired. Turn about and I'll unfasten you."

Her traveling frock was modest, keeping all of her skin except for her face and throat from view. Perhaps that was the reason that as the fabric parted to reveal what had been hidden, he pressed his mouth against her warm flesh.

"I thought you were dead tired," she said, but he heard a hint of teasing in her tone.

"Mmm. But it seems a shame not to take advantage of this time I have alone with my *wife*."

She released a giggle, a tiny giggle, that seemed so out of place coming from her, and yet it caused the weariness to evaporate and desire to ratchet through him. He wondered if she was uncomfortable with the thought of marriage because it had once been something of which she dreamed, something that had been snatched away, something she had accepted as an impossibility. If she was nervous now because she was striving not to allow those dreams to reawaken.

He did more than unfasten her frock. He assisted her in divesting all of her clothing. When she was bared, he didn't know why he'd thought he'd sleep beside her without touching her. After removing his trousers, he took her hand and led her toward the bed. "I'm no longer tired."

ESME FOUGHT NOT to envision how marriage to him would involve many nights like this: of his undressing her and taking her to bed. His referring to her as his wife shouldn't give her the thrill that it did. Instinctually she knew he would marry for love, would adore his wife, would make her grateful every night that she was his.

When he pulled her down onto the bed, she gladly went, finding herself on her back as he trailed his mouth over her skin while his hands stroked her, igniting the flames of her desire. This wasn't their usual frenzied lovemaking. It was lazy and slow. With him, it was always different and yet the same. She scraped her fingers along his hard muscles, relished the way they bunched with his movements. She'd never had a man as fit as he was, of such strength. He was spoiling her. After him, how could she possibly find satisfaction with anyone else?

He rolled onto his back. When she straddled him, he cradled her hips between his large hands, digging his fingers into her soft flesh, stopping her when she would have mounted him. She lifted her gaze to find his eyes smoldering with want and need.

"Come up here," he rasped.

She furrowed her brow. "I'm not quite sure—"

Gently he pulled on her. "I want to taste you."

Heat like molten lava sluiced through her. He nudged her again while circling his tongue around his lips. How could she refuse such an invitation? She worked her way past his chest and shoulders until her knees rested on either side of his head. He eased her down and licked. Nibbled. Licked again.

With a low moan, a soft sigh, she dropped her head back and absorbed the incredible sensations coursing through her.

"Play with your breasts," he ordered in a strangled voice.

Doing as he bade, she kneaded her breasts, pinched her hardened nipples, and soothed them with circular strokes while he plundered. She'd never felt so unfettered and free. With a movement of her hips, she could increase the pressure or soften it. She could direct where he should lick. He unerringly followed her direction, but it wasn't enough. It was all for her and she wondered if she could drive him as mad as he did her.

Lowering her hands, she threaded her fingers through his hair and lifted her hips until she could meet his gaze. "I'm going to turn about."

She wasn't nearly as graceful as she would have liked, nearly toppling over, but when she was once again situated so he could feast, she bent over and kissed his hip, taking pleasure in his low moan. She licked the inside of one thigh and then the other. He smelled of musky sex. It heightened her own arousal.

She wrapped her hand around his cock and licked the glistening tip. His hips bucked slightly, and his deep moan echoed around her. Yet he didn't stop his ministrations but increased the urgency with which he partook. She was on fire and wanted him burning as hotly, wanted him squirming as she did, wanted all the little sounds of pleasure rumbling through him. So she took the hard length of him into her mouth so her tongue could dance over him.

"Christ, Esme." His fingers dug into her hips as he worked feverishly, igniting such pleasure within her that she thought she might die of it.

She wanted him near death as well. Feeling the tension building in him, she continued to lick, suck, and stroke. She'd never felt more powerful. Or more consumed with pleasure. It took hold and wouldn't let go, building, building until it erupted through her, and she was crying out from the pure ecstasy of it.

Then he was lifting her, turning her, guiding her down, and plunging into her hot, slick wetness.

"Ride me," he growled, pumping into her before putting a hand at the back of her head, holding her as he rose up and took possession of her mouth.

She tasted herself on his lips and wondered if he could taste himself on hers. Then he tore his mouth from hers, bucked, and groaned, his fingers tightening on her hips as he flew over the edge and fell back. Crumpling on top of him, she listened to his harsh breathing and his pounding heart as she was lulled into sleep.

MARCUS HAD SLEPT the sleep of the dead. But then it appeared so had she. He'd awoken to find himself spooned around her and had the absurd thought that he wouldn't mind waking up like that every day for the remainder of his life. But she wasn't keen on marriage. Although perhaps it was just marriage to him.

They'd prepared for the day, enjoyed breakfast in the hotel dining room, and then hired a hansom cab to cart them out to Balmoral, where they'd paid the driver enough so he would stay until their business was completed and he could return them to Aberdeen.

They were presently waiting in the grand entryway while the Queen was alerted to their presence and, hopefully, would consent to an audience with her. He was striving to keep his emotions in check, not to focus on the fact that because of this woman he'd lost so much. It was his father's fault. That was where the blame rested. Yet some compassion on her part toward his family would have been appreciated.

Esme certainly didn't seem nervous. Reaching over, she brushed some lint off his coat. "I didn't think to ask if you've ever met her."

"Once. Some affair at Buckingham Palace that I attended with my father when I was sixteen and Prince Albert was still alive. I don't expect her to recognize me. I've changed since then."

"Haven't we all?"

Hushed footsteps whispered over carpeting just before the butler appeared. "Her Majesty will see you. If you'll be so kind as to follow me."

The stately servant led them through a maze of corridors and into a chamber that no doubt served as her office for receiving official visitors. A rosewood desk was near a window. One wall housed books. Majestic paintings covered the walls, some he noted by renowned artists. There were several sitting areas. Near the one closest to the door stood England's petite ruler.

"Miss Esme Lancaster and Mr. Marcus Stanwick," the butler announced formally before stepping out and closing the double doors behind him.

Esme graciously curtsied while Marcus bowed. "Your Majesty," she said softly.

"Esme, dear, greet me properly."

She rose, glided over to the Queen, took her hand, and pressed a kiss to it as she curtsied.

"You're looking well, child."

Esme straightened. "You're kind to say so."

Then the Queen was studying him. "Stanwick. Not the Duke of Wolfford's heir surely."

Standing now at his full height, he angled his head to the side. "I am his firstborn, yes."

"You no doubt believe you were treated unfairly."

He understood fully that his father's actions, had they been successful, would have carried grave consequences for the nation and the world. But the punishment had caused his innocent family to suffer as well. "I'm not here to question or dissect past actions."

"Then why are you here?" While she seemed to

be asking the question of him, she was once again looking at Esme.

"Mr. Stanwick has been assisting me in my search for the others who wished you harm. We believe we've come up with a plan for drawing them out, but we require your cooperation."

"We'll take tea in the garden to discuss it, shall we?"

Marcus was fascinated watching Esme's interactions with a woman who ruled an empire. He doubted any lady of his acquaintance would be as relaxed as she poured tea for her sovereign or asked after her family. Because of her closer association with the Queen, Marcus remained an observer, allowing her to explain how they hoped to lure the conspirators into revealing themselves. Mary Talbot, the surrogate, would arrive, make a brief appearance without speaking with anyone other than her hosts, declare herself weary, and retire to the wing set aside for her and her ladies—the wives or daughters of peers who served in various positions to see to her comfort. John Brown would need to accompany Mary because no one would believe Victoria would go anywhere in Scotland without him. Using a secret passageway, Marcus and Esme would slip into the designated chamber. Marcus would escort Mary through the chamber to the outside where he, along with Brown, would escort her back to Balmoral. Meanwhile Esme would be waiting for the arrival of an evildoer. He and she had argued extensively about that part of the plan, as he'd wanted to be the one waiting—but she'd insisted it was her duty. In the end he'd let her have her way.

As there was little for him to contribute now, he simply sat back, enjoyed his tea, and took pleasure in observing. The two women smiled, laughed, and seemed to truly care for one another. He supposed the two years that Esme had served the Queen in such a personal capacity had forged a bond between them.

An hour after they'd arrived, he and Esme were in the cab headed to Aberdeen. They were on a train back to London by nightfall.

CHAPTER 20

THE FOLLOWING THREE weeks were the most wonderful of Esme's life. During the day, she and Marcus spent a good bit of time with his sister working out the details of the ball that was to take place at her husband's family estate. Esme helped to design the invitations and addressed them when they were delivered by the printer. As though she were a young debutante enjoying her first Season, she gossiped with Althea and Kathryn, who it was obvious had long been the best of friends.

"I have it on good authority," Kathryn said, "that Chadbourne and Jocelyn are presently residing in different dwellings. I daresay you were fortunate that he tossed you over."

Althea offered Esme a small smile. "I was once betrothed to the Earl of Chadbourne before Father's downfall . . . The earl cast me aside. Jocelyn, a dear friend at the time, took my place."

"She's getting what she deserved," Kathryn said.

"No one deserves to be unhappy."

They spoke of who was courting whom, recent scandals, and the hopes of several unmarried misses. With the passing of each day, she caught a glimpse of what Marcus's life would have been if his father hadn't betrayed his country, precisely how he would have fit into it. The self-assurance with which he laid out their plans, the attention he gave to the details, the manner in which he instilled confidence in the others that they would meet with success. The way he strutted about. How comfortable he was speaking with a man who would one day be duke. It pained her heart to see how suitable he was for a world that had been stripped from him.

And every night when they returned to her residence, they retired to his room and made mad, passionate love. The attention he devoted to her was beyond anything she'd ever known. Or imagined. To give so much of himself to her, he had to care for her to some degree. She would tell herself it was only lust, but then she'd awaken to find him studying her as though he couldn't get enough of watching her.

She halfway hoped that their mission failed, and he'd have no reason to leave her just yet. Then she'd be struck by the selfishness of such a thought. His future had been upended, and she wanted him to find happiness and purpose beyond retribution against those responsible for stealing everything from him and his family. She wanted him to find love, to marry, to have dark-haired sons with his beautiful blue eyes. Sons who would grow up to be as bold and magnificent as he.

She visited her modiste and had a new gown sewn. He went to a tailor to have evening attire fitted to his specifications.

The invitations were dispatched, not through the post, but via liveried footmen who were sent out en masse to deliver each vellum card to every lord and lady in the whole of Britain. A note carefully inscribed in perfect penmanship accompanied each one: *Her Majesty has deigned to honor us with her presence at the ball.*

People would arrive the day of the ball, with accommodations provided so they could stay the night. The following morning would see them sent away after partaking of a hearty breakfast. A great deal of travel for so short a time. It would eliminate those with no interest in either a queen or the newfound son of a duke.

She and Marcus had arranged to arrive the day before it was acceptable for anyone else to make an appearance because they both wanted to explore the residence and grounds to ensure they knew their way around and would be comfortable carrying out their plans while keeping everyone safe.

As the coach in which they'd been traveling came to a stop in front of the massive manor, Esme glanced at Marcus and found him watching her. "You'll soon be free," she said softly.

"What of you?"

"I'll move on to another mission, thank goodness. I've been getting rather bored with this one. There is always some sort of intrigue at court, some information that needs to be gathered about someone. And then there are those who break the law and must be apprehended, and sometimes Scotland Yard requires my services. You would be surprised by all that transpires about which no one will ever hear."

"Will I ever know if tragedy befalls you?"

"By the time it does, if it ever does, you will have forgotten me."

"You're not one to be forgotten, Esme. But we get ahead of ourselves, I daresay. We need this little escapade to work first."

"How right you are."

The coach door opened, but before the footman could hand her down, Marcus grabbed her arm, halting her descent. She glanced back at him.

"I have something for you, to make this all the more believable."

As she settled back on the squabs, she couldn't imagine what it might be.

"We'll need another minute," he said to the footman before reaching for and closing the door to give them a bit more privacy.

Sitting across from her, he took her left hand and slowly began to tug off her glove. Her breath caught as she suspected where this was headed. "Marcus—"

"I should have given this to you sooner. Don't

know why I didn't. The symbolism of it I suppose made me a tad nervous." He raised his eyes to meet and hold her gaze. "Even if it is only pretense."

Her mouth went dry as the kidskin slipped past the end of her fingers. Lifting her hand, he pressed a kiss against her knuckles before removing something from his coat pocket. A simple rose gold band, she realized as he slowly slipped it onto a finger of her left hand, almost a perfect fit, only a little loose. As a girl, she'd dreamed of that happening in a church filled with spectators, joyful at her happiness. She swallowed hard. "You shouldn't have gone to the bother or the expense. I do hope the jeweler will let you return it and give you your money back."

"It was my grandmother's." Her stomach knotted. "My mother had a hidden safe in her bedchamber where she kept her jewelry. I'd forgotten about it until the day you and I went to the residence. In need of a ring, I decided to hell with the Crown's order that we were to take nothing personal. I was quite pleased to discover that those who had removed things from the residence hadn't found the safe—or if they did, they left it as it was. The other jewelry I found within it, I gave to Althea. But this is for you."

"I'll return it to you as soon as all this is over."

"I'd rather you keep it as a remembrance of . . . when you were my wife." Although his lips curled up with a sardonic twist, she wasn't quite certain that he wasn't taking the wife part seriously.

"I don't feel quite right keeping it, but I shall be honored to do so and will treasure it as I treasure your . . . friendship."

He suddenly grinned wickedly. "Is that what you're calling my cock? Friendship?"

"Oh, you beast!" She slapped at his shoulder playfully, grateful the serious moment was behind them because a small secretive part of her wished it was her true wedding band and that when all this was behind them, she would still be his wife.

With a laugh, he shoved open the door, leapt out, and handed her down.

Brewster, who'd been riding up top with the coachman, approached. "That's a monstrosity of a place," he said. "I don't know how you're going to protect the Queen in there."

They hadn't told him the details of their plans, that it wasn't the Queen who was coming. As far as he knew Victoria had contacted them saying she wished to attend the ball and wanted her protector there to ensure her safety. While Esme trusted Brewster, she didn't want to take any chances that a slip of the tongue would ruin things for them. "Speak with the servants, see if you can determine if anyone isn't an admirer of Victoria's. Be subtle. We want people to think that, like her, we're only here to attend the ball."

"Leave it to me. I suppose I'm to haul your baggage up."

She smiled at him. "We'll have footmen see

to it. But remember you are to cast yourself as
Marcus's valet."

He scowled. "Not even a butler. It's insulting."

"It's for only a few days. You'll survive."

With a grunt, he walked away.

"He's an irascible sort," Marcus said.

She wound her arm around his. "He likes to
feel important. I think he objects to my confiding
in you more than him these days—although the
truth is that I've never confided in him fully."

"Do you with me?"

Probably more than was wise. In her occupation it was difficult to trust completely, and yet it
hadn't taken her long to begin confiding in him.
They strolled up the path to the broad steps
leading to the massive door that had no doubt
been originally built to withstand the assault of
battering rams. No one would be surprised that
Marcus was attending an affair hosted by his
sister, although she suspected a few would avoid
him, still suspicious regarding any involvement
he might have had in his father's plans. She expected many a lady would be jealous that Esme
was intimate with this fine specimen of a man.
While his family name might be tainted, she
imagined lying with him was a fantasy for some.
That she was privileged to be doing so brought
her a measure of pride. Rather than answer him
succinctly, she said, "I share more with you than
with anyone else."

"Then I consider myself fortunate indeed."

The door they approached sprung open on well-oiled hinges, and the butler led them into the parlor filled with an assortment of people: the six Trewlove siblings and their spouses, Griff and Kathryn, and a man Esme recognized as being the Duke of Glasford. When she'd worked at the palace, she'd seen him once when he visited the Queen. While he stood as large and bold as his son, beside him was his lovely wife sitting in a wheeled chair.

Althea approached, her husband at her side. "We were beginning to wonder if you'd gotten lost."

"No, we simply got a late start leaving the inn where we stayed last night," Marcus said. A late start that had happened because they'd spent longer than they should have frolicking in the bed.

"My parents insisted upon being here," Benedict Trewlove Campbell said. "Seems they're responsible for the stubbornness I inherited."

"We'll keep them safe," Esme promised before he walked them over to the duke and duchess and made introductions. Esme curtsied. "Your Graces, thank you for allowing us to make use of your magnificent manor."

"More castle than manor," the duchess said.

Esme straightened, aware of Marcus at her side. "Yes, but still magnificent."

"No one would believe this ruse of yours if Mara and I were not here to welcome the Queen," the duke said with his thick Scottish brogue.

"You don't hie off to Europe when royalty comes to call."

"Valid point," Marcus said.

"I've met you before, lad. As I recall your da introduced us at a club some time back."

"Yes, Your Grace. Life was very different then."

"You never know what is in the hearts of men. My own da is a prime example. Hatred had him trying to kill my Mara and my lad. I'm sorry for the course your da put you on."

"He wasn't alone in it, I'm convinced of that. Hopefully soon we'll have answers."

Althea approached and touched her brother's arm. "Come, let me introduce you both to my new family members."

Esme knew those of the Trewlove clan by reputation only—they often filled the gossip sheets and were nattered about. No one sneered at her or gave any indication they considered her beneath them, but then when born out of wedlock or married to someone who was, one tended to have a more accepting nature. They welcomed her and Marcus as equals, and she imagined that in the future he would spend a good bit of time in the company of these people. He'd no longer be the lone wolf set on retribution. He would be further embraced as a member of this family. She wanted that for him, wanted him to once again belong.

CHAPTER 21

MARCUS HAD FORGOTTEN what it was like to be welcomed into the home of a nobleman, to have servants with whom he was not familiar at his beck and call, to sit at a table with an abundance of people and to carry on a conversation with no one making snide remarks about his parentage or his family's fall from grace. To be accepted. To have new acquaintances show genuine interest in anything he had to say.

But what brought him more satisfaction was that they were equally accepting of Esme. And it had to have been so much longer since she'd received such kindness. They'd been given adjoining rooms. Without Laddie about, Marcus had slipped into her bed. He wasn't certain how their relationship might change if they met with success that evening, and he wanted as much time with her as possible.

Following breakfast, they were strolling over the grounds that included rolling hills, the occasional tree, and fields of heather.

"Was your family's ducal estate anything like this one?" Esme asked quietly.

"Not quite as wild. The manor house is more a Jacobean style, huge, built for entertaining, with one wing devoted exclusively to the use of royalty. Apparently, a few of my ancestors were quite favored by their king."

"Did Victoria ever visit?"

"No. May have been for the best, all things considered. Everything about the estate spoke of privilege. In addition to the immense gardens, we had three parks. One was actually fenced off and contained lions. My grandfather had been responsible for their captivity, so they'd been there for a while, twenty years, I think, by the time I came along. I was allowed only to watch them, not play with them. I was about five when the first one died. I thought it a shame that he'd had so many years of not being able to run wild. I began mapping out a plan to set the remaining two free, but alas, my plan was dependent upon my growing up a bit and being stronger. They didn't wait on me before succumbing to old age." He couldn't prevent the disappointment and sorrow he'd experienced at the time from weaving their way through his voice now.

"That must be why you're so good at strategy, having started so young."

He grinned sadly over at her. "When I was old

enough and strong enough, I took one of my an-
cestor's old battleaxes to that fence."

"Were you punished?"

"Oddly no. I'm not even certain Father noticed."

"When you were much, much younger, did
you dream about what you would like to do if
you were not destined to be a duke?"

"It's what I was born for. It never occurred to
me to be anything else. I think that's part of the
reason it took me a while to find my way through
the quagmire once it was no longer my destiny."

"You *wanted* to be a duke?"

He furrowed his brow. "Why would I have
not?"

"It just seemed to me that being an heir defined
one's future, prevented a man from pursuing
other occupations for which he might be better
suited. What if you wanted to perform upon the
stage, for example? Lords do not become actors.
Or physicians. Or chefs, for that matter."

"I never saw all the responsibilities that would
come to me as a burden. I relished the thought
of one day being duke. Not because of the prestige or the power that came with the title but because of what I could have accomplished for the
tenants of the estates, for the estates themselves.
They were all languishing under Father's care.
He lacked imagination when it came to managing them. Another reason I know he was not the
mastermind of this plot."

"I didn't realize an imagination was required
of a lord."

"It's not a requirement but without it, how can one see the potential?"

"What did you see?"

"Ways to improve the lives of the tenants. With education and teaching them more modern methods of farming. Training their children for occupations in the cities. Ensuring there was a path to avoid poverty for the next generation and they were productive members of society. What the land could provide was changing and we needed to change with it. Just as I'd done with the lions, I began planning only this time I was in search of a means to move us into the future. Part of the reason that the Crown taking everything came as such a devastating blow was because I'd sought out no personal avenues of income for myself. I was concentrating on what would one day be mine, unlike some friends who were pursuing their passions until the title came to them. I was so damned anxious to hold it, to be ahead of the game . . . and then my father's actions changed the rules and I lost at the game."

"Perhaps if all goes well tonight, Victoria will consider returning the titles to you."

"No, Esme, the best I can hope for is that people will realize I'm not like my father, that I can be trusted and am an honorable man. And perhaps an article in the newspaper that will bring clients in need of sleuthing skills my way. A bit of positive renown associated with my name wouldn't hurt."

Having walked over the grounds until they

were familiar with the area, they headed back toward the manor. Throughout the morning guests had been arriving. He was rather dreading seeing some of the fellows with whom he'd once played cards or visited at the clubs. He was determined to act as though their refusal to have anything to do with him after his father's arrest hadn't been an unexpected shock that had sent him reeling for a time. The swiftness with which people had turned against him had astounded him, not that he blamed them, at least not deep down. They couldn't risk being suspected of having any sympathy for someone who had wished harm to the monarch. He'd been arrested, questioned, suspected, and that made associating with him a risk that no one was willing to take.

Griff had gained his revenge by snubbing them or charging them a fortune to be members of his exclusive club. When it came to entertainments, they were quick to forget how unfair they'd been to the duke's spare. Marcus doubted they would be as forgiving toward the duke's heir.

CHAPTER 22

$\mathcal{A}$s THE DAY had progressed toward evening, more carriages began arriving at a steady clip until a line of vehicles filled the drive leading to the manor house. It was a lovely day. The air was crisp with the first hint of autumn. People gathered in the gardens for a bit of refreshment and a chance to visit before night and the ball approached. And to have their curiosity satisfied. Not only about the new heir to Glasford, but also the former heir to Wolfford.

Esme had planned to take advantage of this opportunity to speak with the wives and daughters of the various lords, to ingratiate herself to a few in hopes of possibly learning something she hadn't known regarding Wolfford or his friends. She had been trained to mimic those around her, to appear to belong. She was comfortable doing so.

But as she wandered through the gathering striving to determine who might be a fountain of information, some of which might prove useful, she couldn't help thinking that one of the recent debutantes or brides might have made the perfect wife for the Wolfford heir. And she couldn't help wondering if one of them had enjoyed a picnic with him the summer before.

Not wanting to offend the Duke and Duchess of Glasford, the guests welcomed their daughter-in-law, Althea. Not wanting to offend Althea, no one gave a cut direct to either of her brothers. Esme noticed a couple of ladies shyly approaching Marcus with wistful smiles, and it occurred to her that like Griff, Marcus could possibly land himself a lord's daughter when all this was behind him. Or perhaps even if it never was. It was obvious that he'd been liked, sought-after then, sought-after now—even if he was presently believed to be married.

It appeared she'd also been correct that no one recognized or remembered her as the duke's mistress. At least not so far. But then she wasn't brazenly strutting about or striving to draw attention to herself. She was the demure and only recently wedded wife to a man who should have been duke.

She thought of their earlier conversation when he'd shared how he'd been busy preparing to be duke rather than engaging in other pursuits. He had been pursuing his passions, and they had been precisely what the heir to a dukedom should care about. The future of what he would inherit. How she longed for him to have what he'd once been passionate about.

She spoke with one lady about roses, another about her love for tulips. She complimented frocks, asked advice on hiring servants, and discussed books. Being a voracious reader, she was able to contribute to any topic without becoming flustered. She was skilled at directing conversations away from herself. People loved to talk about themselves, and she gave them the opportunity to do just that. So it was that she learned Lady Aubrey was incredibly grateful to be back in Britain after more than a year in France.

"The invitation we received to this affair finally prompted Aubrey to return," she confided now.

"France is a beautiful country," Esme said. She'd once spent a few days along the coast.

"I especially love the wine," the countess said. "But watching the vines grow is so tedious."

"Were you at a vineyard?"

"Oh, yes, did I not say? Aubrey inherited one from a distant uncle. He's become rather obsessed with it. Never wanted to leave, but neither was he willing to give up an opportunity to see the Queen. He'd like nothing more than for his wines to be served at the palace."

It was some time later as she was glancing around that she felt the large, warm hand land against the small of her back and smiled up at her *husband*.

"You should look up at me a bit more ador-ingly," he teased. "After all, I swept you off your feet the moment we met."

She arched a brow. "You did?"

"Mmm."

"Is that what you've been telling people?"

"We're supposed to stick as close to the truth as possible, aren't we?"

"You were insufferable that first night."

Leaning down slightly, he pressed his warm lips against her temple. "And I've regretted it ever since."

"You shouldn't. I was fairly insufferable my-self."

"I hope the gown you're wearing this evening is red. You're irresistible in red."

"I think you find me irresistible in anything I wear."

"More so out of it."

With a laugh, she stepped in front of him so she could face him. "Do you always flirt so at affairs such as this?"

One corner of his mouth hitched up. "I sup-pose I did. I'd forgotten how much I enjoyed them. While we're here on a serious matter, until the Queen arrives, we might as well have a bit of fun."

"We're supposed to be on the hunt."

"I've been on the hunt, but thus far the prey is keeping his distance."

"What do you know of the Earl of Aubrey?"

His smile disappeared and the teasing glint in his eyes turned to steel. "Why?"

"He's been in France for a little over fifteen months, which means he left around the time of your father's demise. Supposedly tending to a vineyard he inherited. But he couldn't resist the opportunity to be in the Queen's presence. The timing seems odd."

He nodded. "I'll have Griff keep an eye on him. Anyone else suspicious?"

"Not thus far. Have you had any luck?"

"No one is as forthcoming with me. Mostly, it's 'Tough luck, old chap.' And then they head off to speak with someone else. But at least they're acknowledging me so there is that."

"You should take the opportunity to let them know if they ever need any sleuthing done, you're their man."

He studied her for a minute, and she wondered if she should tell him that he was her man as well. "We should probably return to our snooping about," she said instead.

"I suppose we should."

"And it is red."

His grin fairly melted her heart. "I look forward to divesting you of it later."

As he strode off, she felt giddy, like a young lady who had never been hurt, or an older one who had decided *he* was worth the risk of being hurt.

MARCUS WAS UNDOUBTEDLY biased but Esme was the most strikingly beautiful woman in the ballroom. It was more than her comely features. It was the demure, welcoming air with which she strolled about, her projection of providing a haven for anyone in need of one. Ladies fluttered about her like butterflies searching for a sturdy blossom upon which to alight for a respite from the harsher elements. He wanted to be her champion, but she served as her own champion. And that increased her attractiveness.

If anyone recognized her as being associated with his father, they kept it to themselves. Absent the red hairpiece, she didn't draw as much attention, didn't stand out as she had when he'd first seen her more than a year ago. He was amazed by her ability to blend so thoroughly into her surroundings. He understood more fully why she was such an asset in her position with the Home Office. He'd wondered if with her success, they'd hired more women or would. She'd made the best of a tragic situation, and he couldn't help but admire her all the more for it. He hoped in years to come, with the success he intended to make of his detective agency, that the same would be said of him.

Although many of his contemporaries were a bit wary around him, most were more welcoming than he'd expected. However, the smile on the handsome face of one of the two men approaching him was exceptionally warm as he extended a glass of scotch toward Marcus.

"King, Knight," he acknowledged as he took the offering from the Duke of Kingsland.

"Stanwick," King said. "I didn't expect to find you here. Thought you'd declared yourself more comfortable in the shadows."

"There are shadows aplenty about. Besides, my sister rather insisted I make an appearance. I see you apparently resolved matters between you and your secretary."

"She's no longer my secretary but my wife." His tone carried an immense amount of joy and pride. "I appreciate your assistance in finding Penelope. She can be quite the stubborn wench when she sets her mind to it. Appears you've taken a wife as well."

Marcus didn't much like lying to a man he admired but took comfort in knowing it was all for the greater good. "I have indeed."

"I've been trying to convince Knight here to give marriage a go."

"Not bloody likely that's going to happen," Knight said.

"Eventually you'll need an heir," King pointed out.

"Deuced stupid reason to marry or have children."

"I agree," Marcus said. "I wonder what idiot came up with primogeniture anyway."

"I hope they flogged him," Knight said. "By the by, wagers are being made that you'll confront the Queen when she arrives."

"Avoid more like," Marcus assured him. "That's where I'd put my money. Are the other Chessmen here?" The moniker was often used when referring to the four friends who were known for their ruthless strategy when it came to investing.

"Bishop and Rook are about somewhere," Knight said, "probably in the cardroom. If you'll excuse me, I believe I'll join them."

As he walked off, Marcus took a small sip of the scotch. He had to keep his wits about him tonight.

King cleared his throat. "If I'm not mistaken, your wife was your father's paramour at one point."

"I was hoping no one would notice."

"I saw them in your father's theater box, next to mine, one night shortly after rumors were flying that he'd taken a mistress. Unfortunately for you, as Penelope will attest, I'm not likely to forget something once I've seen it. Although your wife's hair is a different shade now. The two of you seem an odd pairing."

Marcus shrugged laconically. "I went to see her, hoping Father might have told her something that would help me return honor to the family name. He hadn't, but I found I rather liked her. She wasn't at all as I expected."

"Women seldom are," King said. "But they're nice to have around. Are you any closer to achieving your goal?"

"There are times, King, when I'm not even certain I know what it is I'm searching for any longer. Perhaps you had the right of it that night when you suggested I give up." King had come to him because Penelope Pettypeace had disappeared from his life, and he wanted her back in it. "Being here, among the *ton* once again, I'm questioning whether I ever truly belonged."

"I think we're a poorer lot for having lost you."

While the words touched him deeply, he grinned with a need not to get maudlin in light of all that had transpired. "If you hadn't, I wouldn't have been much use to you when you needed help."

"If I can ever return the favor—"

"You paid me well enough." Coins that he had used sparingly to ensure he didn't have to beg anyone for more. As a footman passed by, Marcus set his empty glass on the tray the servant was carrying.

"Another?" King asked.

"No, I don't need to stumble about like a fool."

"Well, I believe I'll go have a dance with my wife. It was good to see you, Stanwick."

"You as well, Your Grace."

After King walked off, Marcus stayed where he was and continued doing what he'd been doing all along: observing those in attendance, searching for anyone who might appear a bit nervous or tense, anyone who was sweating overly much. It was a cool night. The doors leading onto a terrace were open and a slight breeze wafted through the room. In an alcove, set high in a wall, accessible by a back stairway, musicians played. People danced or gathered in small groups and visited.

In another room, nearby, a feast was being served. Much gaiety was about. It was like every ball he'd ever attended. Nothing seemed amiss.

A young lady stepped in front of him. "Hello, m'lord." She shook her head until her blond curls quivered. "I'm sorry, I got that wrong. It's Mr. Stanwick now. But you still give the appearance of being a lord. I realize I'm terribly bold but wondered if you might dance with me." Giddiness was reflected in her brown eyes.

"How old are you?"

"Almost ten and eight."

A child. "You've a reputation to protect, sweetheart. Dance with another."

"No one is as exciting. They're all such bores, whereas you have an air of danger about you."

"Pip, what the devil are you doing?"

The girl's eyes widened as an older woman—no doubt her mother, based on the same blond curls—descended like an avenging angel. Before her daughter could respond, she grabbed the young girl's arm and glared at him. "She's not for you." Then she was hustling the moping lady away.

"Should I be jealous?"

He glanced over to see Esme and was damned tempted to take her in his arms and kiss that smirk right off those sensual lips. "She's the third to approach me this evening."

"It's the way you prowl through the throng like a ravenous tiger. You make all the other men look dull and unexciting."

"You make the other women look remarkably unappealing."

"Then why haven't you danced with me?"

"A situation I need to rectify straightaway." He held out his hand. "Will you do me the honor of a dance?"

Her gloved fingers landed lightly on his gloved palm, and he wondered briefly why Society was so opposed to skin touching in public. Perhaps because it led to more skin touching privately. He wished they could escape upstairs for a more intimate encounter, but duty called for her, retribution for him. Tonight might provide the answers and an end to his quest, so for now he would be content with a waltz.

"I noticed you dancing with a couple of gentlemen. Did you garner any information?"

"Oh my word, yes. Lord Sayres would like very much to ask for Lady Violet's hand, but he fears a rejection because he has seen her on more than one occasion staring wistfully at Lord Harding, who he considers to be unworthy of her. Lord Harding, on the other hand, did go down on bended knee during the Season and is betrothed but is now having second thoughts, fears he may have acted a bit too hastily because the lady, it seems, has become quite the complainer. To complicate matters, he's recently met an American to whom he's taken a fancy. He wondered if it might be kinder for all concerned if he broke things off."

In amazement, he smiled at her. "How do you

do it? How do you get people to tell you all manner of things?"

"I'm nonthreatening. I hold their gaze and let them know that I honestly care what they have to say. Nothing is trivial because to them all their worries are large. I offer them a place to set them down for a while."

"So you can sift through them in case a treasure is buried within them."

She wrinkled her nose. "That aspect doesn't sound so nice of me, does it?"

"The ends justify the means. Has anyone appeared to recognize you?"

"If they have, they haven't said anything to me."

"The Duke of Kingsland remembers you sitting in a box at the theater with Father."

"That's unfortunate."

"He won't gossip about it," Marcus reassured her. "If anyone else is giving you an interested look, I suspect it's because you're the most beautiful woman here."

She smiled, and it caused a catch in his chest as he fought not to imagine all the future ones that she wouldn't bestow upon him. "You're not giving enough notice to the eligible ladies who will no doubt be vying for your attention once honor is restored to your family name and they realize that you are not in fact married."

"They won't give me any consideration. I'll still be without a title."

"You underestimate your appeal if you think it

is dependent upon you having a title. Regardless, you will be celebrated as a hero, having saved the sovereign."

"And you a heroine for the same reason."

She shook her head. "It would be best if you take all the credit, if none learn of my part in the success of this endeavor. Wherever I go next, it's best if people don't know who I am."

"That hardly seems fair—that you should do so much of the work and receive none of the acclaim."

"I don't do it for accolades. Besides, a good many souls do far more than I and yet no one has ever even heard of their names."

"Like O?"

"He is one, yes. To protect queen and country so much takes place about which so few people are aware. It's really quite remarkable."

"You are quite remarkable."

"While I've never been able to forgive Beatrix for her unkind actions, I do owe her for leading me to a life that is far more than I ever expected it to be. Without her shenanigans, I doubt you and I ever would have become friends."

"Is that what we are—friends?"

"And more."

"What will we be when this is over, Esme?"

As she gave her head a slight shake, her gaze slid past him. Her eyes widened, her brow furrowed, her steps faltered. "Oh my God."

He brought them to a halt, and they weren't the only couple to favor ignoring the music to look toward the doorway. To his surprise, he stared at the petite woman, flanked by a tall gentleman on one side, and several ladies on the other. "My God, you were right. Mary Talbot could pass as the Queen's twin."

"That's not Mary. Unfortunately, it is indeed Victoria."

CHAPTER 23

*W*HAT A BLOODY disaster!

Esme couldn't very well march up to the Queen and demand to know what the hell she was doing here when they'd agreed she would remain in residence at Balmoral and send Mary in her stead. John Brown was beside Victoria, and Esme tried to draw some comfort from knowing the Scot would lay down his life for the woman it was obvious to anyone with a keen eye he loved.

"How do we handle this?" Marcus asked.

"She is safe as long as she is in this room. Anyone who wishes her any harm isn't going to attack her with so many potential witnesses about."

"Unless they're planning to follow Guy Fawkes's plans and blow the place to smithereens."

"If that was their plan, they would have done it before now at Windsor, Buckingham, or Balmoral. No, if there is any danger at all, it is to her alone. When she retires, you will need to get her out of her bedchamber as quickly as possible."

"I'd rather stay with you," he said, not for the first time.

"That's not the plan."

"Then you take her," he whispered near her ear in a manner that no doubt had others believing he was taunting her with sensual promises.

"We've discussed this before. It's my job."

"Are you going to speak with her?"

"Only a polite greeting from the receiving line because one does not chastise Her Majesty." People were already beginning to queue up.

The Duke and Duchess of Glasford, as well as their son and his wife, were greeting the Queen and her escorts.

"I suspect Victoria will snag at least one dance with John Brown before retiring." Although the Queen continued to dress in mourning attire, she wasn't dead and John Brown was a fine, strapping man.

"Do you truly believe the Queen is having an affair with her servant?" Marcus asked in a low voice.

The orchestra had gone completely silent, and Victoria was being led to a massive chair that Esme suspected had been designed generations ago for visits by the monarchs. "I won't be surprised if, decades from now, writings unearthed in the royal archives will reveal quite a bit of naughtiness going on between those two."

"Is that one of those secrets to which you're privy?"

She gave him a saucy smile. "Wouldn't you like to know?"

"I'd wager, with the proper use of my tongue, I could have you revealing all."

Dear Lord, but she was going to miss him when they were finished here. "I dare you to try."

He arched a brow and gave her a sensual smile. "With pleasure. Although it would no doubt behoove us to stay in this chamber for the present."

"Indeed. We should separate now and eavesdrop on conversations to see if we can discover anything of import. We'll join the queue once it's not so long."

The Queen's ladies-in-waiting who now surrounded her were not the same ones who'd been at the palace when Esme was there. Victoria often changed them out for variety. But even if they had been the same, it was unlikely they'd have remembered Esme because no one paid any attention to servants and it had been well over a decade since she'd resided at the palace.

As she made her way around the room, listening to conversations, she used her ability to blend in to ensure she continued to go unnoticed.

"¶ DARESAY THE Queen's imposter does a spot-on imitation of Victoria," Griff said, standing with Marcus near a virtual jungle of fronds.

Marcus had walked slowly around the perimeter of the dance floor, catching snatches of conversations, but they were all related to speculation about the Queen's arrival and why she had chosen to honor this family with her presence. It seemed that many had not expected her to show, but most were striving to determine what it might mean for the Duke of Glasford's future as well as that of his son. Marcus had heard a couple of wagers being made as to whether Victoria and Brown would dance; if they did dance, would it be a waltz or a polka? How many times would they dance? But he'd heard no mutterings that threatened the sovereign's life, not one word hinting at dissatisfaction with the monarch. If there were people here who wanted her done away with, they were certainly hiding themselves well.

"Unfortunately, it *is* the Queen."

"I thought the plan—"

"Apparently she changed it," he said in exasperation.

"Then you'd better bloody well hope she doesn't get killed while she's here. They'll say you arranged it and chop off your head."

"Hanging is more like."

"Christ, Marcus—"

"I know." He didn't need to hear his own qualms voiced aloud by his brother. What would it mean for Esme to be partnered with him, to have trusted him, to have arranged all this with him without consulting with O or the Home Office? If something went wrong, might she be blamed? Might she find a noose around her neck?

"There's going to be another change in plans, and I need your help with it."

"Whatever you require."

In spite of all his father had set into motion with his actions, Marcus couldn't help but believe some good had come of it by bringing the siblings closer. "I was to secrete the Queen out through a hidden passageway that connects with her chambers and see her safely returned to Balmoral. But I dare not risk leaving Esme to face whatever blackguard might be intending to take advantage of Victoria's presence here tonight. I'll escort the Queen down the passageway, but I want you waiting at its entrance to take her to Balmoral. I have some weapons in my bedchamber you can use so you won't be unarmed and Brown will be there with you." By the time Esme learned he'd altered their strategy, it would be too late for her to argue about it. She'd be forced to accept his appearance at her side.

"I brought my own weapons."

He shifted his gaze from those milling about the Queen and Esme, who was standing casually nearby, her eyes like those of a hawk. She was discreetly keeping watch. He arched a brow at Griff, who merely shrugged.

"Since we roamed the darker corners of London together, I always keep weapons at the ready. Never know when someone might come for us, and I'll be damned if they'll touch a hair on Kathryn's head."

"Are some on your person now?"

"Yes. You?"

"Absolutely."

"Do you think there will ever come a time when we don't expect the worst?"

He turned his attention back to where Esme stood, somehow managing not to draw attention to herself as she assessed those visiting with the Queen. When he was with her, he didn't expect the worst, even if it was hovering nearby. She made him feel that they had the power to conquer it, defeat it. Even now, with the unexpected arrival of the actual Victoria, he believed that if someone made a play to assassinate the queen, the action would result in failure. Esme wouldn't accept any other outcome.

He wanted a lifetime of sharing picnics with her, myriad opportunities to hold her in his arms, a thousand waltzes across parquet floors, and endless strolls through heather-coated fields. He wanted her smiles, her laughter, and her passion. If honor was restored to his family name, would it be enough to keep her at his side? He'd considered himself nothing without a name to be proud of because presently the name marked him as his father's son and branded him the offspring of a traitor. But if he could break free of the shackles that chained him to the past and kept him anchored to his father's actions, could he have a future with Esme?

Victoria suddenly stood and Brown held out

his hand to her. Together they made their way to the center of the dance floor as people backed away to its edge to give them room. She signaled to the orchestra and the lilting strains of a waltz filled the air.

"I just won twenty quid," Griff said.

Marcus grinned. Of course his brother would have made a wager. His tendency to gamble had provided him with the means to establish his club. A few people began to join the couple on the dance floor. "If you'll excuse me, I'm going to take advantage of this moment to dance with Esme." He was relatively certain she'd want to be in close proximity to Victoria.

"By all means. Think I'll do the same with my wife."

Esme must have been anticipating his move because she met him halfway and glided smoothly into his arms. Following her lead, he swept her into the circle of dancers.

"Did you hear anything of note?" she asked.

"Mostly wagers being made. You?"

"Nothing of any significance."

"What if they're not here, the others who wished her harm?"

She smiled softly. "Then I had the opportunity to waltz with you."

As much as it pleased him that she should feel that way, he was hit with other concerns. "I'm serious, Esme. Where would we go from here?"

"I don't know. Perhaps it was only your father

and there's naught to the other rumors floating about. Or it doesn't involve the nobility. I truly don't know, Marcus."

He'd no doubt be branded a traitor if anyone at all could read his present thoughts because he was praying that someone tonight would in fact try to kill the Queen.

CHAPTER 24

*B*ECAUSE ONE DID not yell at royalty, Esme was keeping her tongue in check and would not grant it freedom anytime soon, although she was rather put out that Victoria had not gone along with their plans to the letter. The whole point of strategizing was to avoid being taken by surprise, and it certainly didn't help matters when the one she was charged with protecting placed herself in peril.

It was nearing midnight before the Queen and her entourage bid good night to everyone and made their way to the wing that had been set aside to accommodate them. As a result, Esme was now ensconced in a dimly lit hidden passageway, her ear pressed up against a concealed door so she could hear the scurrying about happening in Victoria's bedchamber as her servants—who had been welcomed via the servants' entrance and been waiting to be called upon—prepared her for bed and made her comfortable. To increase the chances of this endeavor working, it was imperative that no one in the entourage or among her servants know that she would be secreted away. Her ladies-in-waiting were wives or daughters of noblemen, and it could be possible one of them was involved in the plot. After all, it would be beneficial to have someone who was complicit working on the inside to provide information regarding the Queen's comings and goings.

Marcus was at her back, his hand resting against the curve of her waist. She wasn't quite certain he was aware of how often he touched her. The way his hand always found its way to her seemed so natural and unaffected, as though she was the moon and he the tide. She rather liked the artlessness of it, the unconscious need he had to connect with her.

She became keenly aware of the quietness emanating from the other side. "The others have left," she whispered before pressing on the latch that swung open the hidden panel. She'd barely stepped into the room before dropping into a deep curtsy at the sight of the small woman, wearing her nightdress and wrap, standing beside the bed. "Your Majesty."

"Is that pique I hear in your tone, Esme?"

Aware of Marcus, stone still, beside her, she straightened. "No, ma'am."

"Did you truly believe I would send someone into harm's way in my stead?"

"I'd hoped"—she shook her head—"it doesn't

matter what I'd hoped. We need to get you out of here posthaste. Mr. Stanwick is going to escort you to safety."

"I saw his father hanged and his inheritance stripped from him. Do you truly think he will have my best interest in mind?"

"I trust him with my life," she stated vehemently, "and with yours. As we told you when we met with you at Balmoral, he is not his father. And Mr. Brown is waiting for you outside."

The Queen nodded. "Very well then. Let's see this done. Nothing quite as unsettling as having a death sentence hanging over your head. I'm ready to be rid of it."

"This way, Your Majesty," Marcus said, bowing slightly and sweeping a hand toward the passageway.

As the Queen ducked through the doorway, he grabbed Esme and slashed his mouth hard and quick across hers. "Stay safe until I return."

Then he was gone, the panel sealing them away, beyond the reach of anyone who might enter the bedchamber through the door. She desperately wanted Marcus here with her, which was ridiculous. She was a woman who'd learned early on to depend upon no one other than herself.

Quickly, she crossed over to the bed, threw back the duvet, and placed pillows along the mattress's center. Tossing the duvet over the makeshift body, she set a braided hairpiece, which matched the shade of Victoria's hair, against the pillow so it appeared the Queen was on her side sleeping. She blew out the lamps, leaving only the flames dancing on the hearth to provide the light. Although the shadows placed her at a disadvantage, they would do the same for whoever entered the room. If anyone did.

Slipping behind a thick and concealing frond that had been placed beside the wardrobe that morning, she had a clear view of the doorway, the window, the bed, and the remainder of the large chamber. The clock on the mantel ticked, ticked, ticked. An irritating sound. She should have stopped it from marking time before she'd taken up her position. Normally she enjoyed the crackling of a fire, but even that soft murmur was grating on her ears. This was her least favorite part of any hunt—the wait.

She didn't feel in control, couldn't rush the perpetrator into attending to his task. She was at his mercy for when things would be set into motion.

And then she heard it. The *click*.

The door would have been locked, so someone was tinkering with it. Another *click*, slightly more ominous than the first, and then the door was opening on silent hinges. The gloom prevented her from seeing anything except the silhouette of a figure that quickly entered and sealed them in together. Short in height. For some reason she was surprised by that fact.

Whoever it was possessed the skill of moving without creating a sound. She tracked his—or her—path to the bed. She had to be sure, so she waited for an action that would offer proof that a dastardly deed was on the verge of being committed.

She saw the firelight glint off the edge of a blade, watched as the knife sliced down, heard the muttered profanity as feathers flew. A calmness settled over her as she stepped out from behind the frond, brandishing her revolver. "Don't move."

But he did. Quickly. And she found herself facing *his* revolver. She stared at him, unable to believe her eyes. "O?"

THE QUEEN WAS acting like they were on a bloody holiday, taking her time, cautiously placing one foot on a step, following it with the other, before attempting to navigate the next roughly carved bit of stone that would lead her out of this blasted place. Marcus was holding the lantern over her head so she could see clearly but that didn't seem to make any difference. Of course, she was a good twenty-five years older than he was, but still . . . Esme was up there alone, waiting for God knew who or how many.

He was tempted to hand the lantern off to Victoria and tell her to make her own way, but he knew Esme would never forgive him for such an action, especially if some tragedy did happen to befall the woman. If she fell, or God forbid, someone other than his brother and Brown were waiting at the entrance. And one certainly couldn't tell the Queen to get a move on.

Ah, but he was sorely tempted. What worse thing could she do to him? She'd already deprived him of everything of any consequence. Although he supposed she could have him imprisoned. Or hanged. The risk was worth it to return to Esme. "Your Majesty, perhaps we could move a tad more quickly."

"I'm not as spry as I once was, young man." Then she stopped, bloody stopped, and faced him. "What is Esme to you?"

"Presently, to me, she is in danger."

She flicked her hand toward him. "Then head back up."

"She'd never forgive me for abandoning you." Then another idea struck him. "Would you hold the lantern?"

She took it with the enthusiasm of someone picking up offal. When she had it firmly in hand, he lifted her into his arms and began hurrying down the steps.

"What the deuce are you doing?" she screeched. "You're not allowed to touch your queen without permission, and you most certainly can't treat your sovereign in such an undignified manner."

"You're welcome to hang me later for the offense, but I'm doing what I must to save you and—" *the woman I love.* He nearly stumbled and sent them both tumbling down the stairs. When had he come to love Esme? Yet there was not a single doubt that he did, with everything within him. She was the sun and the rain, the moon and the stars. She was the reason that he was presently risking incarceration or death by touching a woman whom no one was supposed to touch. Well, except for her husband. Prince Albert had obviously touched her or they'd have not had all those children.

Children Esme couldn't have, which made her unmarriageable in his former world. But now . . . now he had to get back to her as quickly as possible. He wondered why when he'd followed this route that morning, he hadn't realized traversing the passageway was akin to traveling to the Isle of Wight. It went on for bleeding forever.

Then finally, he saw the open doorway and Griff standing in it.

"I was beginning to worry—"

He shoved the Queen into his brother's arms without explanation or letting him finish his sentence. Grabbing the lantern, he raced back up as though his very life depended on it—because it did. How would he survive if anything tragic happened to Esme?

CHAPTER 25

ESME STARED AT the man to whom she'd been assigned, who gave her the orders she was to follow. "How did you even know a ball was being held here and the Queen would attend?"

"Brewster told me. He reports to me as well, you know. Unfortunately, I thought you were coming here only to protect the Queen. I didn't realize you were using the opportunity to uncover who wanted the troublesome woman dead. You didn't tell Brewster everything, did you?"

"I never tell anyone everything." Except Marcus. No, she hadn't confided everything to him, she hadn't told him that she loved him. "Why do you want to end Victoria's life?"

"Because she is no longer serving as queen. She's hidden herself away. The country is in shambles, and she mourns her dead love rather than seeing to her duty. I must protect England.

It will be much better off in the hands of a king. In my hands. Because I am the true and rightful heir to the throne. I can trace my bloodline back to Richard the Third. Look at me. I even inherited his deformity."

While Shakespeare had described Richard III as hunchbacked in his play, Esme wasn't certain if he truly had been. She was beginning to suspect, however, that O was quite mad. "How did you convince Wolfford and Fotheringham to go along with your plans?"

"They believed as I do: that she was bad for the country. I convinced them of my claim to the throne and promised them more wealth and power than they could ever hope to hold otherwise. And then the damned Home Office assigned you to me."

Her breath caught. "Oh my God. I wasn't the decoy. Wolfford was. You had me get involved with him so he could keep tabs on me and report to you. Not the other way around."

"Precisely. Your reputation preceded you. Left to your own devices, I knew it wouldn't take you long to ferret me out. So I gave you a diversion. I thought once you were publicly associated with him, the Home Office would assign you to something else, but you stuck to it. I needed it to appear I was doing my job, so I made a sacrifice to the greater good."

"You're the one who had Wolfford arrested. You didn't fear he would tell them everything? No, no, you made sure he wouldn't. You threatened him with something. You killed Fotheringham."

He shrugged, and in that action, she saw the truth of the matter. It had been no riding *accident*. Somehow, he'd managed to make it look that way, but it had been murder. "When you came on the scene, he began to get scared that we'd be caught before I was in power and could protect us all. I couldn't risk him mucking things up. So I got rid of him, which turned out to be fortuitous because it proved I was willing to do anything to achieve my ends. When Wolfford was arrested, I told him that if he gave anyone my name, his heir would suffer the same fate as Fotheringham."

So the Duke of Wolfford had held his tongue and gone to the gallows as a traitor in order to save the life of his son. She wondered if Marcus would take any comfort in knowing. "And Podmore? Why send me to his party with instructions to search his desk?"

"Those papers meant nothing. I needed to place you somewhere within a particular time frame so my *associates* could dispense with you because you're too smart for your own good, girl. I put my plans on hold for an entire year waiting for the Home Office to determine you were of better use elsewhere. I'd grown tired of the delay in claiming what was mine, and I needed you gone. I'd not counted on blasted Stanwick getting involved that night."

Although she wanted to believe she could have

defeated those four men, she very much doubted it. Not with her rapier against all those knives. Without Marcus fighting beside her, her life probably would have come to an end.

"I shouldn't have provided you with the answers," he said drolly. "Hell would have been pure torment for you with all those questions swirling about."

"The gunfire will bring people to this room so you can't shoot me."

"On the contrary, m'dear. As I've long suspected, you are a traitor and were here to kill the Queen."

He fired.

ESME FLUNG HERSELF to the floor before realizing that Marcus had rejoined her and was flying toward O. What the hell? Did no one understand the importance of sticking to a bloody plan? Before she could begin to worry about where the Queen was, Marcus had crashed into O and taken him down. Only he didn't move as O struggled to squirm out from beneath that massive body.

The bullet. The bullet must have struck Marcus. The fury that poured through her turned her into a she-devil. She jumped to her feet, darted across, grabbed O, dragged him out from beneath the man she loved, and pounded her fist into O's face once, twice, thrice, taking satisfaction in his grunts of pain.

As she'd suspected, the gunfire had the ladies-in-waiting and their husbands, if they were in attendance, barging into the room. Along with Glasford and Benedict, who'd also taken rooms on this wing in case they were needed.

"She was planning to kill the Queen," O shouted or tried. The words were rather unintelligible since she'd broken his jaw.

"He's lying," she and Marcus said at the same time. She jerked her attention over to see him, thankfully, sitting up, leaning against the bed, one hand to a shoulder, blood oozing between his fingers, the other holding O's pistol directed at those standing stupidly just inside the doorway.

"Don't try to stop Esme from her purpose," he ground out. "She has the Queen's blessing on this."

Roughly, she rolled O over and began tying his hands with a length of rope she'd stored in her pocket.

"Where is the Queen?" one of the men demanded.

"She is here," a regal voice announced, and Esme wanted to scream. Did no one care about their own safety?

The crowd parted and the Queen strolled in, Brown and Griff in her wake. "Oglethorpe."

"She is the traitor, Your Majesty," O blurted. "Look at the bed. You can see where she tried to stab you in your sleep."

"If she was going to stab me, she'd have done it while I was alone in the room with her earlier. I'm so terribly disappointed in you, Oglethorpe.

I shall have to cancel my plans for your knighthood. Your man seems to be injured, Esme. Attend to him while Mr. Brown and Mr. Stanwick see to the traitor in our midst. I'm certain this castle has a room somewhere that was set up to hold prisoners at one time."

"Indeed it does, Your Majesty," Glasford said. "'Tis rather cold, damp, and uncomfortable, I'm afraid."

"It sounds like perfection."

Leaving O to be handled by the others, Esme moved over to crouch beside Marcus. "What the devil did you think you were doing, bursting into the room like that, hurling yourself at O? That was not the plan. You were supposed—"

Placing the revolver at his hip, he wrapped his hand around the nape of her neck and brought her in for a searing kiss.

CHAPTER 26

WORD OF THE happenings within the Queen's wing spread through the castle-like manor with amazing speed, and before Esme knew it, she was in the grand parlor with Victoria, who had decided to delay her departure for Balmoral until everyone saw that she was uninjured and could be reassured that all was well in hand. Because of her fear of illness, she never traveled without a physician, and he was now attending to Marcus.

Esme wished he was here with her because she was rather uncomfortable with all these people gathered around inappropriately in their nightclothes, listening intently as Victoria regaled them with the truth of her visit and how very close she'd come to death.

The Queen's ladies and any of the husbands who had seen the aftermath of what had transpired had been sworn to secrecy regarding what

had truly happened and who had been involved.
Marcus was being given all the credit for stopping the assassination attempt, which Esme knew
would probably not sit right with him, but it was
best that her involvement be limited to being the
wife of a hero.

In the event she ever needed to investigate or
gather information from those in attendance tonight, she needed to be forgettable. Once she was
forgotten, Marcus could claim to have hired an actress to assist with his ruse. He could carry on with
his life, and so could Esme.

Word had been sent to the Home Office and once
all of the guests departed, O would be brought out
of the dungeon and transported to London under the watchful eye of the Queen's guards. Esme
could only hope that the Home Secretary wouldn't
be too upset with her for striking out on her own
and not keeping anyone there apprised of the situation. But based upon how it had all turned out—
that one of their own was untrustworthy—surely
they would see the wisdom in her strategy.

Footmen who looked as though they'd recently
been roused from their beds were passing by with
trays laden with brandy. Esme grabbed two drinks
before walking over to Brewster, who was standing near a window looking like a puppy who had
just been kicked. Or perhaps he was contemplating
leaping through the glass to make his escape. She
offered him a snifter.

Ducking his head slightly, he shook it. "I told
him everything. O. I was assigned to him as well,

but he would only ever meet with you. When he sent word that he wanted an audience with me, I have to admit that my head swelled. I thought at long last I was being recognized."

"I'm sorry if I made you feel unimportant."

"No, it was him, not you. Then when he wanted me to keep him apprised of what you were doing, I thought it was because of Stanwick, that O trusted him no more than I did and that he thought Stanwick might be turning your head or distracting you from our purpose. It never occurred to me that he wished you harm or that"—he looked toward Victoria—"he was the one all along, the one we were searching for."

"Obviously it didn't occur to any of us. When I reflect on where he wanted to meet, how eerie he made things—Marcus described the catacombs as practically medieval, and I have to agree with him now. I thought O was simply eccentric, but I believe he might be living in the past." She nudged the snifter against his hand until he finally took it.

"You didn't tell me everything about what was going on tonight. It was right for you not to trust me."

"It wasn't that I didn't trust you, Brewster. But I learned long ago that the fewer people who know everything—the safer it is for everyone."

"I shall resign after this. I think I make a better butler anyway."

She smiled. "You can still be my butler."

"After I nearly got you killed? I told him you were going to Podmore's, the night you found the lad dead. That might be the reason he had him killed. I've never had actual blood on my hands, but I feel like they're coated in red now."

"You shouldn't. It's not your fault. And I do hope you'll reconsider staying with the Home Office. You have experience and knowledge that is of real value."

He gave her a sad nod. "O ruined a lot of lives. I suspect more than we'll ever know."

SITTING UP IN his bed, Marcus sipped on the scotch the Queen's surgeon had left for him. The bullet had done no real damage, having gone into the meat of his shoulder. He'd chosen to have the lead removed without the benefit of ether or chloroform. He'd also declined the use of laudanum before or after. He didn't want to be drowsy or fall asleep. He wanted to find that damp, cold chamber where they'd taken Oglethorpe and beat the hell out of him until he cried for mercy—and only then would Marcus decide whether to grant it. The man had pointed a revolver at Esme and fired! He'd tried to kill her. Marcus was still consumed with such rage that it was a wonder he didn't ignite.

He'd taken some satisfaction in seeing Esme landing blows against the man's jaw, but it wasn't enough. He wanted to deliver a few jabs himself.

Hearing the door that connected his room to hers click, he glanced over to watch her entering. She was still wearing her red gown. Her hair was slightly askew, but it only made her all the more appealing. As she lowered herself to the edge of the mattress, she didn't appear to still be cross with him. Instead, she reached out and gently touched the bandage. "Must your shoulder take the brunt of all the attacks?"

Leaning in, she pressed a kiss there, and something inside him seemed to come undone and bloom throughout. What he felt for this woman was terrifying.

After setting his glass on the table beside the bed, he threaded his fingers through her hair. "He was going to kill you."

"I anticipated it and was already moving out of the way. But when I saw you lunging at him—I'd have never forgiven you if you'd died."

Her words shouldn't have brought him solace, and yet they did. They proved she cared for him. At least some. "Better me than you."

She took the hand of his injured arm and wrapped both of hers around it, holding it firmly. "You should know that O threatened to kill you if your father told them anything at all about their plans. Marcus, he could have received leniency if he'd confessed all. I think he didn't in order to protect you."

Dropping his head back, he stared at the ceiling. "It doesn't negate that he wanted to kill the Queen."

"No, but perhaps you can find some comfort in knowing he wasn't completely rotten."

Perhaps in time. "So many people were hurt, Esme, suffered. Lives were changed." He turned his attention back to her. "The odd thing is, I no longer resent what happened to me because I came to know you."

Drawing her near, he claimed her mouth, pouring all he felt for her into the kiss, hoping she would interpret what he feared saying aloud because he wasn't certain she'd accept the words. The words that had rushed through his mind in the stairwell. He loved her, this woman who claimed marriage was not for her. Could he convince her that it was, that her future should contain something other than a pretend marriage?

Or had the intensity of his life since he'd walked through her door caused him not to see things clearly? Too many times, just like tonight, they'd come close to death and narrowly escaped its grip. But the nearness of it heightened emotions, made one aware of the fragility of life, and caused a need to cling to that life with fervent intensity.

Perhaps that's what he'd experienced earlier tonight: the rush of knowing all could be lost and a need to hang on to the familiar. Just as now he wanted to feel alive, wanted this woman to feel alive. He needed to shake off the lingering cold fingers of death.

And so he took the kiss deeper.

ESME KNEW SHE should leave him to rest, that he needed to lie quietly and put no strain on his shoulder, but with his luscious mouth moving so provocatively and enticingly over hers, she could no more return to her bedchamber than she could fly to the moon.

His quest had come to an end. Her assignment was finished. Nothing remained to hold them together, to keep them in close proximity. He could carry on with his life now, do whatever he desired, be whatever he wanted. She wished the very best for him: a woman who loved him, a family, success, happiness. All he deserved.

So now, tonight, was her last chance to be with him. She wasn't certain he'd quite grasped that reality, but she had. She knew that when a mission was done, she couldn't linger. She needed to move on as quickly as possible, and it was better with no goodbyes, no regrets, no what-ifs.

And so she eased back, slid off the bed, and, with her gaze latched on to his, slowly began removing her gown and all that was beneath it, taking absurd satisfaction in the darkening of his eyes and the quickness with which his chest began to rise and fall.

"I think I will never grow tired of seeing you bared," he rasped when the last of her clothing was pooled at her feet.

Reaching up, she began removing the pins from her hair. "We'll have to take care with your shoulder."

"To hell with my shoulder."

She laughed, soft and low. "You may have need of it someday."

When her hair finally tumbled around her, she returned to him and saw to the removal of his trousers. She stroked his muscled thighs, his flat stomach, his broad chest. "I'll never grow tired of seeing you bared."

But in the future, she would see him only in her imagination. At that moment, she wanted to make love to him for all the times she wouldn't. She couldn't envision that any other man would ever mean to her what he did.

She became lost in the sensations as he touched and cajoled pleasure into blooming forth. He rolled her onto her back and came up on his good arm, using the other to stroke, knead, and squeeze. He gave so much of himself. Even now injured, he gifted her with all his attention, all his focus when she wouldn't have complained if he'd simply lain back and taken.

Reaching down, she wrapped her hand around his cock and did her own stroking, delighted by his low, torturous groan. His heat and hardness, the rumble in his throat and chest heightened her own pleasure. Giving, receiving. They were so well matched. She loved him for it, for the way he allowed her to be in control and set the tempo. And then ensured that he followed her lead, that she was never left wanting.

Lowering his head, he circled his tongue around her nipple. When she moaned, "More," he closed his mouth over the pearled peak. Heat consumed her as he suckled and soothed.

Cradling his jaw, she brought his mouth back to hers, pouring all that she was into the kiss, afraid it might be the last, concerned she might not realize the last kiss was the last kiss until it was too late.

Gently, she nudged him onto his back and trailed her mouth along his throat, down his chest, and across to his nipple where she returned the favor of licking it over and over before closing her mouth around it and giving it a little nibble.

With a low growl, he plowed a hand into her hair and tilted her head back until he captured her gaze. "I'm near to bursting, Esme. Ride me, sweetheart, ride me hard and fast."

Lifting herself, she straddled his hips and positioned him at her entrance. This, she was fairly certain, would be the last time and she wanted to remember every second of it. Slowly, so slowly, inch by glorious inch, she lowered herself until he filled her to the hilt.

For a heartbeat, two, she remained still, relishing their joining, recalling how she'd once believed they didn't fit, but now it seemed perfection. Then she began to move, meeting his thrusts with an increasing urgency as the pleasure built. She watched all he was experiencing cross over his features like the pages in a book, a story told if one took the time to relish all that was revealed.

"Don't close your eyes," she ordered.

The fire in his eyes set her ablaze, igniting her nerve endings, her skin, her very bones, until stars burst through her. His cries mingled with hers, their names intertwining like some ancient Celtic knot.

Mindful of his wound, she eased down until she was nestled along his uninjured side, his arm holding her against him.

"It's damned good to be alive," he said between harsh breaths.

She smiled. "Yes."

"Even better to have you here with me."

I love you, her mind, body, and soul screamed, but she wouldn't give voice to the words, wouldn't let her heart have the final say. It would only serve to make the parting that was to come that much harder.

CHAPTER 27

MARCUS STOOD IN an antechamber at Balmoral awaiting an audience with the Queen, his arm in a sling and his shoulder hurting like the very devil. Esme had been sent for as well and was presently with the Queen. Apparently, Victoria wanted to speak with each of them separately, while he thought they should be addressed together. After all, they were a team. They'd worked in tandem to bring things to an end.

When they'd gone down to breakfast, they'd been warmly greeted. He'd received a few slaps on the back and reassurances that he'd never been suspected of being involved in the conspiracy with his father. He was struggling with what Esme had told him about the threat Oglethorpe had made to his father. Might the duke have been spared the hangman's noose if he'd confessed all?

He heard the tinkling of a bell and the footman standing at the door disappeared inside. Shortly afterward, he reappeared. "Her Majesty will see you now."

Straightening his spine, he marched into the familiar room where he and Esme had met with the ruler a few weeks earlier. Her hands clasped in front of her, Victoria stood within a foot of the same chair she had upon their last visit. He bowed. "Your Majesty."

She gave a nod and waited until the footman had closed the door with a *snick* to say, "I should have you flogged for daring to touch my person in such an unseemly manner when we were making our escape last night."

"My sincerest apologies, but I thought haste was of utmost importance."

"You were worried about Esme."

He allowed his gaze to scour the room, searching for fronds behind which she might be hiding or shadows within which she could melt. "I didn't see her leave this chamber."

"No, she left through another exit." Did all these Scottish castles have hidden doors and passageways? "She thought it for the best."

His gut clenched so tightly that it nearly doubled him over. "Why would she think that?"

Elegantly, Victoria lowered herself to the chair and indicated the one closest to her. "Please sit, Mr. Stanwick."

What he wanted to do was go tearing out of this

room and through all the others until he discovered where she was.

"You won't find her." The Queen's tone was laced with utter conviction threaded with a measure of pity. He wanted to prove her wrong. "Sit," she repeated.

Would she see him hanged if he didn't obey her order and instead stormed out? Was it worth proving himself a disloyal subject after spending the better part of more than a year striving to prove the opposite? He dropped into the chair, suddenly taking no satisfaction in the accomplishments of the night before because he was beginning to suspect success had come at a cost he hadn't been willing to pay.

"Esme thinks very highly of you," Victoria said.

"She is an incredible woman."

"Do you love her?"

Before they were even spoken, the words tasted bitter on his tongue because he should have admitted it to Esme before he did anyone else. "With all my heart."

"I have known her for a good many years now, and she has always served me well. But this latest mission . . . I do not think it was particularly easy. I feel that I owe her more than I can ever repay. I offered to give her anything in the kingdom that she desired. I hope you are deserving of it, Marcus Stanwick."

He shook his head. "I don't understand."

"She wanted the Duke of Wolfford's titles and

properties to be returned to his heir." Reaching for the bell on the table beside her, she gave it a ring. "I bid you good day, Your Grace."

MARCUS HAD NEVER exited a room so quickly in his entire life.

"Have you seen Esme . . . Miss Lancaster?" he asked a maid.

"No, sir."

It was the same answer he got whether he asked the question of a footman, another maid, the cook, or a stableboy. Or John Brown when they crossed paths.

"Sorry, lad," he said.

"She can't have simply disappeared." But even as he said it, he knew she could. The question was why? Why would she not even give him the courtesy of a proper goodbye?

"The carriage is waiting to take you back to Glasford's," Brown said.

The royal carriage that had arrived with the Queen's summons and brought them. He didn't even bother to hope that Esme would be inside waiting for him. As it carried him back to his brother and sister, he stared out the window knowing that he should feel elated. He was a duke, the Duke of Wolfford. He was where he'd always thought his life would lead him, to holding the titles to a dukedom and an earldom. He would now be responsible for managing estates, would take his place in the House of Lords. His life was back on track; he'd been returned to the proper path. Yet everything about it felt wrong. Because of Esme. Because she wasn't there to celebrate it with him.

When the carriage rumbled to a stop at the Glasford castle, he saw his brother leaning against the wall, one foot crossed in front of the other. Griff approached as Marcus leapt out.

"How did things go with the Queen?" Griff asked. "What did she want?"

"To return the titles and properties to me."

"Bloody hell!" Griff laughed loudly and boisterously, his grin broad. "That's an outcome I didn't expect. Congratulations, brother. Or I suppose I should say, 'Your Grace.'"

"Brother will suffice."

You have me at a disadvantage as I don't know your name.

Esme will suffice.

Would everything always remind him of her?

"You're affected as well, Lord Griffith," Marcus said. As was Althea, although he suspected she would prefer to be associated with the forms of address that came with her marriage to an earl who would one day be duke.

Griff's eyes widened. "I hadn't considered that. Will come in handy should I have any daughters. Kathryn will be pleased. She is still recognized as a lady because of her father but now it can be because of her husband. I very much like that notion."

The door opened, and Althea began prancing down the steps. "I heard the commotion. What's happened?"

"Marcus is the bloody Duke of Wolfford."

"Oh my God!" Her arms were suddenly around him, and he couldn't remember her ever hugging him or showing such jubilation. Releasing her hold, she smiled up at him. "I'm so glad. You went on a circuitous route, but being duke was always your destiny."

But he wanted Esme to be his destiny.

"Did Esme not return with you?" Griff asked.

The question hurt and his chest tightened until he thought it might cave in on itself. "No, she apparently needed to be elsewhere."

"I'm not surprised," Althea said. "Before you left to meet with the Queen, she gave this to me and asked me to give it to you when you returned but not before."

When she unfurled her fingers, Marcus saw the rose gold wedding band.

"She said it belonged to our grandmother," Althea said, a slight question in her tone.

"Yes, we were using it as a prop since she was pretending to be my wife. You should have it."

"Perhaps you should take it for the next Duchess of Wolfford."

He shook his head. "No, you should have it."

"I'll treasure it."

Which was more than he could say for Esme. He'd wanted her to keep it. And now he was left to wonder if he'd ever meant anything at all to her or if their time together had been merely a result of her work for the Home Office. Had it all been a lie?

CHAPTER 28

MARCUS HAD BEEN in London for two weeks before he finally knocked on Esme's door. The London residence was nearly put to rights. He'd been hiring servants, going over the books from the estates, familiarizing himself with all the changes that had transpired since his life had taken a detour. And every day he sent her a dozen roses with a card that simply had *M* written on it.

While he expected nothing of her, he needed her to know how much he appreciated the request she'd made of the Queen, and he wanted her to see the residence returned to its former glory. It was the reason he'd begun with it and not the estates. She could more easily visit the London manor.

As soon as the door began opening, he braced himself for his battle of wills with Brewster.

Only it wasn't Brewster who stood there, but an older man with silver hair and a slender build whose posture was ramrod straight as though he was expecting a military inspection to take place at any minute. Had they let Brewster go because he'd trusted Oglethorpe?

"Yes, sir, may I help you?" the butler asked.

"I'm here to see Miss Esme Lancaster."

He tipped his head slightly. "I believe you have the wrong residence."

"I'm quite certain I don't. Announce to the mistress of the house that the Duke of Wolfford has come to call."

"There is no mistress, Your Grace. Only the master."

What the devil? Shoving his way past him, ignoring his protests, Marcus charged into the parlor. Everything looked the same. The carpeting, the furniture, the paintings on the walls.

But where Esme should have been standing was a man: tall, broad-shouldered, immaculately dressed in black trousers, a dark blue coat, and a light blue brocade waistcoat.

"My apologies, sir," the butler stammered, "but he simply barged in. Says he's the Duke of Wolfford."

"It's quite all right, Collins, I suspect this is the chap who's been sending us the lovely flowers. I'll handle things from here," the man said before bowing his head toward Marcus. "Your Grace, how might I be of service?"

"Where is Esme?"

"I'm afraid I don't know of whom you speak?"

"You're not acquainted with Esme Lancaster?"

"No, Your Grace."

Marcus walked farther into the room. Only a faint wisp of her fragrance remained, but still he filled his lungs with it. "How is it that you live here?"

"My employer has generously made it available to me as I have some work to do in the area and this abode was conveniently vacated recently."

Marcus slammed his eyes closed. "You work for the Home Office."

Silence greeted his statement. Opening his eyes, he saw the resolve set in his opponent's— because that was how he thought of him now— chin. The man wasn't going to confirm the statement. "Do you know where I'll find her?"

"As I said, I'm not—"

"Acquainted with her. Yes, I heard you, but that doesn't mean that you don't know her by reputation or that you don't know where she is now."

"I don't have the information you seek but you might find it helpful to know that I have a personal residence. As do most of those with whom I work. Perhaps the woman you're looking for does as well."

Turning on his heel, Marcus headed for the door.

"Does this mean you shan't be sending us flowers any longer?" the blighter called out after him.

"Go to the devil."

THE FIRST NIGHT of November, Marcus wandered through the London residence. Colder weather had arrived. Every fireplace was lit, the flames dancing on the hearth in each room he passed. He'd visited both his estates and set out tasks to be handled by the individual estate managers, but he couldn't seem to stay away from London for any length of time. No doubt because he wanted Esme to be able to find him easily if she had a change of heart.

With a bit of sleuthing, he'd managed to confirm that the Home Office owned the residence in which she'd lived, so he was rather certain the man he'd met there was also an agent. He supposed the government had properties all over London. For times when they needed to hide someone away, perhaps. Not that it mattered. What mattered was that she was no longer there, and he still had yet to determine where she might be. Maybe she wasn't even in London but was living elsewhere.

As he was now a duke again, with some prestige and power, perhaps he'd simply ask the Home Secretary where she was.

He finally made his way to the library and poured himself a scotch.

I believe your preference is scotch.

He could seldom go an hour without something reminding him of her. Glass in hand, he walked over to the fireplace, leaned the shoulder she'd once stitched up against the mantel, and sipped his favorite whisky while he waited for his guests to arrive. He was having Althea and Griff, along with their spouses, over for dinner now that the residence had finally been returned to what it once was. Slipping the hand not holding the glass into the pocket of his coat, he skimmed his fingers over the painted wooden soldier. He carried it with him not as a reminder of his father, but as a reminder of *her.* Esme. Because she had found it, because her fingers were the last to touch the toy before his. It was all he had of her. By not keeping the ring, she'd ensured she had nothing of him. The knowledge shouldn't make him so sad, but it did.

He would be wise to stop thinking of her, and yet when he walked anywhere through the residence, he saw her there, scouring through nooks, crannies, and drawers. He even imagined, in spite of all the dusting and polishing that had been done, that he could still smell her fragrance from time to time wafting about him. She haunted this residence, haunted him. If only he'd had a chance to say goodbye . . .

It would have made no difference. He still would miss her.

He took the soldier from his pocket and studied it. It was such an odd thing for his father to hide away in a cubby. If something ridiculous like the toy had been placed in Podmore's hidey-hole, she might have been on her way out the door before Marcus entered the room. She wouldn't have been standing there taking photographs, and he never would have received that first kiss. But Podmore's hidden compartment had been used as it was meant to be and so something believed to be of significance had been found. The duke had not been so wise—

"Christ. Maybe he wasn't hiding you away. You were a message." After setting his glass on the mantel, he dashed across the room, nearly ramming into his butler, who was leading his guests into the library. "Make yourselves at home. Pour them a drink, Smithers. I won't be long."

"Marcus!" Althea called after him, but he didn't respond.

He merely raced down the hall and up the stairs to his bedchamber. He hadn't been able to bring himself to use the master's bedchamber but still slept in the one he'd occupied since he was a boy. Hanging on the wall was a wooden rectangle inside which was a series of cubbies. Each had provided a home for his soldiers when he wasn't playing with them. He'd been meticulous about keeping them properly aligned, never leaving them out. He always put them away. To make it easier for him, the box came off the wall and could easily be hung back on it. Even after he no longer had the soldiers, he'd kept it on the wall as a symbol and reminder of what his father had taken from him.

He lifted it off the nails and turned it over. The edge of a folded note had been tucked up into the corner, so it was held in place. He pulled it free, set aside the box, and with trembling hands carefully unfolded the foolscap.

Marcus, my boy, some years back I gambled away an entire fortune and was in dire need of funds. I borrowed from my old friend—a fellow named Oglethorpe. We'd gone to Cambridge together. He told me not to worry. Some day he would collect what was owed. I managed to get our coffers back to rights. I had the funds to pay him, but he wanted a favor instead. He would tell me when the debt came due. Eventually it did. To make a lady believe I wanted to kill the Queen and to convince others she was my mistress. He has shown me the evil men can do and left me no choice but to honor his demands in order to protect my family from that evil. I have made a deal with Lucifer and I fear no good will come of it.

Regretfully,
Father

"Marcus?"

Glancing over at Griff, he extended the foolscap toward him, watched as his brother took it and then read it.

"Jesus," Griff muttered before lifting his gaze. "He was innocent?"

"It appears so. I know Oglethorpe threatened to have me killed if Father gave him away after he was arrested. He may have confessed, hoping to save his family."

Tears welled in Griff's eyes. "He wasn't that good of a father."

"Esme once told me that the Home Office takes care of a lot of dangers about which we never hear anything. Perhaps the same is true of parents."

Griff turned his back on him, his shoulders rising as he inhaled a deep breath, striving to regain control of his emotions. His hand came up and Marcus assumed he was dispatching the dampness in his eyes. When he spun back around, his jaw was set. "I wish they'd hanged the bastard."

Oglethorpe had been found guilty of attempting to murder the Queen, but he had also been declared insane and sent to an asylum where he would live out his remaining days.

"I'll take the letter to the Home Office, see if there's anything that can be done to set the record straight. At the very least, it needs to be chronicled in the family records, so our descendants know the truth."

"No wonder he would get livid when I gambled. It feels odd to think we may have shared something in common."

"Perhaps you'll take pity on firstborn sons now and let them into your club."

"Never."

Marcus took back the letter. "We should let Althea know. And your spouses. Strange, I suddenly feel as though a heavy burden has been lifted."

"Do you think Mother knew? I hate knowing that she may have died thinking the worst of him."

"I hate all of it." Except for the tiny soldier. The one his father, for some unknown reason, had kept through the years after tossing out all the others. The one he'd stored in a hidden cubby in his desk, perhaps out of fear that if he placed the letter there, Oglethorpe would find it and destroy it. The tiny soldier that a lady with a knack for discovering secrets had found. However, she hadn't known enough about the duke or his heir to unearth what it meant. But then neither had he. Maybe if he hadn't been consumed by rage, if he'd only thought it through—

He knew his answer wasn't what his brother needed to hear. "I hope she knew the truth, although I don't know if it would have made anything easier for her."

"You're probably right." Griff pointed toward the letter. "You'll want to share that with Esme as well."

Carefully refolding the missive, he slipped it inside his jacket. "I've yet to find her."

"Now that you have your estates in order, perhaps you can focus on what truly matters: being with the woman you love."

"I didn't think you liked her."

"You deserve a woman who loves you, Marcus, and she does."

"How do you know that?"

"Because I saw the way she looks at you. It's very much in the same manner that Althea looks at Trewlove and Kathryn looks at me. She would fight to the death for you. And considering our family history, that's the sort of woman you want to hold close."

CHAPTER 29

CHRISTMAS EVE WAS Esme's favorite night of the year, when the carolers were out singing, filling the air with hope and joy and love. She always spent the evening in her small home with its small lawn and gardens near the park where she'd brought Marcus that lovely afternoon eons ago. She'd almost shared her dwelling with him then, but she'd known a time would come when their paths would diverge, and it would be easier if he didn't know where to find her.

She liked this area of London that Mick Trewlove had refurbished. The less affluent lived in the nearby town homes but as their fortunes increased, they were often able to move in to the larger ones he built. The more affluent resided, as she did, in homes with no one else's walls touching theirs. But even those houses ranged in size from small like hers to grand.

But because she lived alone, she had no use for the larger dwellings. Not quite alone. Laddie was with her. He enjoyed the carolers as well. He would begin barking as their voices grew louder and he could smell their approach.

She opened the door to greet the group of half a dozen children lifting their voices to the heavens. Laddie rushed out, sniffed around their feet, and rushed back in. Snow was lightly falling. An inch or so had already gathered, painting everything in pristine white and making it seem so peaceful.

Her life had been much the same since Scotland. Serene. O's position couldn't be offered to a woman and so it had gone to Brewster, in spite of his lamenting he would do better as a butler. Esme had taken a much-needed respite from working in the shadows and striving to uncover traitors or those who wished to undermine the government. Her superiors were toying with the idea of sending her abroad. She rather liked that idea. It removed all temptation of showing up at Marcus's door late at night when she missed him the most.

She had clandestinely watched him a few times: leaving his residence, attending the opera, riding through Hyde Park. If the articles written about the man who'd saved the Queen were any indication, he was settling well into his role of duke. It would be more difficult to read about him during the upcoming Season when the ladies would be vying for his attention in the hopes of becoming his duchess.

The carolers finished their song. Reaching into her pocket, she withdrew a handful of half crowns, gave one to each of the children, and wished them a happy Christmas. Murmuring joyfully, they began wandering over to the next house.

Closing the door, she picked up Laddie and walked into her parlor where only an hour earlier she'd finished decorating the small tree that sat on a table near the window. No gifts beneath the boughs, but then she'd already received the best gift of all: knowing that Marcus was back where he rightfully belonged.

She heard the next set of carolers coming up the street, their voices growing louder as they neared. She lowered Laddie to the floor. He scrambled to the front door, barking exuberantly. "These voices are a bit deeper, probably adults. I'm not certain they'll be as happy with you sniffing about."

Still, she opened the door and gave him his freedom. He bounded out and headed to one of the men at the back, who crouched and gave attention to her spaniel as he deserved. But there was something about the fellow that caused her heart to beat erratically. His head was bent, his beaver hat hiding his face, but the breadth of his shoulders, the size of his gloved hands, the grace with which he'd lowered himself—

Then he looked up, captured her gaze, and slowly straightened to his full height. Her heart nearly stammered to a stop and her lungs seemed to have forgotten how to draw in air. His black outer coat molded perfectly over his broad shoulders. He wasn't singing but she imagined his voice, deep and rich—

No one was singing. After reaching into her pocket, she began dispensing the half crowns. "That was lovely. Thank you. Happy Christmas."

And then she waited, waited until the carolers wandered away and he remained. Waited as he strode forward until he was so close that she could smell the bergamot and spicy scent of him. Waited as he swept his hat from his head. "Hello, Esme."

She curtsied. "Your Grace." *I expected you sooner.* When she'd tried not to expect him at all. "It's a bit nippy out here. Would you care for a bit of scotch to warm you before you go on your way caroling?"

"I wasn't caroling. I just didn't know if you'd open the door if you saw it was only me waiting out here."

"I've never been a coward."

"I beg to differ. You left without saying goodbye."

"I thought it would be less painful."

"You were wrong." As though she didn't bloody well know that. "But, yes, I'll take that scotch."

She led him into the parlor and carried on to the sideboard with its assortment of decanters, wishing her hands weren't trembling as she poured them each a glass of the amber liquid.

"The Queen indicated you thought being a duke would suit me."

Damn Victoria for not keeping secret that Esme had asked for the dukedom to be returned to him. "Based on what I've been able to gather from the articles that have appeared in the newspapers, I had the right of it, and it does suit you."

He glanced around. "Was this residence a gift from Victoria?"

"No, I actually purchased it some time back. I reside here when I'm not needed elsewhere. How did you find me?"

"I have my ways." He set down his glass on a table, removed his coat, and tossed it onto the sofa. She did wish he hadn't done that. His clothes were perfectly tailored, a black jacket, white shirt, pristine white cravat, and a silk waistcoat of emerald green, no doubt a nod to the season. From inside his jacket, he retrieved what appeared to be a missive. "Something the Home Office needs to see. I was hoping you might be good enough to deliver it for me."

So he was here because of her occupation. She was relieved. Immensely. *Liar.*

"You should read it," he said.

Carefully she unfolded it and scoured the words before lifting her gaze back to his. "Where did you find it?"

"The toy soldier you discovered was a message to me that I was too . . . angry to interpret. But in my bedchamber is a small shelf where I kept my soldiers. It was behind that."

"O told me your father believed his claim to the throne, but I suspect he was either lying or delusional. I lean toward delusional. He was quite mad. To get the duke to participate in his scheme, he must have shown your father an outcome that was worse than hanging. I'll see that this is delivered to the Home Secretary." After setting it on a table, she turned her attention back to him. "I'm glad you were right. That he didn't want to kill the Queen."

"Still, he did play a role in it, so he's not completely innocent. Why did you leave me, Esme?"

Swallowing, she cursed the tiny tremors cascading through her. "It would have happened sooner or later. Sooner seemed for the best. You're a duke, and I'm still an agent for the Crown. You have your duties and I have mine."

"You should see my London residence now, free of all its tarps and coverings, servants scurrying about, lights lit—almost returned to what it once was. Except what it once was . . . was an unhappy place. That is not what I want for it." He took a step forward. "Presently it is a lonely place, and I don't want that either."

"The next Season should remedy that situation. The young ladies will be falling all over themselves to become your duchess."

"I don't want a woman who falls all over herself. I want one who stands on her own two feet, steady and sure. A woman who desired me when I had no title, no honor to my name."

"Marcus—"

"You also returned the ring I gave you."

The abrupt change in subject took her aback.

"It was an heirloom. It should remain with the family."

"I don't think it fit all that well anyway. I brought you something more appropriate to replace it." Reaching into his jacket, he brought out a small velvet box. A tiny box. A very tiny box. He held it out toward her.

"You don't need to give me a gift."

"I think you'll like this one. I had it made especially for you. It's not at all what it appears to be."

Now he'd piqued her curiosity. Setting her glass aside, she took the box from him, opened the lid, and studied the rose gold band with pure gold around the edges and gold dissecting the ring in several places, creating small tiles upon which had been painted tiny, delicate roses. "It's a very beautiful ring."

"Study it carefully." After she picked up the ring, he took the box from her and set it aside. "It is the sort of thing that an agent of the Crown might find useful."

She examined it, running her finger along the smooth inside and then the outside—

Her fingernail caught on something. "It has a very miniscule latch."

"Hidden compartments for storing messages. Open it."

She did, pulling back one of the tiles to reveal the tiniest scrap of paper. Carefully she withdrew it to uncover etched in the gold in delicate script *I love you*. She lifted her gaze. "Marcus—"

"Read the note."

With her heart in her throat, she did. *Marry me in earnest.*

She squeezed her eyes shut, finding it incredibly difficult to breathe. Opening her eyes, she shook her head. "I can't. You must know I can't."

"I spent more than a year striving to regain what I'd lost and having finally acquired it and more, I discovered that I sacrificed the only true joy I've ever known. You. Marry me, Esme."

Her heart cracked. It was unfair of him to ask this of her. "As duke, it is your duty to provide an heir and I can't . . . I can't give that to you."

"When you asked the Queen to place the dukedom within my care, you did so with the expectation that it would mean that we couldn't be together."

Holding the ring tightly, she clutched her hands together to stop herself from reaching for him, from skimming her fingers over his beloved features. "Not as man and wife, but we could be lovers, I suppose."

"Having witnessed what my mother endured when we all thought my father had taken a mistress, I could never be unfaithful to my wife."

She nodded. "It's one of the reasons I care for you as I do."

"So I will not take a wife."

Had he suddenly struck her, she would not have been more shocked. "You must. A duke must have a duchess."

"In my heart I already have one, and she is you.

Whether or not it is sanctioned by the church or recognized by Society, you are my duchess."

"Marcus, don't be absurd." She began pacing.

"Do you love me, Esme?"

She came to an abrupt halt. "Until you, I didn't know what love was—to love, to be loved."

"Until you, neither did I. If I have to choose between the dukedom and you, I choose you. If your only objection to marrying me is that I need an heir, I have a brother. Perhaps he will provide one. If he does not, I have cousins aplenty. I don't expect you to give up your position with the Home Office. Being married to a duke could give you access to information or people you might not have had otherwise. And who would suspect a duchess of being a spy?"

She turned to him. "You're making it very difficult for me to say no."

He grinned. "Good."

Tears welled in her eyes. "I have missed you so much. I love you so much. I want you to have everything you deserve."

"Then let me have you."

"Yes, a thousand times yes. However you want. As often as you want. But only if you're sure you'll have no regrets."

His arms came around her. "How can I regret having happiness and joy and the woman I love at my side?"

"We'll scandalize a few, I'm certain."

"Your mother sent you to finishing school

and then to work in the Royal household hoping you'd find yourself a gentleman. I'm so grateful you didn't. Because you, Esme Lancaster, are going to marry a duke."

He cut off her laugh by blanketing his mouth over hers. Ah, yes, she was going to marry a duke, but more importantly, she was going to marry Marcus Stanwick.

Epilogue

London
Some Years Later

LONG PAST MIDNIGHT, pacing within her bed-chamber, Esme had never known such wretched nervousness. Marcus had left for Kent that morning and his delay in returning had her worried that something terrible had happened. She should have a horse saddled or a carriage readied and go in search of him. If she'd not had an urgent appointment with the Queen that afternoon, she'd have accompanied him to begin with. She should have headed out straightaway when she left Victoria, but she'd been so certain he would return at any minute.

Slowly she began turning the ring on her finger, a habit she'd developed over the years whenever danger was afoot or a drastic decision needed to be made. Within each compartment was etched *I love you*. She always drew strength from the words, feeling as though he was right beside her.

She had discovered that the ring was not only good at concealing messages but poisons as well. She'd once used one of the compartments to deliver a powder into the wine of an enemy of the Crown. The man had become ghastly ill. Certain he was on the brink of death—no doubt because Esme had told him so—he'd revealed the names of his cohorts in exchange for the remedy she promised would save him. It had been only sweetened water, and as it would have without her *remedy*, his stomach upset eventually dissipated.

When the situation warranted, Marcus would assist her with her assignment. Doing so satisfied his craving for the shadows and danger that sometimes haunted him. He straddled the two worlds well, and she was certain there was no finer duke in all of England.

The door to her bedchamber burst open and in he strode, her tall, dark, and magnificent love, taking her into his arms and kissing her passionately as though they'd gone years without seeing each other rather than hours.

When he drew back, he cradled her face and smiled brightly. "After three daughters, Kathryn finally delivered a son to my brother."

Tears welled in her eyes. "You have your heir."

"We do." Lifting her up, he swung her around before setting her back on her feet. "I apologize for my delay in returning but Griff was beside himself while she was in labor, and I had to keep him calm. Then afterward, we had to drink a toast to the Wolfford heir."

She pressed her palm against his cheek. "You're truly happy."

"I am. I have you. The title will pass through to my nephew. Ironic, since my brother always considered himself the spare, held in reserve. Now his son will inherit. All is as it should be."

"I love you so much."

"And I have missed you too much." Sweeping her into his arms, he marched over to the bed, tossed her onto it, and followed her down, half covering her body with his own. "What did Victoria want?"

"She would like me to begin working for the War Office, specifically the Intelligence Branch. It would mean spending considerable time in Europe, gathering information. It would no doubt prove helpful to have a powerful and influential duke at my side."

"Mmm." He began nuzzling her neck. "At your side, at your front, at your back. Wherever you need me, love."

"At the moment I need you inside me."

He laughed. "I'm always happy to accommodate your needs."

As she was his. What a circuitous route they'd traveled, and yet she couldn't help but believe that they were both exactly where they were always meant to be. Within each other's arms.

AUTHOR'S NOTE

I'M OFTEN ASKED where I get my story ideas. They come from so many different places, and the smallest thing can trigger them or can give me the idea for a character.

When this series first took shape in my mind, I envisioned it involving two brothers who had lost everything and how they each adapted. However, when I finished Griff's story, I wasn't quite certain of the details regarding Marcus's story. Fortunately, the Duke of Kingsland, a character I introduced in Griff's book, took over and insisted I write his tale next. While I was working on *The Duchess Hunt*, searching for something on the Internet for that story, I ran across an article about the Lancaster watch camera, made in 1886, that looked like a pocket watch but was really a carefully hidden tiny camera. While it was made twelve years after the setting of my story,

I decided a spy in 1874 might have had access to a prototype. And with that little bit of information, I realized that Marcus's story would involve a female agent for the Crown. From there, Marcus and Esme's story unfolded, helped along when further research fortuitously introduced me to Kate Warne, the first female detective to work at the Pinkerton Agency in Chicago. She was hired by Allan Pinkerton after convincing him that a woman had the means to gather information in situations where a man couldn't, that a woman was able to project sympathy and understanding that would cause others to confide in her more quickly and easily. To her advantage, she would not be suspected of being a detective because the profession was considered the purview of men. She was credited with being instrumental in collecting information that prevented an assassination of Abraham Lincoln in 1861. Following her death in 1868, she came to the public's attention in the United States and Britain when various newspapers expounded on her incredible accomplishments. The articles led to a greater acceptance of women as detectives and sleuths in both countries.

The ring that Marcus gave Esme is based on one that is on exhibition at the Victoria and Albert Museum.

I have always been saddened by the story of Lady Flora Hastings, an unmarried lady-in-waiting to Victoria's mother, the Duchess of Kent. When her abdomen began to grow, rumors flew that she'd had an affair and was with child. No one would believe her denials. Unfortunately, the young Queen Victoria took delight in the gossip, and it caused her to face harsh criticism. Not until Lady Flora died was it discovered she had a tumor. So, Esme traveled a similar path with a more sympathetic queen, and I gave her a happier ending.

I hope you've enjoyed the Once Upon a Dukedom series. Now I'll be turning my attention to the Chessmen, who are masters not only at investing but at the game of seduction.

Happy reading!

Lorraine

If you've enjoyed
The Return of the Duke,
don't miss *New York Times* bestselling
author Lorraine Heath's

THE COUNTERFEIT
SCOUNDREL

The first book in her
exciting new spin-off series
The Chessmen: Masters of Seduction.

Available everywhere February 2023

REL 0722